PRAISE

RIDING ON

"Kudos and beyond for Ms. Burton's best book yet! I cannot wait to see what comes next!" —*Fallen Angels Reviews*

"Everything about *Riding on Instinct* is picture-perfect and I stayed up half the night, unable to put it down until finishing the very last word." —*Romance Junkies*

"Another smokin'-hot Wild Riders story you will love reading." —*Fresh Fiction*

"Jaci Burton's *Riding on Instinct* took me on the ride of my life." —*Wild on Books*

"Thank you for giving us a love story where there is room for compromise and the good guys not only win, they take down the bad guys with a minimum of bloodshed and loss of innocent life." —*Night Owl Romance*

RIDING TEMPTATION

"Full of intrigue, sexual tension and exhilarating release. Definitely a must-read." —*Fresh Fiction*

"*Riding Temptation* has it all—action, suspense, romance and sensuality, all wrapped up in a story that will keep you on the edge of your seat and have you clamoring for the next story in the Wild Riders series!" —*Wild on Books*

"Kudos to Ms. Burton for creating this exciting new series!" —*Romance Junkies*

continued . . .

RIDING WILD

"A wild ride is exactly what you will get with this steamy romantic caper. This sexy and sizzling-hot story will leave you breathless and wanting more."
—*Fresh Fiction*

"A nonstop thrill ride from the first page to the last! Grab a copy of *Riding Wild* and take your own ride on the wild side of life!"
—*Romance Junkies*

"What an exciting and wonderful book!"
—*The Romance Studio*

"*Riding Wild* is a must-read for anyone who loves sexy romances filled with plenty of action and suspense."
—*Kwips and Kritiques*

"Burton delivers it all in this hot story—strong characters, an exhilarating plot and scorching sex—and it all moves at a breakneck pace. Forget about a cool glass of water; break out the ice! You'll be drawn so fully into her characters' world that you won't want to return to your own."
—*Romantic Times*

WILD, WICKED, & WANTON

"*Wild, Wicked, & Wanton* starts off with a bang and never lets up!"
—*Just Erotic Reviews*

"This is the best erotic novel I have ever read! I absolutely loved it!"
—*Fresh Fiction*

"Jaci Burton's *Wild, Wicked, & Wanton* is an invitation to every woman's wildest fantasies. And it's an invitation that can't be ignored."
—*Romance Junkies*

FURTHER PRAISE FOR THE WORK OF
JACI BURTON

"Realistic dialogue, spicy bedroom scenes and a spitfire heroine make this one to pick up and savor." —*Publishers Weekly*

"Jaci Burton delivers." —*New York Times* bestselling author Cherry Adair

"Lively and funny . . . The sex is both intense and loving; you can feel the connection that both the hero and heroine want to deny in every word and touch between them. I cannot say enough good things about this book." —*The Road to Romance*

RIDING THE NIGHT

JACI BURTON

HEAT | NEW YORK

THE BERKLEY PUBLISHING GROUP
Published by the Penguin Group
Penguin Group (USA) Inc.
375 Hudson Street, New York, New York 10014, USA
Penguin Group (Canada), 90 Eglinton Avenue East, Suite 700, Toronto, Ontario M4P 2Y3, Canada
(a division of Pearson Penguin Canada Inc.)
Penguin Books Ltd., 80 Strand, London WC2R 0RL, England
Penguin Group Ireland, 25 St. Stephen's Green, Dublin 2, Ireland (a division of Penguin Books Ltd.)
Penguin Group (Australia), 250 Camberwell Road, Camberwell, Victoria 3124, Australia
(a division of Pearson Australia Group Pty. Ltd.)
Penguin Books India Pvt. Ltd., 11 Community Centre, Panchsheel Park, New Delhi—110 017, India
Penguin Group (NZ), 67 Apollo Drive, Rosedale, North Shore 0632, New Zealand
(a division of Pearson New Zealand Ltd.)
Penguin Books (South Africa) (Pty.) Ltd., 24 Sturdee Avenue, Rosebank, Johannesburg 2196,
South Africa

Penguin Books Ltd., Registered Offices: 80 Strand, London WC2R 0RL, England

This book is an original publication of The Berkley Publishing Group.

Copyright © 2010 by Jaci Burton.
Cover art by S. Miroque.
Cover design by Rita Frangie.
Text design by Kristin del Rosario.

PRINTING HISTORY
Heat trade paperback edition / September 2010

Library of Congress Cataloging-in-Publication Data

Burton, Jaci.
    Riding the night / Jaci Burton.—Heat trade pbk. ed.
        p. cm.
    ISBN 978-0-425-23656-7
    1. Government investigators—Fiction.   2. Motorcycle gangs—Fiction.   I. Title.
    PS3602.U776R57 2010
    813'.6—dc22

                                                                    2010012980

PRINTED IN THE UNITED STATES OF AMERICA

10 9 8 7 6 5 4 3 2

To the readers who've loved the Wild Riders—
the Wild Riders and I thank you,
from the bottoms of our hearts. This one's for you.

acknowledgments

To my editor, Kate Seaver. Thank you for your guidance, for the plotline assists and for the ever helpful editorial comments.

To my agent, Kim Whalen, the calm in my daily storm.

To Fatin, a wonderful, warm, sweet soul who helps me keep my sanity. I couldn't do it without you.

To a few of the people in my life who let me cry on their shoulders and whine incessantly, and who love me anyway—Angela James, Shannon Stacey and Maya Banks.

And as always, to Charlie, who doesn't mind occasionally having cereal for dinner so I can finish a book. Thank you for loving me enough to put up with it all.

PROLOGUE

TEN YEARS EARLIER

THEY'D PARKED ON A TREE-LINED HILL OVERLOOKING THE CITY. Private. No one came up here anymore. AJ had taken his stepdad's truck because it had the bench seat and was roomier than his car. He was gonna be in deep shit for taking the truck without permission. What else was new—he was always in trouble over something, and he didn't give a shit about the consequences. Not today.

Today was Teresa's eighteenth birthday and he wanted it to be special for her. They rarely got time alone, had to sneak off whenever they got a chance because her parents didn't approve of her seeing him. Not that he could blame them. And his fucking stepdad was on his ass all the time to make something of himself, to get a decent job and quit staying out all night long.

He was already somebody, so the old man could kiss his ass. He was going places, making money. If it wasn't quite legit . . . well, tough shit. He was his own man, and soon enough he wouldn't have to answer to his asshole stepfather anymore. And his mother had never stood up for him—not once in all the years she'd been married to that dickhead. She'd always taken the old man's side, too weak to defend her own son even though he saw the apology in her eyes. Well, screw her, too. Soon as he got enough money in his pocket, he was gone. And he'd take Teresa with him when he left.

But tonight was all about Teresa, the beautiful raven-haired girl who made him feel clean, made him feel like he could conquer the world. For the past two years she'd been the light and soul of his life, the only reason to make him smile. What she was doing with him he could never figure out, but for some reason she liked being with him. She sat next to him on the bench seat of the old pickup and smiled at him as she opened her present.

"It's not much," he said, feeling like he should apologize. "I'll get you something better soon."

She turned her emerald eyes on him and smiled. "I'm sure it's perfect, AJ. Thank you."

"You haven't opened it yet."

She leaned up to feather a kiss across his lips. "It doesn't matter what it is. You thought of getting me a gift. That's what matters."

She carefully pulled the tissue paper apart and gasped when she saw the sterling silver chain. It had cost him a month's worth of wages at the shop, but he knew it would look perfect against her olive skin.

"Oh, AJ, it's beautiful. Put it on me?"

She handed him the necklace and half turned, raising her hair so he could do the clasp in back, then turned around to face him, fingering the necklace. "How does it look?"

It was perfect, the pattern sexy and delicate, just like the girl who wore it. "It looks good on you."

"Thank you." She climbed onto his lap, straddling him and placing her hands on either side of his face. "I love you, AJ."

Every time she said those words, his gut clenched. He didn't deserve her. What did he have to offer? "I love you, too, Teresa." He laid his hands on her hips, his cock hardening as she kissed him, moved against him, rubbing her breasts against his chest. A rush of heat enveloped him just as it always did whenever she looked at him, touched him or kissed him. He wrapped his arms around Teresa's back, pulling her flush against him.

She made him feel whole. The only time he felt good was when she was in his arms. He slid his hand under her T-shirt, loving the softness of her skin, the way her belly trembled when he touched her there.

"Let me see you," he said.

She did, resting her back against the steering wheel. He shifted, reaching down to push the seat all the way back, giving them room before lifting her T-shirt.

"Nice bra," he said, smiling up at her as he fingered the see-through silk and lace and the soft flesh rising above it. She had great tits, dusky nipples visible through the fabric. His dick pounded against the denim of his jeans, demanding release.

Yeah. Soon. He couldn't wait to be inside her, had waited two damn years for this night. He could already imagine how tight she'd feel, how wet, how good it was going to be to come up inside her.

She dropped her lids partway down and tilted her head to the side. "I bought it for you."

He cupped his hands behind her back and brought her forward, placing his lips over her bra, feeling her nipples harden through the material. He pulled the cups down and put his mouth over one bud, needing to taste her. She threw her head back and tightened her hold on his shoulder. Teresa loved having her nipples sucked, and goddamn did he love putting his mouth on them.

"Yes," she whispered, her voice hoarse and broken as he pulled her nipple between his lips. "Harder, AJ."

He sucked her nipple, then bit lightly with his teeth. She cried out and tangled her fingers in his hair, dragging her gaze to his. "Are you going to fuck me tonight?"

He nearly shot off right then, the thought of burying his cock inside her slamming his balls tight against his body. "Yes, I'm going to fuck you. We've done every damn thing together except me being inside you, Teresa."

And he'd loved doing all those things with her. Good girl though she was, Teresa was an explorer when it came to sex. There was nothing she wasn't willing to try, and if it wasn't for him holding out, they'd have fucked already. But he'd wanted to wait until she was eighteen, until she was an adult, at least technically. He wanted her to be sure this was what she wanted.

But yeah, they'd done everything else. She had the mouth of a goddess and went down on him damn near every time they were together. He'd jacked off many times remembering the feel of her hot, wet mouth surrounding him, taking him in, all the way to the back of her throat, until he exploded. And he did the same to her, licking and sucking her pussy and clit. He loved the way she responded, climbing the walls and screaming out when she came with his fingers pumping inside her, feeling how hot and wet she was and knowing how goddamn good it was going to be when he fucked her.

She kissed him, surged against him, her panties wet, moistening the crotch of his jeans. He gritted his teeth and buried his face against her neck, breathing in the sweet, cleansing innocence of her. The innocence he was about to take. He swept his hands over her ass and started to lift her skirt.

"I know. I've been waiting for this for so long. I've waited for you for so long, AJ. We're going to be together forever."

His hands stilled. *Forever.* God, he wanted that so much, could see himself with Teresa for the rest of his life. She was everything he'd ever wanted.

But that was him being selfish, wanting what was best for him—Teresa by his side. What about what was best for her? He'd just gotten hooked up with the south side crew stealing and chopping cars. He'd been lucky to get the gig. Great money, and soon enough he'd be out of his stepfather's reach. He could get his own place—a place for him and Teresa.

Yeah. She could live with a criminal. Great life for her. And what would her brother Joey—his best friend—say about that? Joey would kick his ass if he knew. And AJ would deserve it.

What did he really have to offer her? He could take her virginity, and then what? Invite her to shack up with a high school dropout who stole cars for a living? He was almost nineteen and going nowhere fast except down the road to hell.

He wouldn't take Teresa with him.

He smoothed her skirt down and lifted her off his lap, breathing in and out, slow and easy, trying to calm the hunger that pounded through his blood.

Teresa laid her hand on his arm. "AJ, what's wrong? Why did you stop?"

"Pull your clothes together, Teresa." He couldn't even look at her, at the ripe nipples showing through her bra, at her slim legs and thighs peeking out from under her short skirt. He only had so much self-control and he was no goddamned saint.

She adjusted her clothes and shimmied over to the other side of the seat, staring out the window.

He'd hurt her. That couldn't be helped.

"I'm sorry for whatever I did, AJ."

Her voice trembled. He glanced at her reflection in the side window and saw tears shimmering in her eyes.

Ah, shit.

"You didn't do anything wrong, Teresa. I did."

She shifted her glance to him, forcing him to see the pain and confusion on her face. He'd put it there. He was the worst kind of asshole imaginable.

"I shouldn't have started this tonight, shouldn't have brought you here."

Her fingers drifted up to skim across the necklace he'd gotten her. "Why not?"

"Because this can't work between us. Not anymore. I have . . . places to go and you can't go with me." He put the truck in gear and peeled out, heading back into town.

"I don't understand, AJ."

Her voice was the barest whisper, as if it took every ounce of energy in her body to speak. He'd crushed her. It was going to get worse before the night was over, because he was walking away from her. He was no good for her and he should have realized it before tonight. He wouldn't do this to her. Better to hurt her now than later. He knew what he wanted and where he wanted to go, and no way was he dragging her down with him. His freedom from his family meant sacrifice, and that sacrifice had to be Teresa.

Someday she'd understand and appreciate that he'd let her go.

It had started to cloud over. A storm was coming. He pressed down on the accelerator, hoping he could get Teresa back home before the shit hit the fan.

Losing her was going to kill him.

"Where?"

His gaze drifted to hers. Silvery tears slid down her cheeks. His stomach hurt. "Where what?"

"You said you had places to go that I couldn't go with you. What places?"

He inhaled and let it out, hurting so bad he thought he might be sick. But he was right to do this. He loved her.

"Dark places, Teresa. Really dark places. Places I have to go to alone."

one

"WE COULD BE WINDING THROUGH THE SMOKY MOUNTAINS BY now instead of sweating our asses off at a truck stop in the middle of nowherefuckingville, Missouri."

AJ arched a brow at his best friend, Pax. "This is my hometown you're insulting."

Pax shrugged. "It's still in the middle of fucking nowhere. And it's August. And it's goddamn hot here."

AJ laughed. "Quit whining. We were headed this direction anyway, and I thought we'd stop by and see a few people."

Pax sat on his Harley and took a swig of water, slanting AJ a dubious look. "And where did this sudden pang of homesickness come from? You're about as dedicated to home as I am. Your parents don't even live here anymore, do they?"

"No." Thankfully. AJ could maybe tolerate his mother. Maybe. But he'd mostly given up on her after she married Dale, the man who thought AJ wasn't good enough—for anything. And AJ had spent six years of his life proving Dale right. "My parents moved to New York to be near his family. But some of my friends might still be here."

"You had friends?" Pax arched a brow.

"Smart ass. Yeah, I had a few. A long time ago." People who cared about him no matter what, people he could count on. Like Joey. And Joey's sister, Teresa.

Though Teresa had been much more than a friend. But that wasn't what had brought him back here. It had been ten years since he left. By now, Teresa was probably married and had three kids or something. She'd gotten over him. It wasn't like she'd pine away for him or anything.

But he'd like to see Joey again. He and Joey used to be tight, had shared a lot of secrets—and a lot of trouble. They were close friends, kind of like AJ and Pax were now. AJ had never thought he'd make friends as an adult, had thought himself a badass loner who didn't need anyone. It had surprised the hell out of him when he and Pax clicked when they joined the Wild Riders. But they'd both had major chips on their shoulders, and maybe they both had been licking teenage wounds, too. Close enough in age, they gravitated toward each other and formed a bond that ten years later hadn't yet been broken.

They did everything together, even took off and vacationed together.

A vacation that had been a long time coming, and for AJ, vacation meant climbing on his Harley and riding. He had two weeks to do whatever the hell he wanted.

They'd taken off from Dallas—Wild Rider headquarters—after filing the paperwork on their last case with General Grange Lee, the man they reported to, the one who'd plucked all the Wild Riders from the dregs of their lives as troubled teens and turned them into decent human beings. If it hadn't been for General Lee, AJ would probably be pacing the confines of a prison cell at twenty-nine instead of living the free life and riding his bike. He had a lot to be grateful for. Grange had taken a half dozen raw, angry, messed up teenage criminals and turned them into capable under-cover agents who could slip into any street situation and get the job done. The Wild Riders blended well as a team, which was sur-prising considering their less than stellar backgrounds.

Grange had taught them combat the right way, which meant that every battle didn't have to end with someone dead. He'd taught them how to handle weapons, and he'd worked their asses off, mentally and physically, turning boys into men. When they were finished, they'd become sanctioned agents working for the United States government. Not a bad gig for AJ, who hadn't thought much of himself or his chances at the age of nineteen. He'd blown this small town, thinking he was on the losing end of his future, content to mix with the wrong crowd as long as the money was good and he got it in a hurry. He'd just wanted free-dom and cold, hard cash; he thought they were his ticket to the big time.

He'd been wrong. And maybe he was back to show a few people how wrong they'd been about him. Of course Dale wasn't around these parts anymore. Not that he cared what Dale thought. To his stepfather, no matter what AJ did, he'd never be good enough. And it wasn't like he could tell his family what he did for a living anyway. That was confidential. But maybe he wanted to check on a few people and see how they were doing.

He leaned against the bike, sucked down the last drop of water and tossed it into the nearby trash can, surveying the few cars that traveled the twenty-five-mile-an-hour speed limit down the main street of town. It was after eight P.M. on a Friday. And for a small town, that meant people out and about here in the suburbs, less than an hour's drive from St. Louis. Attractive to those who liked the quiet life, but close enough for those who wanted to work in the city. As small towns went, it was big enough to have a movie theater, a bowling alley and a mall, but small enough that everyone pretty much knew everyone else. He'd liked growing up here—mostly.

And when he'd left, he'd vowed he'd never come back. He wasn't sure what had led him this way when he and Pax decided to take a vacation.

"You ready to ride?" Pax asked. "I'm getting bored watching traffic go by. How about we hit a bar?"

AJ nodded. "I know just the place, if it's still open. It used to cater to bikers." They grabbed their helmets and climbed on their bikes, and AJ led the way out of the parking lot. They blended into traffic, two Harleys mixing in with minivans, SUVs and fuel-efficient commuter cars.

The town had grown in ten years, retail establishments popping up all over the formerly quiet side roads. AJ used to be able to count the retail as he rode by—the dry-cleaner's, hardware store and a single donut shop. Now there were strip malls filled with anything and everything from salons to the trendy coffee shops to big grocery stores. That signaled population growth, which AJ supposed was good for the people.

And speaking of people, there sure as hell seemed to be more of them now than there were ten years ago. Whereas before on a Friday night there might be five or six cars at the single stoplight on the main road in town, now he and Pax were shuffled behind a block of cars, sucking up exhaust while they waited through more stoplights than he could remember.

Progress. He wrinkled his nose at the changes in his hometown and goosed the throttle as they made it through the last stoplight on their way to the outskirts. Even here, new business had sprouted up. AJ doubted the bar still stood.

But as they rounded the bend in the road, he was surprised to see that not only was Greasy Rider still standing, it had grown. Where once had stood a one-room metal building with a tin roof, now there was a building three times its original size, in brick with a shingled roof and a neon sign.

And a full parking lot, loaded with bikes and cars.

They parked and Pax stepped over to AJ. "Pretty big place."

"Bigger than it used to be. When I was here last, it was a hole-in-the-wall shack."

Pax slapped him on the back. "Progress, my man. Everything either grows or dies."

"I guess." They headed toward the front door, where the sound of classic rock music blasted them as they opened it.

AJ blinked to adjust to the darkness in the bar. Smoke only added to his inability to see, along with the black leather uniform of the day.

This place was biker heaven, with wall-to-wall bikers lined up against the long bar, crowded around the half dozen pool tables and taking up seats in the TV area. Yeah, the bar had definitely expanded. Where the hell had all these bikers come from? When AJ had lived here, there were a handful of biker groups and gangs, and they'd all hung out at Greasy's on the weekends. But even when they were all there, the one-room place hadn't seemed congested.

He muscled his way past the crowd, thankful for a good working air conditioner.

"I'll get us some beers," Pax said. "Why don't you put us down for some time on a pool table?"

AJ nodded and headed toward the tables, the least crowded part of the bar. At least it was cooler over there. He put his quarter up behind three others, so they'd have to wait to play. In the meantime, he grabbed a couple of stools and took a seat, waiting for Pax to find him with their beers.

And then he waited a little longer, but still no sign of Pax. Knowing his friend, he'd found some chick to hit on. It never took Pax long to locate the women. He either zeroed in on them right away, or his good looks would attract them like a magnet. And since they often shared women, that worked to AJ's advantage, too, so it wasn't like he minded. And he sure as hell wouldn't mind a little female diversion tonight.

He stood and spotted Pax leaning against the bar, shook his head and smiled. Figured Pax would hit up a female bartender. By the end of the night they'd probably have free drinks and a bed partner. AJ headed over there and slid in between Pax and another guy, shoving his elbow in Pax's ribs.

"I'm dying of thirst over there while you're lining up a date," AJ complained.

Pax turned to him and passed a bottle of beer his way. "Not my fault this beautiful lady struck up a conversation with me."

AJ shook his head, grabbed the beer and turned to the bartender, prepared to work her just like Pax was doing.

The gut punch to his memories almost made him drop the bottle on the bar.

This was no stranger Pax had just hit on.

It was Teresa. Teresa Oliveri, the one person he'd really come here to see.

Ten years had changed her, and all for the better. Raven hair fell long and straight over her shoulders and settled over her generous breasts. Her eyes, still as green as emeralds, widened with the same shock and recognition.

They locked gazes, and time stood still. It was ten years ago, and everything they'd ever been together, what they'd done together, came rushing back in a blast of heated memories.

"AJ?" she asked, her voice unsure and tentative, as if she couldn't really believe it was him.

He nodded, realizing now what an epically fucked-up idea it had been to come back home. "Teresa."

He couldn't take his eyes off her. She had been a beautiful girl at eighteen. Ten years later, she was a stunning woman, the kind of woman men follow with their eyes. Tan, tall, in blue jeans and a midriff-baring top that hugged her breasts, revealed a flat belly and narrow waist, and showed off slim hips and long legs. Three silver earrings dotted each ear, and a piercing sparkled in her belly button.

That was all he had time to see, because she backed away.

"I have customers, guys. I'll be right back." Her gaze lingered on his for a second, then she turned to grab some beers out of the ice, bending over to show a tattoo—a tramp stamp on her lower back—a heart, with a dagger through it and blood dripping off the end. And holy shit she still had one fine ass, one that had aged well over the past ten years.

She moved down the bar with beers in hand, and AJ finally blinked.

"Teresa? *The* Teresa? That's your Teresa, the one you told me about?" Pax asked, leaning over the bar to follow her with his gaze.

"Yeah."

"Dude. You're fucking insane for ever leaving that woman. She's the hottest thing this side of the Red River. Or the Mississippi River. Or any river."

AJ slumped onto the bar stool and took a long swallow of beer to coat his now parched throat. "It seemed like a good idea at the time." He'd had a lot of reasons for leaving her, the least of which was his stepfather. He'd had enough and had to get away from the life he'd been leading. Leaving Teresa had been part of it.

So why the hell had he come back? To kick himself in the gut again and remind himself of all the things he could never have?

"What brings you back to town, AJ?"

Pax kicked him, and AJ lifted his head. Teresa cast inquisitive eyes at him, seemingly friendly and open, but the spark that used to lift him up was gone.

He'd wanted her like he'd never wanted a woman since. But he'd never had her. He'd been proud of himself for turning down the one thing he wanted more than anything else. Why taint her with everything that was bad about him?

God, he'd hurt her. Even now he wanted to fold her in his arms and tell her how sorry he was for walking away from her, from what they could have had together.

But what could they have had?

Nothing. Not then.

And not now.

He shrugged. "Pax and I are doing some riding. We happened to be coming this way so thought I'd ride through and see if anything had changed. I see Greasy's has."

She grinned and put her hands on her hips. "You like it?"

He saw the pride in her eyes. "You own this place?"

"Sure do. Todd got sick about five years ago. I was working for him then, and he said he was going to have to close up. We'd grown so much by then, bikers were crowded in here like sardines. No way was I going to let someone else take all that business, so I got a loan and bought the bar. Made a few changes, things kept going well, so we ended up remodeling last year."

"You've done a great job with it, Teresa. It looks great."

"Thanks." She popped open two more beers and slid them to the guy who'd moved in next to Pax, took the guy's money and made change, smiling at her customer as if he was the only man in the room. No wonder bikers piled in here. Who wouldn't to spend time with Teresa?

But as she moved on to help another customer, AJ finally

opened his eyes to see a couple more bartenders step in. Both women, young and beautiful, wearing tight jeans, cowboy boots and midriff-baring tops. And with great bodies, just like Teresa.

Teresa had always been smart. She had a good thing going here. Bikers with their girlfriends or by themselves having a good time on a Friday night. Music blaring, pool playing, sports on the various TVs set up in the corners, and plenty of drinks flowing. He took a pull of his beer and watched the women work the bar. They smiled at the guys, took no shit from them, in fact threw it right back at them, shoving them and hurling insults at them when they got too close. The men loved it.

Of course they did. Men loved a strong, take-no-shit kind of woman, the kind who could hold her own. She was the best type of biker babe, and those were the types of women men like these guys fantasized about.

Come to think of it, who the hell were all these guys?

"Seems like a pretty small town for all these bikers," Pax said as he leaned against the bar and surveyed everything around him.

"I was just thinking the same thing. Greasy's used to get maybe a half dozen, dozen at most on the weekends." There had to be thirty or forty bikers in the bar right now, and it was still early for a Friday. "I have no idea where they come from."

"We've grown," Teresa offered, obviously overhearing them talk. She kept her voice low and leaned toward them, which made Pax and AJ move in to hear her. "Joey is managing a club on the south side here."

AJ's brows lifted. "Joey leads a club now?"

"Yeah," she said, laughing. "Hard to believe, but he started riding with the Thorns not too long after you . . . left." She let the word trail off. "Anyway, he's been with them ever since, moving his way up as the group expanded. Now he leads the south side."

"And what about the north side?"

She wrinkled her nose. "The Fists. Tough gang. Into some bad shit."

"Like?" AJ asked.

"They're running drugs on the north side. I don't like serving them when they slide into the territory here, but not much I can do about it since their money is as good as anyone else's. They're looking to take over the Thorns."

"Why?" Pax asked.

"They want territory expansion and they don't make any secret of it. It's gotten ugly a few times, but the Thorns try to keep things clean, so the cops have stepped in to keep it cool between the clubs."

"Here?" AJ didn't like the sound of this, or that Teresa was in the middle of it.

"Yeah."

"Not a good position for you."

She grabbed a cloth and wiped up the bar, her green eyes intense as they met his. "I can take care of myself. Been doing it for a long time, AJ."

"I'm sure you can. But what happens when a Fist pulls a knife on you?"

She grabbed his wrist and pulled up on his thumb. AJ winced as she lifted just to the point of pain, just to get his attention. Her hold was firm and strong as she hit all the right pressure points, like someone who'd been well trained. AJ knew a countermove that would lay her flat, but he sure as hell wasn't going to use it on her. She'd made her point. What she knew would take down someone who wasn't trained.

She let go and AJ shook his hand.

Pax laughed. "I guess you *can* take care of yourself, can't you?"

She nodded. "Damn straight."

"Ow."

Teresa rolled her eyes. "Pussy. I didn't hurt you. But I could have if I wanted to."

"I believe you. When did you become a tough girl?"

"When I bought the bar. I was dating one of the local cops who taught me some self-defense maneuvers. They come in handy."

"So do their handcuffs, when used in the right situation." Pax waggled his brows and Teresa laughed.

"Yeah, those can be handy, too."

AJ did *not* want to hear about Teresa dating one of the local cops, or what they did with handcuffs. This whole thing was surreal. She had definitely changed. Grown up. Become a woman. With some other guy, who'd had what he could have had.

Fuck.

"Son of a bitch. AJ Dunn. I thought you were dead or in prison."

AJ flipped around on the bar stool, then slid off and enveloped Teresa's brother Joey in a bear hug. "You asshole. I thought the same about you. I even brought flowers for your grave."

Joey Oliveri took a step back and smirked. "Prick. What the hell are you doing here?"

"Riding through. Teresa's been filling me in on what's been going on around here since I've been gone. I hear you've done well."

"Yeah. Pretty good."

"This is my friend Pax. Pax, this is my former best friend Joey."

Joey snorted and shook Pax's hand. "Any friend of AJ's should have his head examined."

Pax laughed. "I hear you. But somebody has to look after him. Nice to meet you."

"You've gained weight," AJ said, looking over Joey's stomach. "Too much pasta?"

"You know how Italians are. We can't resist spaghetti."

"Doesn't seem to have affected Teresa any."

"She burns off calories working this bar. Me, I just sit on my ass and drink beer and ride." Joey patted his protruding belly.

Joey and Teresa were twins, though you couldn't tell it by looking at them. Same hair and eye color, and that's where the similarities ended. Where Teresa was slender, Joey was filled out all over, and not all of it was muscle. But then again he'd always been a little on the heavy side, and the guy liked his beer.

"So what is this I hear about you leading a club?"

Joey grinned. "Yeah. Imagine that, me at the head of the Thorns. Pretty cool, huh?"

"It is. Teresa told me you have some trouble with a rival gang."

Joey narrowed his gaze. "Yeah. The Fists are in our business, trying to take over our territory."

"Why?"

"Because they're dirty motherfucking drug runners and they want some of the action here."

AJ stilled. "You aren't . . ."

"Nah. No illegal stuff here. We keep it clean and have a good relationship with the law. But our presence keeps the Fists from gaining control in this part of the county, and they see it as a prime opportunity to expand their drug distribution operation. Plus we're situated near the river, which is good for shipping. We have the best territory and the Fists know it. They've wanted it for a while now, but they're not going to get it as long as the Thorns are here."

AJ didn't like the way that sounded. "You need to be careful. Some of these gangs will stop at nothing to get what they want."

Joey nudged AJ on the arm. "I'm not a moron. I've got it covered."

"You and your guys armed?"

Joey nodded. "We'll use 'em if we have to. We protect what's ours."

Pax slanted his gaze at AJ, a look of concern of his face.

Yeah, AJ knew. In their line of work with the Wild Riders they'd infiltrated plenty of gangs looking to distribute anything from drugs to guns. And once these gangs wanted something, they'd let nothing stop them, including people.

"So what are you up to these days, AJ?"

AJ slid his gaze to Pax, then back to Joey and shrugged. "Nothing much. Odd jobs here and there. Pax and I just ride."

"Yeah? Thinking about settling back here in town again?"

AJ noticed Teresa watching him intently. "No. Just passing through."

Teresa averted her gaze and moved down the bar. AJ wondered what her life was like now. Was she married? Did she have kids?

"Teresa's done well. I can't believe she bought this place."

Joey grinned. "Yeah. She's always been damn smart. Smarter than me, that's for sure. When Todd got out, she stepped in and scooped this place up, cleaned it up, hired the sexy bartenders, and bikers started coming in here by the hundreds. She made enough money to expand and it's still going strong."

"Yeah, I can see that." He hesitated, but something drove him to know. "She ever settle down and get married, have any rug rats?"

"You want to know about my personal life, AJ, why don't you ask me directly?"

AJ did a half turn on the bar stool to face Teresa, hadn't realized she'd moved back into earshot again. Shit. "Just wanted to make sure you were doing okay."

"I've always been okay. Since the day you left ten years ago, I've been just fine. I didn't need you then and I don't need you now, so you can quit worrying about me."

TWO

Teresa wanted to wince, to take back what she'd just said. She'd wanted to be cool and calm and unaffected by AJ, not take a bite out of him with her words. She'd wanted him to see her as a success, a woman who met life on her own terms, a woman who didn't need a man—especially him—to be happy. Because, dammit, she *was* happy. Most days.

She'd never expected to see AJ again, figured when he left town all those years ago that was it, the end. When she looked up to see him at her bar tonight, her heart had done a flip-flop, her pulse double-timing it so fast she'd gotten dizzy. For years after he'd left she'd imagined what it would be like if she ever saw him again, had played the scenario over and over again in her mind. And each year that went by she thought of him less and less, until finally he'd disappeared from her thoughts. He was the past and he was supposed to stay there. Until tonight, when he showed up again, and everything they'd ever been to each other came rushing back, bringing with it a tidal wave of emotion.

But she could handle it. She wasn't eighteen anymore and a lot had happened in the ten years since they'd last seen each other. What they'd meant to each other back then meant nothing now. She could smile and be nice to him and eventually he'd leave and everything would go back to the way it was.

She'd been doing just fine until she overheard AJ asking Joey about her, asking if she'd ever gotten married or had kids. Pain had ripped her inside and out, just like it always did when someone mentioned marriage and children, normal things a woman her age should be experiencing. Except there was nothing normal about her life. It brought back memories she fought hard to keep buried.

She pinned AJ with a hard stare, making it clear she didn't appreciate the end run.

"Sorry," AJ said. "I was just curious."

"Not married. No kids. Satisfy your curiosity?"

He didn't answer, just looked at her with sadness and regret in his storm gray eyes. She didn't want his regrets, didn't want to remember how simple and beautiful her life had been when he'd been in it, and how ugly it had gotten after he'd left.

"I didn't mean to pry. It's been a long time, Teresa. You look good."

"She looks better than good," Pax said, focusing a smile on Teresa. "She's damn fine."

Tingles skittered up her spine at the way AJ's friend Pax looked at her. It had been a long time since she'd felt . . . anything. Pax didn't know her past, didn't know what had happened to her. He didn't have preconceived notions, so he couldn't have pity or remorse or revulsion. He just saw her as a woman. A desirable woman. She liked that look in his dark eyes. She liked the way he looked, period, with his spiked dark blond hair and his chiseled features and goatee. He was every inch a rugged, sexy biker. Who didn't know a damn thing about her.

She winked at him, surprised to feel a little rusty in the flirting department. She flirted with her customers all the time, but that was meaningless. This . . . wasn't. It felt like an awakening, which shocked her. "Thanks for the compliment."

"I'll bet you get them all the time."

"I might. But I don't necessarily pay attention to all of them. Or any of them."

"Can't say I'm unhappy to hear that, as long as you pay attention to me." Pax's gaze was intense. A woman could get lost in those whiskey-colored eyes. He could very well make a woman believe she was the only one for him.

"He's full of shit, you know."

Her gaze skirted to AJ, then back to Pax, and she lifted her lips. "I don't doubt that for a second."

"I'm crushed," Pax said. "And AJ lies."

"I don't doubt that, either. And I can already tell you two are dangerous together."

"Darlin', you have no idea." Pax picked up her hand and electricity sizzled up her arm. He pressed a soft kiss to the back of her wrist, then folded her hand between both of his very large ones.

Her belly fluttered, and that long-dormant area between her thighs sprang to life and dampened.

I'll be damned. She might not be dead down there after all. That was the first honest sexual response she'd had since . . .

She slid her hand from Pax's. "I have work, and playing with you boys isn't on my list of things to do."

"We're not going anywhere," AJ said.

That was too bad. Having AJ back in town was bad enough. Even worse would be dredging up memories of what she'd once had . . . what they'd once had. Having Pax with him was a double whammy of testosterone and chemistry that had slammed into her and gotten her attention despite running around tending to her customers and taking care of business.

And if it happened while she was 90 percent distracted, what would happen if she gave them her undivided attention?

Scary. And interesting, too. She really hoped they'd decide to hightail it out of town before her turn on top of the bar tonight.

PAX WATCHED TERESA TEND BAR. SHE SEEMED TO ENJOY HER customers, gave them her attention, laughed with the other bartenders.

That laugh—wow. It was full-on throaty and loud, as if she enjoyed life. And Pax liked a woman with passion.

But there was also something guarded about her, a shadow that crossed over her face in the midst of those happy moments, after she turned away and she thought no one was looking. Pax was always looking. He didn't know what had put that shadow on her face. Maybe AJ had.

And maybe it was none of his goddamn business. They were just passing through. Teresa was part of AJ's past, not part of their future. Playing with and sharing women was a fun way to pass the time for Pax and AJ, but Pax didn't think this woman would be one AJ would want to share.

But Pax sure would. Her first smile had struck the match and lit his fire. Too bad she was AJ's old flame, the one he'd told Pax about, the one woman AJ'd had real feelings for.

And AJ didn't get "feelings" for women any more than Pax did. He liked them and respected them just fine, treated them all good. They both did. But loving them? Pax didn't do the love thing. He enjoyed his freewheeling lifestyle way too much to fall in love with one woman. Not when there were so many women available. Monogamy just wasn't his style, which was probably why he enjoyed sharing women with AJ. Less likely to fall in love with someone—or have a woman think you were going to go one-on-one with her—if you were doing two-on-one.

But he wasn't going to get to do two-on-one with Teresa, so he settled against the bar and just watched her, his gaze flitting to the two other bartenders. They were fine, too. One with short brown hair and a full curvy body, the other a curly headed blonde with big tits and a low-cut shirt that clung to those babies like she was damn proud of them. The blonde gave Pax the once-over . . . more than once.

But Pax's attention kept moving to Teresa, watching her work the bar, her brows knit in concentration as she poured shots or popped open the tops of beer bottles. She laughed with her customers, was good-natured about it when she had to push away guys who got too close, moved in a rhythm that said she was comfortable with who she was. And okay, he liked watching her hips move, the easy way she swayed across the floor. He liked her ass and the sweet spot where her jeans met the skin of her lower back, that pretty tattoo there where he'd like to press his lips.

His jeans tightened as his cock twitched to life.

Down, boy. He took a long cold swig of beer to douse the heat.

"Don't even think about it, man. We're not going there."

He slid his glance over to AJ and grinned. "I know we're not going there. But I'm still going to think about it."

"Yeah," AJ said, shifting his attention to Teresa. "Me, too. But too much history there. It wouldn't work."

"Too bad. Because she is sweet."

"That's the problem. Too sweet for you and me."

Just then the sounds of women squealing and men hollering,

clapping and catcalling drove Pax's attention to the bar, where the beer bottles were being cleared from one end to the other. A new song came up, something sexy with a hard rocking beat, and the blonde climbed up onto the cleared-off bar top and sauntered down to the end, swiveling her hips to the music. As soon as the beat picked up, she headed their way.

The bar soon crowded in with guys pressing up to see the blonde dance in her cutoff denim shorts and cowboy boots, her feet stomping on the scarred wood. She shimmied down to a squatting position, then back up again.

The girl could move her ass. She moved from one end of that bar to another, leaving dragging tongues in her wake as she slid those tanned legs out and shook her ass in front of some hungry faces. Then she jumped off the bar.

And Teresa jumped up.

Though the music was deafening and the noise of the other bikers clapping and shouting around them drowned out just about everything, Pax was sure he could hear AJ's hard swallow as Teresa made her way down to the other end of the bar.

"Oh, shit," AJ whispered, his voice hoarse.

Pax just grinned and enjoyed the show. Where the blonde used her sexuality as a lure, Teresa was more natural when she moved, like she felt the music inside her. She didn't play to the crowd, but kept her focus straight ahead as she swept her hips from side to side, knocked her boots hard on the bar, and stormed her way toward Pax and AJ.

It was only when she got to them that she tilted her chin and looked down, a wicked smile on her face. Pax looked up and grinned at her, letting her know that he liked the show just fine. He'd like to feel her moving against him like that, wanted to feel her hips sway from side to side while he held her against his throbbing cock.

AJ tilted his head back and stared, his expression unreadable.

Teresa cocked a brow, kicked up her heels and shimmied down the bar, lifting her arms over her head and turning her back on the crowd, sliding her ass down to meet the heels of her boots, then jumping off the bar to let the brunette take over and finish the song.

"Damn" was all AJ said as he kept his gaze glued on Teresa. "Never seen her do anything like that before."

"She was a kid when you left here before. She isn't now. Lots of things change when you're gone for ten years."

THREE

ALL AJ WANTED TO DO WAS FIND OUT EVERYTHING TERESA HAD been doing in the ten years he'd been gone. Everything about her was different, from the way she looked to the way she talked to the way she danced to her expressions and demeanor.

Did he seem that different to her? He wanted to ask her. But what did it matter? He and Pax weren't staying. He wasn't taking up with her again, couldn't. He and Pax had places to go after their vacation was over, and that didn't include coming back home and settling in with Teresa, who hadn't made any moves in his direction anyway. She'd been friendly, but wary, just like she would be with any customer.

And what had he expected—for her to scream and cry with joy because he'd finally returned, then throw herself in his arms and declare her undying love?

Yeah, right. Nice fantasy, but what he wanted and what he was going to get were two different things.

Story of his life.

He and Pax finally shoved away from the bar and played pool with Joey and Russ, Joey's good friend and the second in command of the Thorns. AJ had known Russ when they were younger, too. Good to see he'd stood by Joey all these years. Russ hadn't changed much since high school, either, though he was the polar opposite of Joey. Where Joey was short and round, Russ was tall and rail thin, with freckles on his face and his hair a mixture of strawberry blond and brown. Russ still looked like a kid even though he was pushing thirty.

Pax sank the last ball, and AJ grinned at Joey. "You still suck at pool."

Russ snickered and patted AJ on the back. "Some things never change, do they, AJ?"

Joey glared. "I don't suck at pool. Obviously you and your friend have careers as hustlers. And since you and Pax won all our money, you can buy the next round of beers."

AJ laughed and bought beer. Having a pool table at Wild Riders headquarters meant they got a lot of practice. And AJ was pretty sure Pax had hustled pool when he was younger, though Pax denied it. Probably so he could win every time they played.

"Is that how you guys earn a living, sharking us poor unfortunates?" Joey asked as they sat at one of the tables eating pretzels and drinking beer.

Pax raised his brows and, with a smile, tipped the bottle of beer to his lips.

"I thought so."

"And how about you, Joey?" AJ asked. "What are you doing these days?"

"I own that garage down on the corner of Munich and Davis. Russ and a few of the other guys who ride with us work there, too."

"I can't believe you're still at Smitty's Garage. That was the first place you hired on when you were a punk."

"Yeah, and now I own it. So who's the punk?" Joey laughed.

"Did you change the name to Oliveri's?"

"Nah. Everyone around knew it as Smitty's, so I figured I'd leave it. Good for the old-timers who might not take to something different."

"See, and I always thought you were dumb," AJ teased.

"Har har." But Joey laughed and downed the rest of his beer, frowning as he laid it on the table. Russ stood and moved to Joey's side.

AJ turned in the direction of Joey's frown. The door to the bar had opened and a horde of bikers spilled in, all decked out in leathers, the backs of their jackets bearing a fist crushing a bleeding heart.

"Fists, I presume?" Pax asked.

"Yeah. And they don't belong here." Joey kicked back his chair and stood. Russ followed, and they were flanked immediately by two beefy members of their gang. The rest of the Thorns moved with them toward the front of the bar.

The tension in the entire place thickened so deep you had to wade through it. It emanated off everyone wearing leather. You could see it on all their faces, bikers gearing up for battle. AJ looked to Pax, who nodded. They stood and moved behind the crowd of bikers. AJ slid his hand up under his jacket, reached into the back waistband of his jeans, and released the safety on his pistol, saw Pax do the same. They might be on vacation and always undercover, but they were still federal agents. If shit was going to go down, they had to put a stop to it. Or at least put a well-timed call in to the local police. He hoped this would be nothing more than a standoff and that it would just blow over. Or maybe just hand-to-hand combat, not knives and guns.

Teresa didn't need a brawl in her bar. AJ took a sidelong glance at her. She and the other bartenders stayed behind the bar, but

Teresa had placed both hands, palms down and fingers wide, on
the bar, her jaw set firmly. AJ made a move back with his head, and
Pax took a look at Teresa, then back at him.

She looked mad as hell. The one thing they'd learned working cases for the Wild Riders was to watch out for someone with
a hair-trigger temper, and the tension in Teresa's locked arms and
the tight set to her jaw gave AJ the impression she might climb
right over the top of that bar and go after those guys.

"That's not good," Pax whispered.

"No, it's not." AJ skirted in front of Teresa, and Pax followed, making sure the both of them covered the women behind
the bar.

He half turned to Teresa. "Relax. It's going to be all right."

Teresa's focus stayed on the action at the front of the bar, but
she gave him a curt nod, effectively dismissing him.

"Get out, Larks, and take your Fists with you," was all Joey
said to the guy standing at the front of the Fists.

Larks must be the leader of their gang, AJ presumed. He was
broad, not as tall as the two guys flanking him, but he looked like
one mean son of a bitch. He sported a long, white scar up the side
of his left cheek, and except for a few strands of dark, stringy hair,
his head was covered by an all black do-rag. His leather jacket was
thick and only added to the guy's imposing look. The guy had
thighs like tree trunks and big beefy hands. All in all, he looked
like a whole lot of trouble.

"Now, Joey," Larks said, smiling. "As far as I know this is a
public bar. You can't keep us out of here. We're taking a little road
trip this weekend and just stopped in for a quick drink."

"We don't want you in here. *I* don't want you in here mixing
it up with my guys."

"You lookin' for a fight?"

"No."

"Neither are we. Just came in for a beer, then we're on our way."

"There are a lot of other places you can get your beer. Take a hike."

Larks took a step forward. So did Joey.

"Just let it go, Joey," Teresa said from behind the bar. "We'll give them their drinks and they can leave."

AJ turned to Teresa and could feel the anger vibrating off of her, could see it in the upward tilt of her chin, the way she never once took her eyes off Larks or his men. The last thing he wanted was for her to end up in the middle of a gang brawl.

"I don't think so," Joey said.

"Leave it alone, Joey. I mean it. Let's just get this over with."

"Now see? That's what I'm talkin' about. This lady knows how to be hospitable. Besides, we're paying customers and she knows it."

Larks took a step forward. Joey didn't budge. AJ tensed, waiting for it, ready for whatever happened next.

But then Joey stepped aside, and so did his men, opening a path for Larks and his gang to walk through toward the bar. AJ was disinclined to get the hell out of his way. He and Pax stayed rooted to their bar stools, nursing their beers. Larks looked them up and down.

"Who are you?" he asked.

"Who are *you*?" Pax shot back, offering up a lazy glance to Larks.

"You aren't part of the Thorns."

"No, we aren't," AJ said.

"Then get the fuck out of my way."

AJ gave him a lopsided grin. "I don't think so, man. Get your own fucking bar stool." AJ motioned down the row of empty stools to his right. "These are taken."

"You lookin' for a fight?"

"No. I'm lookin' to sit my ass right where it is and drink my beer. So stay the hell out of my space."

He stared Larks in the eye, making sure the guy understood that AJ and Pax didn't want any trouble, but if Larks intended to serve it up, they'd be more than happy to oblige.

Larks shrugged. "Shoot me a cold one, sweet tits," he said to Teresa as he moved a couple feet down the bar and slid onto the stool.

AJ sucked in a deep breath at the insult to Teresa, who started popping the tops off bottles of beer and sliding them onto the bar. She didn't even flinch making eye contact with Larks and his men who sidled up to the bar to grab the bottles. Larks threw money in front of her. "Keep the change, honey."

"Thanks." She moved to the cash register and put the money in, then turned back to face the bikers.

She was pleasant enough, but she was mad as hell.

Did she have some kind of relationship with Larks?

"What's got her so riled up?" Pax asked, clearly noticing it, too.

"I have no idea." He held up his fingers, and Teresa brought them a couple more beers. When he held out the money and she went to take it, AJ slid his hand over hers.

"Are you all right?"

"I'm fine."

Yeah right. She'd barely got the words out through gritted teeth.

"Let's go outside and talk."

Her eyes widened. "Are you insane? Not with them here. I can't leave my girls alone."

He nodded. "Okay. Later then."

"Fine."

She jerked her hand from his and walked away, her gaze never leaving the Fists.

Yeah, something bothered her. Something bothered her in a big way.

AJ wanted to know what it was.

ANGER CLUTCHED TERESA BY THE THROAT, THREATENING TO CUT off her air supply. Sweat poured between her breasts and down her back. She leaned against the front of the bar where she kept the ice, hoping the frigid rising air would cool her off and help calm the adrenaline-fueled urge to take a baseball bat to the bastards who dared threaten her brother as well as her livelihood.

Those scum-sucking sons of bitches knew better than to stroll into her bar. Everything about them threatened her, her girls and what she did for a living. And if that wasn't bad enough, she'd never gotten over the thought that any them could be the ones. She had no proof, they'd never been found, but still, something in her gut said it was the Fists. And she refused to cower in front of them, stared them all down as if daring one of them to say something, to just look at her the wrong way, just once.

She gripped the edge of the bar and waited, sensing impending disaster, refusing to ever again feel powerless. She had the gun tucked away where only she could find it. And she'd damn well use it if she had to.

"Teresa. You okay?"

Her gaze shot to Heather, one of her bartenders. She forced her shoulders to drop and sucked in a breath, then let it out. "I'm fine, Heather. Thanks." She plastered on a smile and patted Heather on the shoulder.

"These guys give me the creeps," Heather said, her back turned to the Fists crowding the bar.

"I know, honey. They'll be gone soon."

"I'm not getting up on the bar and dancing."

"No worries. You don't have to. And neither does Shelley. We'll serve them beer and that's it. Hopefully they'll make their point and leave soon."

"Hey, sweet tits, how about another?"

Larks waved his empty beer bottle in the air.

Teresa wanted to take that bottle and shove it up his ass, but she grabbed a beer and slid it across the bar to him, took his empty and his money and stared him down, daring him to start something.

"You're not very friendly for a bartender. You got something against the Fists?"

As if he didn't know exactly what she had against his gang. Guys like him and his gang who thought they could do anything, that they were above the law. Just like the ones who . . .

"Is there something else you need?" she asked.

"Well, now that you mention it . . ."

"Back off, Larks. You came here for beer, fine. Leave my sister alone."

Please, Joey. Don't start anything. Let them drink and get out of here.

"I think your sister is plenty old enough to take care of herself, aren't you, sweet tits?"

He was baiting her with his insults and she knew it, refused to answer him.

"Are you trying to cause trouble in here, asshole? Because if you are, there are plenty of guys willing to give it to you. Leave the lady alone."

Pax stood and leaned toward Larks, obviously pissed off and ready to do battle.

He didn't know, didn't understand. The last thing Teresa wanted was to start a war between these gangs because of her.

"Pax. It's okay."

Pax kept his focus on Larks. "It's not okay."

Larks must have realized that Pax would be backed up by Joey and the Thorns, because he held up his hands. "Hey, not looking for trouble here. Just want to drink my beer."

"Then drink it and leave," AJ said, moving next to Pax. "I don't think you're that stupid. You have to know no one wants you here."

Larks made a show of heaving a great big sigh. "I guess you're right. Come on, guys, let's go. We know when we're not wanted."

Right. Like they didn't know that the minute they stepped through the door. Teresa didn't care though, because the Fists were leaving, as was the tight band squeezing her chest. She exhaled a breath of relief when the door closed behind them.

"That's done," she whispered to herself.

"Now. You need a break, and we're going to talk."

She hadn't realized when AJ had stepped behind the bar with her, or even that he had. He linked his fingers with hers.

"Okay." She could use some air, even if it was August and the heat and humidity were brutal. "Heather, I'm taking a few minutes."

"No problem," Heather said, waving to her as she carried an armload of beers and started passing them to the customers, obviously as relieved to see the Fists gone as Teresa was.

Teresa followed AJ, and on the other side of the bar they met up with Pax, who apparently was going with them.

"Let's go out the back. There's a table and some chairs there. The smoke hole for the other girls."

She led them through the back door and into the sweltering

heat. There was an old picnic table and a few aluminum chairs out there. Teresa slid into one of the chairs and let the tension drain from her body. It was over. Nothing had happened. It wasn't ever going to happen. Not again.

"You want to tell me what upset you in there?" AJ asked.

"The Fists and the Thorns have a rivalry going for territory and it's getting pretty intense. I worry for Joey and the guys. Plus they were in my goddamned bar. Did you want me to be happy about that?"

"You were tense as hell."

She shrugged. "Who wouldn't be, AJ? I don't want to fight and don't want to be in the middle of a fight. And I don't want my bar wrecked."

"It was more than that."

She turned her gaze to Pax. "Like I said, the whole thing that went down in there pissed me off. They have no right to be here and just wanted to cause shit. I wanted them to leave. Joey being the leader of the Thorns puts him in a dangerous position. I was worried for him."

"Are you sure there's nothing else?"

Okay, enough was enough. She stood. "Who the hell do you two think you are?" Her gaze shot to AJ. "You've been gone ten years and you pop in here for an hour and suddenly you're worried about me? You lost that right the night you dumped me and left town." She shifted her tirade to Pax. "And you don't even know me. I can take care of myself. I'm fine. Both of you leave me the hell alone."

She started toward the door and AJ stopped her. "You're right. We are just passing through. But you're still someone I care about, Teresa."

"You walked away easily enough ten years ago, didn't you?"

She wanted to bite it back as soon as she'd said it, but it was too late. The words were out and she couldn't take them back.

"Ten years ago I was a messed-up kid who didn't know what he wanted."

She laid her hands on her hips. "And now you do?"

"I didn't say that."

She laughed. "I need to go back inside." She pushed past both of them and toward the back door, but Pax moved in front of her.

"Hey. I don't know you at all, but I know trouble when I see it. If you need help, we're here for you."

His body was so . . . big, covering the door frame. He should have intimidated her, frightened her. Reminded her of things all too unpleasant.

But he didn't, because he had his hand on the doorknob, turning it to open it for her, not to stop her.

She gave him a curt nod. "I've got a handle on it."

The air-conditioning inside cooled her off. She felt bad for going off on them, but she didn't need their concern. She didn't need them at all. She didn't want a man looking out for her. It was bad enough Joey practically shadowed her every move. She didn't need AJ and Pax worrying over her, too.

Pax and AJ came in a few minutes after she did. Instead of coming back to the bar, they moved off to find Joey and Russ. They huddled around one of the tables at the back, whispering together, no doubt about the Fists and what had happened. Teresa went back to work, relieved that it was all over.

She expected Pax and AJ to hit the road as it got later in the evening, but they didn't. Weren't they headed off somewhere? Why hadn't they left yet? They'd stayed, played more pool with Joey and Russ, left only long enough to run out to grab something to eat with Joey and a few of the other guys, but then they had come back and now seemed to be having a great time hanging out.

She didn't want them here. Having AJ around . . . and Pax, too . . . made her uncomfortable.

But not uncomfortable in the usual way guys made her uncomfortable.

This was different. AJ was part of her past, the part when she was still interested in men . . . that way. And Pax was just way too much testosterone for her to handle.

They needed to go.

She wasn't ready to dredge up old history . . . or start new.

She just wanted everything in her life to remain as it was right now. She was content, if not happy. And considering how bad things had been a few years ago, content was a damned decent place to be.

A quick glance at the clock told her it was about fifteen minutes to closing time, which suited her just fine. Time to get everyone out of here so she and the girls could clean up and she could close and get home, lock herself in, take a shower and climb into bed, where she could pass out and hopefully fall into a dreamless sleep.

Tomorrow AJ and Pax would be gone and life would be back to normal.

She liked normal.

Aside from AJ and Pax, there were only a handful of people left, all Joey's guys. She knew she could shuffle them out easily enough, so she sent Heather and Shelley home. Hopefully by two she'd be out of there, too.

She had her back turned to the bar and had just finished drying the last glass, about to tell Joey to move his guys out the door, when the front door opened.

"Hey, we're closing," she hollered as she turned around, hitting the main switch to shut off the music.

Dread sent her body into instant tense mode. It was Larks walking through the door, with more than a dozen of his guys.

"We're closed," she said again.

Larks ignored her, making a beeline for Joey, his intention clear on his determined face. He was smiling, but it wasn't a friendly smile. The last guy through the door flipped the lock closed.

Shit.

Her gaze riveted on Joey and Larks, she reached for the phone, intending to dial 911. She yelped when someone grabbed her wrist and jerked the phone from her hand, tossing it across the room.

"No calling the cops, sweet tits. This is private business."

As he moved away with her phone in his hand, Teresa swallowed past the terror threatening to squeeze her throat closed.

This was not going to happen. Not in her bar.

But as Larks jumped on Joey and all hell broke loose, she knew it already had.

FOUR

AJ AND PAX HAD BEEN IN BAR BRAWLS BEFORE. AJ KNEW THEY could handle themselves. Biker gangs often got into tiffs over territory. This wouldn't be a first. And since they were here, they were going to get into the middle of it.

The middle of it happened fast, because Larks's guys were in the door throwing the first punches before any of Joey's guys could even blink. Joey and Russ and the others pushed right back. It didn't take but a fraction of a second before Joey and Larks went at each other. Suddenly the shit was going down. There'd be no talking them out of it now. There was no way AJ and Pax could stay out of it, either, and it was a given they were going to take Joey's side, especially since the Thorns were outnumbered two to one, since most of Joey's gang had already left for the night.

AJ pulled a guy off Joey's back so he could be free to fight Larks.

Man, he didn't want to be doing this, but they had no choice. Bringing the cops in would just put the Thorns in trouble, too, and AJ didn't want that—not if they could put an end to this fast. He threw a punch and ducked as one came flying his way. He missed seeing a fist flying from his left, though, and took one to the chin. He winced and shook his head to clear the pounding. Son of a bitch, that hurt.

But he had to admit, fighting exhilarated him. It had been a long time since he'd gotten into a fistfight, and it felt damn good. AJ caught sight of Pax, who had hold of two guys. Pax was good with martial arts. When they'd learned it at Wild Riders, Pax dove in and earned his black belt, which he was putting to good use here by kicking the shit out of a guy. He swiveled and knocked the dude behind him in the back with a hard shove from his boot. The guy crumpled, the wind knocked out of him. Pax knew not to give a lethal kick unless his or someone else's life was threatened. The idea was to defuse the situation.

AJ knew Pax could take care of himself.

But the Thorns were outnumbered and the situation was not anywhere close to being defused. If anything it was getting worse. Bodies were everywhere in tight piles, fists flying.

AJ's gaze skirted to the bar. Unfortunately, Teresa was stuck behind it. He couldn't tell if she was scared or not, but she wasn't moving. Her exit was blocked with fighting at either end, so she couldn't get out of there, but he'd make sure no one touched her.

He made eye contact with her, signaled her to stay where she was. She nodded. Then someone landed a punch to his back and he winced, his kidneys throbbing. He pivoted and two guys slammed into him.

After that he had no idea what was happening, because it was one giant pile-on, the entire fight moving to the middle of the bar. All AJ knew was that he was getting pummeled and he was fighting one guy after another. He couldn't check on Teresa or even Pax and Joey. All he could do was try and hold his own. His knuckles hurt, his ribs hurt, he was pretty sure his nose was bleeding, but he was giving as good as he got. And no shots had been fired, so his gun was still in the holster at his back.

Then he heard the sirens and the squeal of tires.

Shit. That's not what he wanted at all. So much for defusing the situation without the police getting involved.

The cops busted through the door before anyone could make a break for it. Someone must have called it in, because there were about a dozen cops in riot gear breaking things up. AJ shoved one of the Fists away from him, backed the hell out of the way and raised his hands, wanting to let the cops know he was ready for this to be over with. They were all pushed outside in a hurry.

Everyone was patted down and weapons were confiscated. AJ could have pulled his federal ID, but he wanted to avoid that if at all possible. They'd get their weapons back soon enough.

He stood outside with the rest of the Thorns and took in heaping gulps of hot summer night air to clear his head. His muscles hurt, his knuckles were raw and bloody, and his lungs ached from the effort it had taken to fight the Fists. He wiped the blood from his nose and did a quick search for Joey, didn't find him. "You seen Joey?" he asked as Pax came up alongside him.

Pax shook his head, his gaze scanning the parking lot. "Maybe he's inside with Teresa because she hasn't come out yet, either."

That wasn't good. He and Pax went to the door, but a cop blocked his way. "You can't go in there."

"My friends are in there."

The cop looked down on him. "You can't go in there. Everyone's going into the station to give statements. Permits for weapons confiscated need to be checked. Some of you will be arrested."

A van pulled up and started hauling both Fists and Thorns into the van. And in the meantime, Joey and Teresa were still inside the bar.

"What happened in there?"

The cop stood at the door and remained mute. AJ saw a couple cops go in with police tape, followed by a van pulling up with the word "Coroner" stamped on the side.

Coroner? Son of a bitch! AJ turned to Pax, who shook his head and shrugged. "No clue, man. It was a major fucking brawl in there, but I didn't see anyone go down. Then the cops came and pulled us all out of there."

"Teresa and Joey are still inside."

Pax's expression was grim. "I know. We need to get in there."

"IDs?"

Pax was already pulling his out of his back pocket. "It's the only way."

Grange was going to have their asses for blowing cover. At the moment, AJ didn't care.

AJ flipped his open at the same time Pax did. "Federal agents. We're working a case here." An outright lie, but the police officer guarding the door didn't know that.

The cop scanned their badges, looked at their faces, and nodded, stepping aside to let them in.

The crisp smell of blood filled the air inside. The place was a wreck, with chairs and tables strewn everywhere, some broken. AJ's boots crunched on shattered glass as they walked across the floor. His gaze zeroed in first on the body on the floor. He didn't exhale until he saw it was Larks, then he spotted Teresa sitting at one of the tables being interviewed by one of the detectives that had gone in earlier. Joey sat at a table across the room.

His friends were alive. That was good. Now to figure out what happened. He went directly to the suit interviewing Teresa. The guy stood.

"Who the hell are you?" he asked.

AJ flashed his badge. "AJ Dunn. Federal agent investigating the Fists. This is my partner, Pax Hudson."

The guy arched a brow, examined their badges and looked them up and down. "You in the middle of this?"

"The fight, yeah," Pax said. "We were trying to maintain cover so we had no choice. Didn't know it was going to end up with a murder."

"So you didn't see what happened to that guy?"

AJ shook his head. "We got hustled out of here when your black-and-whites showed up. Didn't see him go down. We weren't even aware there was a dead guy."

"Detective John Warren. Why don't you tell me what you're working on?" AJ explained what they were doing there, though he embellished a bit about working an undercover case on the Fists so they could stay.

"No one knows your situation?" John asked.

AJ shook his head. "This is my hometown, so I'd appreciate keeping it on the down low." Though he was afraid it was already too late for that. Teresa had seen him flash his badge and had frowned in confusion. He was going to have to explain to her who and what he really was. And since the Wild Riders kept their identities secret, that wasn't going to make General Lee very happy.

"So what happened here?" Pax asked.

John looked down at the body. "It appears the leader of the Thorns stabbed the leader of the Fists. Not surprising considering the clashes these two gangs have had with each other over territory."

Shit. Joey was being pinned for the murder? "Witnesses?"

"No. Well, one, though I question her reliability. Oliveri's sister claims to be a witness. Said someone else did it. We're going to bring Joey Oliveri in and take samples. I'm sure the blood on him will be the victim's."

AJ needed to talk to Teresa. And Joey. Figure out what happened. "Can we question the suspect and the witness? This could have direct bearing on our investigation."

"As long as one of my guys is present, fine."

AJ nodded and went over to Teresa, who stood and flew into his arms, burying her face in his neck. AJ felt wetness against his neck, knew she'd been crying. He put his arms around her. "It's going to be okay."

AJ flashed his badge to the officer sitting with her and explained that the detective had given his okay.

She pulled back, and Pax moved to her side. "Tell us what happened."

The officer in charge of her stood and let Pax and AJ sit, but he stayed close to Teresa.

"Larks and Joey were going at it," Teresa said, her face pale and streaked with tears. She clasped her hands together and laid them in her lap. "I kept my eye on them because I was afraid for Joey, scared Larks would pull a weapon."

"Did he?" Pax asked.

She shook her head. "No, but there was so much going on around them, others fighting. It was hard to see, so I moved around the bar."

AJ winced. "You could have gotten hurt."

Her gaze shot to his. "I was fine. I can take care of myself."

Pax leaned over and rubbed her back. "It's okay. Go on."

She swallowed and nodded, then wiped her palms on her jeans. "Joey didn't kill Larks. One of his own guys did."

"What? Did you see who?"

"Yes. But I don't know any of their names. All I saw was this guy come up behind Larks and shove a knife into his back. Then he disappeared into the crowd."

"Did he drop the knife?" AJ couldn't believe this. One of the Fists killed their leader? Why?

"Not that I could see."

"Could you pick this guy out again?"

She nodded.

"Stay here with her," AJ said to Pax. "I'm going to talk to Joey."

Detective Warner was with Joey, so AJ stood back and listened while Joey recounted the fight.

"It was physical, his fists and mine," Joey said. "And that was all. I took a punch and went down. Then Larks went down on top of me. I thought he was attacking me, but he was deadweight. I felt something wet covering me. It was blood. A lot of blood. I threw him off me, but he didn't move."

Detective Warner wrinkled his nose. "But you didn't see what happened."

"Hell no." Joey laid his head in his hands. "Larks rang my bell with that punch. I was trying to get my bearings again, swaying a little, and holding my arms up to ward off the next punch. By the time I cleared my head enough to get up, he was falling on top of me."

"You moved him?" the detective asked.

"I had to move him to get him off me. But then when he didn't come after me again—he was just lying there—I rolled him to the side, saw a rip in his jacket and blood pouring out. I guess he got knifed by someone. I laid him back down and felt for a pulse." Joey held up his hands. "My hands were covered in blood. I knew it was bad. He was gone. That was right when you guys came in."

Detective Warner stood as a couple uniformed cops appeared. "Take him to the station for further questioning. I want his clothes and hands tested. He's already been read his rights."

The cops nodded and grabbed a handcuffed Joey.

"AJ."

AJ went over to Joey.

"Yeah?"

"I didn't do this. On my mother's soul, I didn't do this. I don't know who did, but it wasn't me."

AJ patted Joey on the back. "We'll figure it out." AJ leaned in further and whispered in Joey's ear. "And don't say anything else until you get a lawyer."

After Joey left, AJ went back to Teresa. The cop watching her was talking to someone else. Pax and Teresa were huddled together, their heads bent, nearly touching. AJ pulled up a chair and Teresa cast a worried gaze at him.

"What did Joey say?"

"That he didn't do it."

"Did he see the guy?"

"No. He said Larks punched his lights out for a second. When he came to, Larks was already down. But he didn't see who knifed him. He just turned him over and saw the blood and the hole in his jacket."

"Damn." Teresa dropped her chin to her chest and wrapped her arms around her middle. "This is bad." She lifted her gaze to both Pax and AJ. "They aren't going to take my word for it because I'm Joey's sister. They think I'm lying to protect him."

"I'm sure they're going to question everyone who was here. Maybe someone else saw what you did."

Detective Warner came back. "Ms. Oliveri, we'd like you to come down to the station and try to identify the man you say knifed Larks. We're going to run through all the Fists we've recovered from the fight, see if you can pull any of them out of a lineup."

"That's fine."

"We'll come along, too," Pax said.

Warner frowned. "You got a personal stake in this case?"

"We know the people involved, but our vested interested is in the Fists and their hierarchy. There's a reason their leader was killed."

Warner nodded. "Let's go. Ms. Oliveri, you'll have to come with us."

She gazed reluctantly at AJ.

"It's okay, Teresa. We'll meet you down there."

After they left, Pax turned to AJ. "You think she's telling the truth?"

"Yeah. Teresa loves Joey, but she wouldn't lie to protect him. She'd hate that this happened and she'd stand by his side, but she'd never lie for him."

"You're sure?"

AJ didn't even have to think about it. He knew. "I'm sure."

"Let's go, then."

AJ knew Pax wouldn't wonder why they were getting involved. He understood friendship and bonds, knew AJ would do the same for him. It's why they'd stayed friends for the past ten years. They had each other's back, no matter what.

And it looked like they might be hanging around here for a while.

So much for vacation.

FIVE

TERESA GAVE HER STATEMENT AT THE POLICE DEPARTMENT, taking it slowly and step by step, recalling everything she'd seen since the fight broke out. She put herself in that place and time, visualizing everything.

It wasn't the first time she'd been here, giving a statement. She knew how this went.

"The tattoo I saw on the guy was very specific. There was a tribal pattern that covered his entire neck almost up to his jaw. And he had a scar on the right side that went through part of the tattoo."

"That's pretty observant."

She lifted her chin. "When someone's stabbing someone else in the back, you kind of pay attention to that person, you know?"

The detective nodded. "I suppose you would. And you'd be able to identify the tattoo again if you saw it?"

She nodded. "Definitely. It was unusual and it covered his neck all the way around."

The detective nodded. "We'll enter the specifics in the database. If he's got a record, it'll come up."

They had to believe her. Joey didn't kill Larks. It didn't matter that she was his sister. Fact was fact and Joey would be proven innocent soon enough.

After she gave her statement, she was allowed to leave. AJ and Pax were waiting for her outside the room, the looks of concern on their faces the only comfort she'd allow herself. What she wouldn't give to step into their arms.

But that wasn't who she was, wasn't what she'd allow herself. She wrapped her arms around herself instead.

"You okay?" AJ asked.

"Fine. I told them what I saw, what really happened."

"That's all you can do. What about the lineup?"

"Detective Warner said he'd come get me when they were ready."

"Can you identify this guy?" Pax asked.

"I'm sure of it. I already gave the detective a description of him. Of course they all wear the Fist leathers, and so did he. But he was totally bald, with pretty specific neck tattoos. Shouldn't be hard to ID."

Pax nodded. "I saw a few guys like that in the bar."

"So did I," AJ said. "At least it reduces the number of Fists in the lineup."

"True." Exhaustion weighed her down. She wanted to go home, crawl into bed and sleep for days. But she had to stay here for Joey. "Do you know anything about Joey?"

"His lawyer's with him now."

"Good. I hope this is over with fast."

Detective Warner came out and motioned to Teresa. "We're ready for the lineup, Ms. Oliveri."

Teresa nudged to her left at Pax and AJ. "They're coming with me."

"Fine, as long as they don't speak."

They stepped into a room with a long, darkened window. Detective Warner stood at the window. "The men will be on the other side. You can see them but they won't be able to see you. I'll call them to step toward the window one at a time. After you look at them you can tell me which one is the one you think stabbed Larks."

"Okay."

The room was icy cold and she rubbed her arms. Suddenly a leather jacket was placed over her shoulders. She glanced around at Pax. "Thank you." She slid her arms into the jacket that was miles too big for her, but it was warm from his body heat, and at least she wasn't shaking anymore.

The room on the other side of the window brightened. Four bald guys stood there, all wearing leathers. Detective Warner called each one to step forward.

Teresa studied each face carefully, noticing the hands and the tattoos on their necks. When they had all stepped forward and back, the detective turned to her.

"These were the only bald guys belonging to the Fists that were present at the scene. Is one of them the guy you claim stabbed Larks?"

Disappointment filled her. "No. He's not there. Are you sure that's all of them?"

"Yes." The detective cast her a sidelong glance, as if he didn't believe her story.

"I know what I saw. And who I saw. None of those guys was the one who stabbed Larks. He had a distinctive tattoo on his neck. I'd recognize it again if I saw it."

Detective Warner nodded. "Thank you for your time."

"That's it? We're done?"

"For now."

"What about my brother?"

"For the moment, he's our best and only suspect. We'll wait for the testing on his clothing and body to come back."

"You're going to check out that tattoo I told you about, right?"

"Yes, ma'am."

Teresa could already tell from the look on Warner's face that they believed Joey was the killer. "The guy used a knife to kill Larks. Did you find it?"

"We took weapons off several people in the bar, including your brother. We're testing all of them."

She inhaled, let it out on a shaky sigh.

"Come on," Pax said, pulling her against him. "Let's go get something to drink."

"I'm fine here. I want to wait for Joey."

"He's in with his lawyer right now. After that he's going to be processed. You won't be able to see him until tomorrow."

Teresa closed her eyes, feeling the distance between Joey and her. She didn't like it. With their parents both dead, it was just the two of them. They took care of each other, watched out for each other. She felt responsible for making sure Joey got out of this.

"We'll be back in the morning," AJ said.

Detective Warner shrugged. "Suit yourself."

After he walked away, Teresa looked at AJ. "What does that mean?"

"It means they won't have all the evidence compiled against Joey by morning. But they won't be able to stop you from seeing him."

"I need to go back to the bar, clean everything up."

"No good," Pax said as they stepped outside the front door of the police station. "It's a crime scene now. They're going to have it roped off and shut down."

Tears pricked her eyes. "It's my business, the only job for the girls. What are they going to do?"

AJ slid his hand on the back of her neck, his touch comforting—not demanding anything of her. "I think that's the least of your worries right now. They'll manage. We'll take you home."

"You can just drop me at my car."

Pax slid his hand in hers. "We'll take you home. If you did see the guy who killed Larks, he might have seen you, too. And he might be looking for you."

That hadn't occurred to her. "You think I'm in danger?"

Pax shrugged. "Don't know yet, but it's a possibility. We're coming home with you."

She stopped dead, her gaze flitting between them. "No. I'm fine. I can take care of myself."

"We're coming home with you," AJ said, affirming Pax's statement. "If you don't want us inside your house, we'll hang outside. Either way, we're staying at your place to keep watch over you."

Part of her warmed at the thought of AJ and Pax being there. Another part of her prickled with unease—and something else she thought long dormant—at having both of them inside her home. It implied an intimacy that both intrigued and unnerved her.

Ridiculous. She was worrying needlessly. All they wanted to do was protect her. But she didn't want babysitters. She'd long ago learned to look out for herself.

"I'll go home alone."

AJ tilted his chin down, his gaze direct. "We'll be following you, like it or not."

She blew out a breath, knowing it was useless to argue. "You don't have to stay outside."

"We'll take you back to your car, then follow you to your place," AJ said.

Teresa went outside with them and looked at the bikes parked in the lot.

She hadn't been on a bike in five years. Not since . . .

"You can ride with me," AJ said, pulling her away from thoughts she shouldn't be thinking. So she was going to climb on a bike again. Big deal. She wasn't going to be alone this time.

She put on the helmet he handed her, and realized she'd have to lean against him and hold on for the short ride over to the bar. She could do this. It wasn't intimate contact. Just . . . contact. And wasn't it time she got on with it, anyway?

AJ got on his Harley and she climbed on the back. He half turned and gave her a smile. She started out leaning against the backpad, but it had been a while since she'd ridden, and she was used to riding on her own bike, not on the back of someone else's. This was entirely different and she felt a little off balance. And AJ was a bit of a speed demon on the roads, especially since the hour was late and the streets deserted. She adjusted her position and leaned against his back, tentatively wrapping her arms around him. He felt solid and steady, comforting as the bike dipped to the side around the bend in one of the roads. She closed her eyes and let the speed and the wind flow through her, feeling weightless and unburdened for just a few moments. It felt right to be pressed against a man again, to breathe in the earthy scent of him, to feel the hard push of his muscular back against her breasts.

It had been so long. For a moment there she allowed herself to just . . . settle.

This is what she wanted, what she needed. A man again. A man who knew nothing about what had happened to her, who wouldn't make judgments or be wary.

They pulled into the parking lot of the bar, the entire front area surrounded by garish-looking police tape pronouncing her pride and joy as a crime scene. Teresa got off the bike, wanting nothing more than to go inside and clean up the blood staining her wood floor.

AJ moved up beside her. "You can't go in."

She continued to stare at her front door. "I know."

"Come on. It's late. Let's take you home."

They drove the three short blocks to her house—formerly her parents' house. Joey liked his condo, where he could hang out with his friends, have barbecues and use the pool. After their parents died, he'd insisted Teresa take the house. She offered to sell it and split the equity with him, but he didn't want it. He had a job and his own place and wanted Teresa to have it. Admittedly, she'd always loved the old place and it reminded her of everything safe. And if that meant she was clinging to a lifeline, then she'd take that small comfort.

AJ and Pax pulled their bikes in right behind her car in the covered carport. She unlocked the front door and waited for them to come up onto the cement porch, each of them toting one bag. She cocked a brow. "That's it?"

"We travel light," Pax said with a grin.

She couldn't imagine taking a road trip using only one bag, but they were guys. They probably only had a change of underwear and a razor. She flipped on the light switch and held the door open for them. Their presence seemed to dwarf her tiny living room. She remembered AJ being here with Joey when they were younger. Not much had changed since then, other than a few pieces of furniture. Teresa had stripped off the threadbare wallpaper and painted, brightened the colors up a bit. Otherwise it was just an old house that she loved.

"Bathroom is down the hall to the left."

AJ turned to her. "I've been here plenty of times, Teresa."

"Oh yeah." She'd forgotten how often AJ used to come over to hang out with Joey. This had been like a second home to him, since AJ and his stepfather never got along. And her parents had loved AJ like he was one of their own kids, so he had always been welcome there. Which meant Teresa got to see a lot of him, too, something she certainly hadn't minded since she'd always been madly in love with him, from the time she was twelve until he disappeared off the radar when she was eighteen. She wanted to ask him where he'd been. And those badges he and Pax had flashed . . .

"So are you and Pax cops?"

AJ skirted his glance to Pax.

"Come on, honey," Pax said. He took her by the hand and pulled her onto the sofa. "Let's sit down and we'll explain it to you."

"I'm sorry." She dragged her finger across her forehead. "My manners suck. Would you like something to drink?"

AJ sat at her other side. "We're fine. You look like you're about to drop. You need some sleep."

"I can't even think about sleeping right now. My mind is filled with visions of the fight, of what I saw. I keep replaying it over and over in my head. I'm sure I'm right."

"We're sure you are, too," Pax said. "You did everything you could. You told the truth. Let the evidence uncover the rest."

She lifted her hopeful gaze to Pax. "Do you think the evidence will point to the guy who actually killed Larks?"

"I don't know. We'll just have to wait and see. But AJ is right. You look tired."

"I'm not tired. I'm tense as hell."

"Turn around."

She cocked a brow. "Why?"

"I'll rub some of that tension out of your shoulders, help you relax a little. Maybe you'll get sleepy."

He didn't have a leering grin on his face, just concern. Teresa turned, facing AJ. This would be a good test. She was alone in her house with two men. She hadn't had any man in her house except Joey. Not since before . . .

No use thinking about that. She was tense enough already.

AJ watched intently as Pax laid his hands on Teresa's shoulders. He pressed in light and gentle, using just his fingertips along the muscles between her neck and shoulder.

"You *are* tight."

"Been a rough night," she said.

He moved along those muscles, then to the nape of her neck, sliding his fingers into her hair, the palm of his hand resting on the back of her head. Tiny pinpricks of sensation skittered along her skin. Relaxation warred with distinct interest, and she was shocked to discover she enjoyed Pax touching her. She dropped her chin to her chest and he increased the pressure, moving from her neck to her shoulders again.

"AJ, why don't you rub her neck while I do her shoulders."

"Sure." AJ scooted in, lifted her legs and draped them over his lap. "Rest your head against me, honey."

She did, letting her head drop against his chest. He slid his fingertips against her temples, making gradual circles there. Teresa didn't want to say a word. This just felt too good. AJ in front of her making magic movements with his fingers, erasing all the tension from her head and neck, and Pax behind her working kinks out of her shoulders.

She was surrounded by two men, caged between them. And she wasn't freaked out, wasn't panicking, was allowing them to touch her freely. In fact, she became more aware of Pax's warm breath caressing her neck and the feel of AJ's steely thighs under hers. Despite the arctic temperature of the room from her well-running air conditioner, she was flushed with heat. Not panic hot, just . . . hot. Every time Pax's fingers sailed along the naked flesh of her shoulders, her nipples tightened, and the feel of AJ's hands in her hair caused goose bumps to break out across her skin.

"Does it feel good?" Pax asked.

"Yes. It feels great." Really great. She felt like the sea, undulating waves crashing lazily against the shore. She let out a soft moan, loving their hands on her.

And then they stopped. AJ stood and moved away.

Dammit. They didn't know, couldn't know.

"How about something to drink now?" AJ asked.

His voice was laced with something Teresa couldn't quite comprehend.

"Um, okay."

She stood and went into the kitchen, not understanding what had changed.

SIX

Pax peered into the kitchen to make sure Teresa was occupied before leaning close to AJ. "What the fuck was that about?"

"We can't do this."

"Do what?"

AJ tilted his head. "You know what."

Pax tried to remember what he'd done when he was touching Teresa. Nothing. He'd massaged her shoulders and that was it. "I was giving her a back massage. She looked tense as hell."

"And you know damn well what that leads to. We're not going there with Teresa."

"Jesus, man, do you think every time I touch a woman it's because I want to fuck her? I was trying to offer her some comfort."

"Right. And you asked me to join in. Don't play the player, Pax."

Pax shook his head. Maybe AJ was right. Consciously he wasn't even thinking about that, but there was no doubt he was attracted to Teresa. Maybe without even thinking about it . . .

"I know where we stand with her. But maybe you can leave it up to her."

"I don't know, Pax. She's been through enough tonight. And it's not like we're going to stay and . . . well, you know."

Pax flopped onto the sofa and laced his hands together behind his head. "I'd like to. Stay. And well . . . you know. With Teresa." He waited for AJ's reaction, figuring his friend would get pissed off. Instead, AJ just cocked his head to the side and slid a glance into the kitchen.

"You want to stay here? Just like that? What about the road trip?"

"She's in trouble. So's Joey. You know how it is. You take care of your friends. I just figured you'd want to hang out until this was settled. And it's not like we had a destination in mind."

"Okay. Good. Thanks."

Pax shrugged. "I believe Teresa. I think someone in the Fists did the deed. But why would someone kill the leader of his own gang?"

"Because he wanted to become the leader?"

"Maybe. There are a lot of ways to oust a gang leader without killing him."

AJ stood and paced the room. "If the majority of the gang agrees."

"So what you're saying is that maybe this was a coup of sorts. That not everyone wanted Larks taken down."

AJ nodded. "It could have been a spur-of-the-moment thing. Hell, for all we know whoever killed him had a personal beef. We just don't know the why of it."

"Or maybe someone has a vendetta against my brother and Larks," Teresa said as she reentered the room. "Killing Larks and making sure the murder is pinned on Joey kills two birds with one stone."

Teresa brought the tray filled with drinks into the room and set it on the coffee table.

"It could be that, too," AJ said. "Whatever the reason, someone in the Fists wanted Larks dead."

She didn't seem upset about them pulling away, but what did he know? They barely knew each other so he was going to have to let AJ lead on this one, and the warning look AJ sent his way said now wasn't the right time. Still, there was something vulnerable in her eyes, a wariness there. Pax would like to know why.

Maybe that's what attracted him to her—she was a mystery. He liked mysterious women. Too many of them were open books, wanting to blurt out their entire life stories the first night you met them. Pax liked a woman who kept her cards close to her chest. It made him curious enough to want to peel back some of the layers.

Teresa took the chair next to the sofa. Safe territory, not near AJ or him. Pax didn't think he and AJ had come on strong. They usually saved that for women who knew what was up, who welcomed the challenge. All he'd been doing was offering comfort, nothing more. And maybe she was pissed off that she had gotten into their touch and they pulled back abruptly. She didn't want to get burned again. He couldn't blame her. Women didn't take rejection well. Problem was, they hadn't rejected her.

"So why would someone in Larks's group want him dead?" Teresa asked. "Unless they're trying to pin this on Joey."

"It might be just that," AJ said.

"That seems pretty extreme, even for the Fists. Besides, Larks is their leader. He would be in on any scheme to take down Joey."

"He wouldn't have been in on this one," Pax said.

Teresa nodded. "Obviously."

"Do you know of anyone on the Fists who has it out for Joey?"

She turned her attention to AJ. "Individually? No. Of course, none of them like the Thorns on principal. The whole rival gang thing. And Joey as the leader puts him front and center. But I can't see how taking Joey out of the equation this way serves their purpose. Because now Larks is out, too."

AJ shook his head. "And that leaves both gangs vulnerable."

"Right," Pax said. "Now you have the Fists' gang leader dead, and the Thorns' leader is accused of killing him. Who benefits?"

Teresa clasped her hands together and leaned forward. "I don't know. This doesn't make sense. Why would this guy want his own leader dead? That's the key question we need to find the answer to."

"Whoa. Who's this 'we' you're referring to?"

"You, me and AJ."

Part of him wanted to grin at the thought of the three of them trying to figure this out. The other part of him didn't want Teresa involved in this at all. "No. Too dangerous."

"I agree with Pax. This guy who killed Larks—did he see you?"

"No. I was on my way over to put a stop to the fighting. I'd had enough, especially when Larks coldcocked my brother. Joey went down, and that's when I saw the bald-headed guy pull the knife and stab Larks in the back. I was afraid he was going after Joey next, so I grabbed my gun and ran like hell toward Joey, but the guy who stabbed Larks made a dash out the front door right after that without once looking back. He never saw me."

"You have a gun?" Pax asked.

She nodded. "I keep it hidden under the bar."

"Got a permit for it?"

"Of course. And in answer to your next question—yes, I know

how to use it. And I would have, too, if that guy had gone after my brother."

So she was tough. And not afraid to defend the people she loved. "What you did wasn't a smart move. Someone could have stabbed or shot you."

"I was aware of my surroundings. I'm not a moron, Pax."

"I definitely don't think you're a moron." He liked the way her cheeks turned pink and the exasperated look on her face. "So how far away were you when he stabbed Larks?"

She frowned. "I don't know exactly. Six feet maybe? The whole place was chaos. I just saw Joey fighting with Larks and instinct kicked in. We look out for each other, always have."

"You could have gotten hurt, Teresa. What were you thinking trying to get into the middle of a gang fight like that?"

She lifted her chin, her gaze skirting AJ's. "I was thinking I was going to do whatever it took to protect my brother. And when that guy pulled that knife, I was certain he was going to defend Larks and use it on Joey."

"Would you have used that gun on Larks?"

"On him or anyone else who threatened Joey's life."

"You shouldn't have put yourself in the middle of a dangerous situation like that," AJ said.

Teresa looked down for a second, then lifted her gaze to AJ's. "I've been in worse and survived."

"What kind of 'worse'?" Pax figured that was an opening, and despite AJ's warning to back down, Pax was going to take the opportunity to ask.

"Nothing." She stood. "I'm really tired. There are two extra bedrooms where you guys can sleep. Come on, I'll show you."

"You need to show us your room," Pax said.

Teresa stilled, that look of wariness shadowing her face again. "Why?"

"Because we need to know where you sleep so we can protect you."

Her lips lifted and she let out a short laugh. "You're not sleeping in my room."

"Didn't say that we were. We'll be taking turns sleeping tonight. We can't protect you if we're both asleep."

She cocked her head to the side and looked at both of them. "I don't really think I'm in any danger."

"You let us worry about that," AJ said. "Just show us where your room is. We'll make sure it's secure in there, then we'll get out of your way so you can get some sleep."

She took a few seconds to look them both over. Pax wasn't sure if it was because she didn't trust them or because she didn't really believe anything bad could happen to her. Finally, she turned and moved to the end of the hall and opened the door to her bedroom.

She flipped on the lights and AJ stepped in, Pax right behind him. Queen-sized bed covered in a brown and yellow quilt. Windows on either side. Pax took one side and checked the latches, while AJ did the other. "Secure over here," Pax said.

"Same," AJ said, then turned to Teresa. "Are there any other points of entry into this room?"

"Just a small window over the tub in the bathroom."

"I'll get it." Pax went in the direction Teresa pointed. The bathroom was small, as was the window over the tub, but the window was big enough to get a body through. He double-checked the closure and came out. "Okay."

Teresa was sitting on the side of the bed. "You never told me who you two really are."

AJ crooked a smile. "Well, honey, you've known me a long damn time. You know me."

She rolled her eyes. "That's not what I meant. All this security stuff, and those badges you flashed at the bar to get past the cops. What do you do for a living?"

Pax moved into the room and knelt in front of her. "We're agents with the U.S. government."

Her brows rose and her gaze shot to AJ. "Really?"

AJ DIDN'T REALLY WANT TO GET INTO THIS WITH TERESA, BUT HE knew they wouldn't be able to avoid it forever. "Yeah. But who we work for is kind of confidential, so we'd appreciate if you didn't go telling everyone in town."

"Of course. Wow. That's wonderful, AJ. I never thought . . ." She stopped mid-sentence, her cheeks flushing. "I'm sorry. That wasn't what I meant."

AJ sat next to her on the bed. "Hey, don't worry about it. I wasn't exactly an altar boy when I left here."

"You had potential. I always believed in you."

Something warm settled in his chest. He brushed it off. "I didn't give you any reason to believe in me. I was a mess. That's why I left."

Her gaze was warm. "But look where you ended up. You did good."

"Thanks."

"What kind of federal agent stuff do you do?"

"Whatever the government needs us to do. Mostly undercover work where bikers or guys who look like us can fit in," Pax said.

"Is it dangerous?"

AJ shrugged. "It can be sometimes."

"Wow. What an awesome job." Teresa's gaze shifted to AJ. "Do your parents know what you do for a living?"

"No. I don't talk to them anymore. They don't even know where I am."

She frowned. "For how long?"

"Since I left home."

"Oh, AJ. Why not?"

"You know why not." Because they wouldn't care. Because it was too late for that kind of family relationship. Because he didn't want it, and they didn't, either. They'd made their choices a long time ago. So had he.

"I'm sorry." Teresa raised her hand and laid it on AJ's shoulder. He pulled it off and laid both his hands over hers. "Get some sleep and try not to worry about anything. Pax and I will take care of you."

AJ stood, and Pax led the way out of the room. They closed the door behind them and took a seat on the sofa.

"Do you really think someone could come after her?" Pax asked as he pulled his Glock out of the back of his pants and laid it on the table.

AJ shrugged. "I don't know. Teresa might not think anyone saw her, but until we know why Larks was killed and for what reason, we need to keep her safe. She's the only one who can ID the guy who really did it."

"And one way or the other, that makes her a target."

AJ nodded and blew out a breath. Not exactly the vacation he was looking for.

Or the kind of hometown reunion he'd had in mind.

seven

DAWN HADN'T YET FILTERED THROUGH THE BLINDS ON TERESA'S windows, only shades of gray announcing it was morning but too early to get up.

It didn't matter. She hadn't slept much anyway, had tossed and turned, wondering what Pax and AJ were doing, coupled with random thoughts about the bar fight, what she'd witnessed, and her worry about Joey's welfare. None of that added up to the ability to get a restful sleep.

She took a shower and got dressed, opening the bedroom door and moving into the living room, surprised to find both the guys there. AJ was asleep on the sofa, Pax sitting in a chair near the front window. He turned to her and smiled, grabbed the pistol sitting on the table next to him and slid it into his pants.

For some reason, knowing they were armed comforted her. Besides, there was something sexy as hell about a guy carrying a weapon who knew how to use it. Not for show or to look tough, but because it was part of his job.

"Heard anything from the police station yet?"

Pax shook his head. "Nothing, but it's early." He came over to her, brushed his knuckles along her cheek. "Too early for you to be awake. You didn't get much sleep."

She took a step back, not used to the little thrill that shot up her spine at his touch. She liked it, which made her uncomfortable as hell. "I'm fine. I'll go make coffee."

"It's already made."

"It is?"

"Yeah. I brewed a pot a little while ago. Go kick the couch and wake up AJ. I'll start breakfast."

"You don't have to do that."

He gave her a look over his shoulder, and a smile that made her toes curl. "I want to."

A guy who made himself at home in her kitchen. That was also a little disconcerting. And comforting. And sexy.

It had been five years. And maybe it wasn't freaking her out as much as it used to. She'd wanted to get back in the game again for a long time now. She was tired of being afraid, of letting what had happened rule her life. She wanted to be a woman again, and damn if she was going to let those guys ruin her. Every man wasn't like they had been.

Every guy wasn't going to hurt her. And maybe every guy wasn't going to run away when he found out the truth about her.

She moved over to the sofa. AJ was too big for her average-sized couch. One arm was slung over his head, his booted feet hung over the edge of the arm. Beard stubble peppered his jaw, making his face look dark and ruthless. AJ had never been ruthless. A bad boy, yes, but he'd always been the fun kind of bad boy.

And he'd never hurt her.

Once, he'd loved her. And she'd loved him. But that love hadn't been enough to keep him out of trouble. They'd just been kids, on the verge of adulthood. Neither of them had known what they were doing back then. It had been innocent and intense, as all teenage romances are.

Ten years later she still didn't know what she was doing. Nor did she know who AJ really was now, other than he was one of the good guys.

She smiled. She liked that he was one of the good guys. It suited him. But he still carried an edge of danger that fit him well, too.

"You're staring."

Startled, she jumped back, realizing he'd moved his arm and his eyelids were partially open, revealing smoky grays studying her. She tried to calm her racing heart. Goddammit, when was she going to relax? "Sorry. I debated waking you."

"I was already awake. Pax walks like a herd of elephants."

"Fuck you," Pax said from the kitchen.

AJ sat up and swung his legs over the edge of the sofa and planted his feet on the floor. "Plus, I smelled coffee." He dragged his fingers through his hair, winked his sleep-laden gaze at the window, then turned his attention on her. "It's still dark out. Why are you up?"

"I slept enough."

He tilted his head to the side, examining her with his intense gaze, then stood, came closer. He reached out and grasped a strand of her hair in his hand. He held it lightly, not demanding, just let it sift through his fingers, his gaze focused on her face. "You look tired."

She inhaled, let it out on a shiver of awareness. What was it about these guys that got to her, that made her so cognizant of them as men? Her usual wariness was absent when they were around, the blocks she put up nonexistent. She knew AJ, but he'd been gone a long time. She didn't know Pax at all. And yet she'd let them stay in her house last night.

None of this made sense. She was usually a lot more guarded.

"Who's hungry?" Pax called from the kitchen.

AJ's lips curled in a way that made her stomach tumble and made heat flush her skin.

"I'm hungry," AJ whispered, so only she could hear.

He let go of her hair and walked away.

Her heart was pounding and her palms were sweaty. But it wasn't from fear.

She took a full minute to get her body and emotions under control, then went into the kitchen to join Pax and AJ.

BY THE END OF THE DAY, THE NEWS FROM THE POLICE STATION wasn't good. Teresa was strung out and ready to pull every hair out of her head.

Blood samples on Joey's clothes matched Larks's blood type, though DNA matching would take a little longer. Since Larks and Joey had been engaged with each other the entire fight, Teresa already knew what it would show—it would be Larks's DNA on Joey's clothes. With no murder weapon and no one else in Larks's proximity, and of course the rest of the Fists loudly pointing to Joey as the one who had stabbed Larks, there were no other suspects. It wasn't looking good for her brother.

Russ hung out there with them that day, worried as much about Joey as they were.

"You know anything about the Fists?" AJ asked him while they waited in the cafeteria.

Russ shrugged his wide shoulders and chewed the hell out of a toothpick. "Not much. Larks was a dick. I'm glad he's dead."

Pax snorted. "Some of them need killing."

"Yeah well the whole Fists gang needs killing."

"Who takes over now that Larks is dead?" Pax asked.

"Walter Rinks. He was Larks's right hand."

AJ slung his arm over the brown metal chair where Teresa sat. An unconscious gesture, but she felt the heat of his body against her back. "Walter have any reason to want Larks dead?" he asked.

Russ shook his head. "They were tight. Like brothers. Like me and Joey."

Teresa described the guy who she saw kill Larks. "Does that match Walter Rinks's description?"

"Not at all. Walter is skinny with long dark hair. No ink on his neck. His tats are on his arms."

She knew it had been foolish to hope it would be that easy. "What about on our team, Russ?" Teresa asked. "Anyone with a personal grudge against Larks?"

"Nah, honey. Not any more than the usual. We follow Joey and are loyal to him. We defend what's ours and will retaliate if we're hit, but we don't instigate for no reason. Murder isn't our style."

She blew out a breath. "Until now. Someone killed Larks and wants the police to think Joey did it."

IT WAS AFTER NINE WHEN AJ AND PAX FORCED TERESA OUT of the police station and made her go home. Again, they had followed her there, though she honestly didn't think anyone intended to do her harm. Wouldn't someone have made a move already if he thought she'd seen who'd killed Larks? Not that she wanted someone to, but she figured if someone had seen her, he would have wanted to get rid of her right away.

She didn't want to think about the possibility at all. But she of all people knew that being prepared and on your guard was the smart thing to do. So like it or not, she still had bodyguards. And as bodyguards went, they weren't too much of a hardship to endure.

When they got inside, Teresa tossed her purse on the table near the front door, then collapsed on the sofa and swept her hands through her hair. She was drained, physically and emotionally; she felt powerless to do anything to help her brother and didn't like being in this position. She'd always been proactive, always known what to do to step in and fix things when something went wrong.

This she couldn't fix and she hated it. There had to be another way.

Pax flopped down on one side of her and AJ on the other.

"Joey's attorney said the evidence was circumstantial, since no one witnessed Joey actually stabbing Larks, and they still haven't found a murder weapon."

Teresa turned to Pax. "Yes, and I know why. The murderer has run off with the knife he used to kill Larks."

AJ rubbed her back. "You need to let the police do their job."

"They're not going to find the guy. They're not even going to look for him."

"You gave them a description of him."

She laughed. "Right. Like they even believe me. You know as well as I do they think I'm making up the other guy to save my brother. The detective said no one with the tattoos I described came up in their database."

"You don't know that's what they think," Pax said. "Not every biker has a police record. Obviously that's why the guy you spotted didn't pop up in the NCIC. They'll follow every lead."

Teresa lifted her chin. "You put too much faith in law enforcement because you're one of them."

Pax laughed. "Honey, I'm hardly one hundred percent on the side of truth, justice and the American way. But you have to give them the benefit of the doubt until they do something to fuck things up."

Her lips lifted. "I know. I just don't want to do nothing and wait while Joey sits in jail. Not when I could be doing something to help."

Pax arched a brow. "What do you think you can do to help?"

"I could be out there finding the guy who stabbed Larks."

"Really. And how are you planning on finding him?"

She looked away for a second, then back at him. "I haven't figured that out yet. But he's wandering out there getting away with murder. And I'm the only one who can identify him."

Pax stood. "Okay. Let's go."

Teresa tilted her head back and stared at Pax. "Go? Go where?"

Pax smiled. "For a bike ride."

"Why?"

"Let's go find the Fists and see if you can spot your guy."

She stood. "Really?"

"That's a good idea," AJ said, already grabbing his helmet and heading to the door.

"Wait. We're just going to ride up into their territory?"

AJ shrugged. "I don't see why not. They rode into yours, didn't they?"

"Yeah. With a gang. We can't just—"

AJ put his arm around her. "Yeah, Teresa. We can. Don't worry. Now, go put on some boots and let's take a ride."

She hurried to her room, put her hair in a ponytail, grabbed her boots out of the back of her closet and shoved them on, her heart pumping double time as she did.

She really didn't ride. Not anymore. But for the second time in twenty-four hours she'd get on a bike again. For Joey, she'd do anything.

AJ and Pax were on their bikes as she closed the front door and headed out to the driveway. Pax had an extra helmet in his hand, so she went over and put it on, forcing her pulse to stop jackhammering.

"You look a little scared. You've ridden before, haven't you?"

She gave him a quick nod, hating the paralyzing fear that always came over her whenever she thought about climbing on a bike again. She was just going to have to suck it up and deal with it. "Of course."

"She's been riding for years," AJ said to Pax. "We used to ride dirt bikes together when we were kids. Then Teresa and Joey both got Harleys." His gaze slid to hers. "You sell your old bike?"

She climbed on behind Pax and nodded at AJ. "Yeah, I sold it a while back." There was no need to explain further.

Teresa leaned against Pax as they took off, inhaling the scent of his leather vest. The night was hot. He certainly didn't need to wear anything but his T-shirt, but as she pressed closer, she felt the telltale bulge of his gun and realized the leather hid the weapon he carried. Since AJ also wore a vest, he must be armed, too, which both comforted and worried her.

The Fists weren't a huge gang, but their numbers weren't small, either. And heading into their territory wasn't just a simple drive-by. Bikers riding into the northern territory who weren't part of the gang were going to be noticed and watched to see if they were out for a joyride, or something else.

It took only about a half hour to reach the northern part of the city where the Fists territory began. Teresa directed Pax to the gang's local hangouts, since she'd often listened in when Joey and the guys talked about riding around in the Fists' area. He'd tried to maintain peace between the gangs, but had finally given up when it became clear that Larks had delusions of becoming huge in the area and he wanted to take over the southern territory. Joey had told Larks to stay the hell out or suffer the consequences.

Larks had suffered all right, but it hadn't been at Joey's hands, or the hands of any of the other Thorns. And now it was up to

Teresa to find the man who did it, so her brother could get out of jail.

The problem was, none of the Fists were at any of their typical hangouts. They rode around to the bars, the bowling alley and the pizza place Teresa knew they frequented, and there wasn't a single bike—or biker—around. It was like they were hiding out. Or simply not there.

After an hour and multiple trips, Teresa tapped Pax on the shoulder. "Give it up. They're not here."

Pax nodded and led them out toward the highway and south, back to Teresa's place. She realized as Pax pulled the bike into her driveway that she'd been so preoccupied with finding the guy who stabbed Larks, had been so worried about Joey, that she hadn't once thought about being on a bike again.

One test passed with flying colors, at least.

They went inside. Teresa pulled a few beers out of the refrigerator and brought them into the living room, stopping for just a moment before she stepped fully into the room, still taken aback at the sheer size of the two men who stood there.

A normal woman would have died to be in the same room with these two men.

A normal woman would have.

She craved that feeling, wanted it more than anything. All it took was some determination and she'd have it.

She relaxed her shoulders and brought the beers in, handed them off and took a seat on the chair across from the sofa. Putting herself in between them was just too much. She was already aware of herself as a woman whenever she was with them, and she wasn't ready. Or maybe being with them made her feel more ready than she had been in years, and diving into that scared her.

Coward.

"So the Fists were nowhere to be found," AJ said, his gaze fixed on Teresa. "Maybe they were out riding."

"If they were riding in their own territory I would think we'd have run into them," Teresa said. "I think they were somewhere else."

"Or in hiding," Pax said.

Teresa screwed the top off her bottle of beer and took a long swallow, letting the cool liquid coat her parched throat. She leaned back and kicked off her boots, pulling her feet underneath her. "Why would they be hiding?"

"To protect the guy who killed Larks."

She hadn't thought about that. "You might be right."

AJ leaned forward. "What about Joey's guys? They might know."

"They might." She pulled out her phone. "I'll call Russ and see if he knows anything."

She dialed the number. After a few rings, Russ answered, the sound of loud music in the background. Teresa had to yell for Russ to hear her. Obviously, he was in a bar. But not her bar, since it was still closed. She grimaced at the thought of all that lost revenue and waited while Russ stepped outside, away from the noise. She could tell from the sound of his voice he wasn't happy to hear she had been on a ride up north. Then again, all the guys were protective of her.

Russ had no idea where the Fists could be, but he spent some time spewing invectives about his dislike of the gang and pointed the blame at them for Joey being in jail. Teresa didn't disagree.

"He couldn't shed any light on where the Fists might be," she said as she slid her phone onto the coffee table.

"They can't hide forever. Once they surface, we can go looking for the guy who stabbed Larks. If they're protecting him, we'll uncover him." AJ leaned back against the sofa and propped his feet on the coffee table.

While AJ and Pax sat quietly drinking their beers, Teresa studied them side by side. AJ, with his dark good looks and smoky gray eyes, had always made her heart tumble. He had that sexy, bad-boy quality about him that would make any woman look twice. Pax had dirty blond hair that he wore short and spiked, a dark goatee lining his jaw, his body all lean muscle, the kind of body a woman would want to run her hands all over. The two men were a study in contrasts—so different and yet so similar. Both screaming masculine and sexy, commanding a woman's attention in ways that were elemental and yet inexplicable.

And she suddenly pictured herself between those two men, their hands gliding over her naked body, their lips pressed against her skin. Being sandwiched between them, touching them in turn, allowed access to their bodies, sliding down to worship their cocks—first one, then the other. They stood still and allowed her to touch, to taste, and only when she'd satisfied her curiosity did they pull her up and turn her face to each of them and kiss her. She wondered about their mouths, their tongues, the different tastes and textures, what it would be like to have that sensation of both of them kissing her, both of them doing . . . everything to her, with her.

Heat settled between her legs, a pounding ache and awareness and need that hadn't been there in far too long. Her breasts felt full and her nipples tingled. She blinked and looked in the direction of the men of her fantasies, and found both of them staring right at her.

They knew. Somehow they knew what she'd been thinking about. It reflected back to her as they looked at her. AJ's eyes had gone even darker, a storm on the horizon as his gaze locked with hers. Pax's gaze was molten heat, all directed at her in a blast as hot as this August summer.

She should look away, move, get out of the room. But she was melted to the chair, unable to break the spell that tied her to these two men. And when Pax stood and moved toward her, her heart knocked against her chest, but it wasn't fear shaking her—it was desire, curiosity, the need to continue to experience the sensations and emotions she was feeling.

Instead of looming over her, he dropped to his knees at the side of her chair. Teresa inhaled the scent of leather, of sweat, of man. She wanted to reach out and trace her fingertips over his goatee, but she didn't, her hands gripping the chair arms so tight her muscles protested from the effort.

Pax smoothed his hand over her head, down along her hair, gently reaching the ponytail holder and drawing it down, releasing her hair. He didn't say anything, just slid his fingers through her hair, draping some of it over her shoulder. She didn't consider anything he did to be out of bounds or dangerous. Except the look in his eyes, the deliberate sensuality she saw there—which he let her see—screamed danger at the highest decibel level.

She heard AJ rise from the couch. From the corner of her eye she saw him move toward her—toward them. He slid to his knees in front of her chair and laid his hands ever so lightly on her legs, pressing in just enough so she knew he was there.

Oh, she knew he was there. She was surrounded by two men who had awakened her libido to a screaming frenzy.

But could she do anything about it? Did she dare?

"There's something you want that you're denying yourself."

Teresa shifted her gaze to Pax. She swallowed, her throat so dry she was afraid she wouldn't be able to speak.

AJ slid his hand to her knee. Easy, a nonthreatening touch. "You're skittish. Do we scare you?"

She turned her focus to AJ, forcing the words out. "No. You two don't scare me at all."

She felt the movement of Pax's hand against her neck, lightly teasing her hair, massaging the tight muscles there. He leaned in and his breath caressed her ear. Her chest tightened as he pressed a kiss to her neck. She closed her eyes as desire flooded her.

AJ moved his hands further along her legs, light and easy movements, his fingers dancing along the denim to her ankles. He pulled her feet out from under her and let her legs drape over him, rubbing her calves with his strong fingers while Pax slid his tongue along her throat. Her breasts strained against her bra, her nipples tight with agonized pleasure. She fought for breath as delicious sensation danced along her nerve endings.

She wanted this so much, yet even as she did, the images assaulted her. She was on the ground and someone was spreading her legs, holding her down, tearing at her clothes. She fought to get away.

The heat and delicious sensation shattered as cold fear took hold of her.

Anger battered her, that even now, five years later, it still haunted her.

"I can't do this. Not yet." She pushed, and AJ released her as Pax backed away. Teresa stood and turned to them. "I'm sorry. I'm sorry." She couldn't even look at them, had to get away. She went to her bedroom and shut the door, felt foolish even as she locked it, but couldn't help herself. She still needed that barrier of safety between her and them.

Between her and men.

eIGHT

AJ WATCHED, STUNNED, AS TERESA LEFT THE ROOM. HE WENT to the hall to follow her, but she shut the door and he heard the snick of the lock, effectively shutting him out.

He walked back into the living room and stood there.

"Damn" was all Pax said.

"Yeah." AJ sat on the sofa and grabbed his beer, finishing it off in two swallows. "You want another?"

Pax nodded, and AJ went to the fridge and grabbed a couple bottles, handed one off to Pax. "I don't get it."

Pax shook his head. "She was fine one minute. I felt her, man. Her body was hot, liquid relaxed and responding to us. The next second she froze up, went stiff and pale and shot out of here like she was spooked."

"A lot of women can't handle two men."

"True enough. But it was more than that. Way more than that."

AJ knew Pax was right. The problem was, what were they going to do about it?

"You need to talk to her."

AJ's brows lifted. "Me? Why me?"

"You have the past with her. You know her better than I do. She might be more comfortable talking to you."

"I don't think so. Leave it alone."

"There's something wrong. This went way beyond a simple 'Hey, I just don't want to be with two guys' kind of thing. She's afraid and I don't want to leave it alone."

AJ took a few swallows and pointed his beer at Pax. "That's your problem and always has been. You push when you shouldn't."

"You lay back because you don't want to confront. Some things are better out in the open."

"And some things are better left alone."

"We aren't talking about how fucked up you are, AJ. We're talking about Teresa."

"You're the one who wants to psychoanalyze everyone, Pax. So you go talk to her."

"Fine. I will." Pax disappeared down the hall. It took AJ a few seconds of fuming, just like it always did when he and Pax got into it. Then he stood and met Pax at Teresa's door.

Pax was leaning against the wall, his lips lifted in a knowing smile. "I waited for you," he whispered.

"Asshole." AJ knocked on the door, light and easy, not wanting to make her think he was demanding to be let in. "Teresa? Can we talk to you?"

No answer for a minute or so. AJ was about to knock again.

"It's not locked anymore. You can come in."

He cringed at the softness in her voice, sensed her reluctance. He didn't want to do this, but Pax was right—they needed to know if there was something they'd done wrong. AJ turned the knob and pushed the door. It opened. The room was dark. Teresa sat in the window seat, the moonlight casting a silver glow over her. Her knees were drawn to her chest, her arms wrapped around them.

"It is okay if Pax and I come in?"

She nodded, still looking out the window. AJ came into the room, Pax behind him. He circled around the bed but stopped there, not wanting to make her feel cornered.

"Five years ago I was riding my bike home after I closed down the bar. It was . . . two-thirty, three A.M., something like that," she said, not looking at them. Obviously she was ready to talk, though. AJ took a seat on the corner of the mattress. Pax leaned against the wall.

"Front tire went down midway home. I tried calling Joey, but didn't get an answer. He was out riding, so he didn't get the call. I didn't want to leave the bike on a deserted stretch of road, but I didn't have much choice. I called for a taxi and waited. Meanwhile, a couple of bikers came by. I was hoping it was some of the Thorns. It wasn't."

AJ wanted to ask questions, wanted to say something, but this was Teresa's story to tell.

"I don't know who they were. They wore full face helmets with dark face shields and were dressed all in black. They pulled over and I told them my tire was shot."

Her face had gone a pale silver, and he knew what it cost her to tell this story. He also knew he wasn't going to like what he was going to hear next.

"They didn't care about the bike, or my tire, or about helping me. They didn't want to hear the word 'no.'"

"Son of a bitch," Pax mumbled from the darkened corner of the room. AJ agreed. It took every ounce of willpower he had not to go to Teresa and fold her in his arms.

"I prayed the taxi would show up, but you know how it is in this town. And it was a game night. Every taxi was in the city. I knew it was going to be a long wait. I told the guys someone was on the way to pick me up, but they didn't listen . . . didn't care. And I had broken down near this deserted shopping center, lots of nooks and crannies and places to hide . . ."

She sucked in a shuddering breath, then continued. "They dragged me over there, behind the buildings, threw me on the ground. They tied a foul-smelling rag around my eyes so I couldn't see. One held me down while the other pulled off my jeans and boots, tore my panties . . ."

Her lips trembled and silvery tears slid down her cheeks. "I kept saying no. Over and over again, I said no. They never responded, never said a word. They took turns violating me." She pulled her legs tighter to her chest. "At least it was over fast. Then they left me lying there, half-naked and sobbing."

She finally turned her tear-streaked gaze to AJ. "I said no. I pleaded with them. But they didn't stop."

Rage tore at AJ. He wanted someone dead for hurting her. But now wasn't the time for that emotion. And it wasn't the time for her to feel alone. He went to her, pulled her off the window seat and wrapped his arms around her.

Then Pax was there, too, on the other side of her, holding her, caressing her hair.

"We're not going to hurt you, Teresa," he said. "Not like that. Not ever."

She buried her face against his chest and shuddered. "I know that. Logically, I know that. Getting my psyche to understand it is something different."

"We aren't going to hurt you," Pax reiterated. "You have a right to say no. Every woman does."

AJ drew her back and cupped her face in his hands. "Did you go to the police?"

She nodded. "Of course. It did no good. Whoever did it, they wore condoms. Never took their helmets off. Their bikes were nondescript and I didn't get license tag numbers. I have no idea who they were. Still don't."

"Christ, Teresa. I'm sorry. I'm so sorry this happened to you."

She managed a smile. "I'm angry it happened to me. I'm furious at them for thinking it was okay to take what wasn't offered to them."

"So the case is still open?"

She shrugged. "Not that it does much good. They'll never be caught. No DNA. No repeat rapes before or after mine. It was an isolated incident. Cops said maybe they were drunk or high and it was just a one-time thing."

"So no one pays for that crime except you," Pax said.

Teresa's gaze lifted to his.

"You've been in a kind of prison, haven't you?" he asked.

She leaned against him. "Yes. I guess I still am. You saw that tonight." She pushed past him and sat on the window seat again, lifted her gaze to him. "I'm not . . . normal anymore."

Pax took a seat in the chair next to her. "It could take a long time. Have you had counseling?"

"Plenty. And it helped me a lot, especially in the beginning. But it can only help me so much. At some point I have to let a man, or men, touch me again."

"The right man. Or men," AJ said. "Ones who'll be patient with you. Ones who'll understand what you've been through, who know you need time to take this slow. Baby steps, Teresa."

She tilted her head to the side. "You understand."

"That you were violated? That your body still rebels against being touched?" AJ nodded. "Yeah, we understand. We may be guys, but we're not dense, Teresa. Any man should understand that what you need most is time, patience and TLC. You have to do this on your own timetable, and in your own way."

"I want to be whole again," she said. "You have no idea how much I want that. But the guys around here . . . they know what happened and treat me differently because of it. They think I'm some china doll who's going to break if touched. They give me a wide berth. They're afraid, which in turn makes me feel damaged."

Pax smoothed his knuckles over her cheek. "We're not afraid of you, Teresa. Or of your reactions to us. Good or bad. And we sure as hell don't think of you as damaged. What happened to you wasn't your fault. You didn't cause it."

She inhaled, let it out on a shaky sigh. "Don't I know it. I'd like an hour in a room with those two sons of bitches who did this to me."

"Me, too," Pax said, smoothing his hand over her hair. "The easiest way to get past this is to be with someone you trust. When you're ready."

The way she looked at Pax, her gaze so trusting, was like a gut punch to AJ. "I am ready."

Pax smiled at her. "I think tonight proved you're not ready yet."

She sighed. "Well, goddammit, I want to be ready."

Pax took her hands between his. "Give yourself a break, honey. There's no hurry. Or timetable."

"Most men—"

"We're not most men." AJ sat next to her. "You need to understand that. We're not going to pressure you. Ever. You want one of us, both of us, that's your call. On your timetable. You don't, we're still here for you."

Pax lifted her hand to his lips and kissed her palm. "We're on vacation. We'll be hanging around for a while. You can count on us, Teresa, no matter what you need. If all you want is a couple of friends, that's what we'll be for you."

TERESA HADN'T INTENDED TO SPILL HER STORY TO AJ AND PAX. She never liked talking about it. Talking about it was like reliving it, and she'd rather have a hot poker stuck in her eye than experience that night again.

Yet as soon as Pax and AJ had come into the room, the story had spilled out. It was as if she'd needed them to hear it. She'd wanted them to know why she'd run out of the room. It was important for them to understand they'd done nothing wrong. It hadn't been them; it had been all her fault—her issues. It was important they know.

And maybe she'd wanted to throw down the challenge, see if they'd run like the others had. She'd told a couple guys about the rape before, guys she'd dated for a while and had tried to get close to.

They couldn't handle it, had closed up on her, pulled away, and she hadn't seen them again.

She supposed she understood why. A woman who'd been raped and hadn't been sexually active since was more trouble than she was worth, especially a woman a guy was just starting to date. She was a mess of emotional scars, terrified of being touched again, yet craving that closeness with a man. That was one hell of a commitment most guys weren't the least bit interested in making.

A man would have to be crazy in love with a woman to make that kind of sacrifice, and no man had gotten close enough to her to fall in love with her. She hadn't allowed it. All the guys in the Thorns knew about the rape, but dating them wasn't an option. They had circled around her after it happened and become family to her. They treated her like a sister, someone to protect. She valued them and loved them all, but she couldn't fuck any of them. And she doubted any of them saw her that way, either.

But she would have never made it through without the Thorns. Their anger and need for retribution for what had happened had allowed her to pull herself together. Then she had been the one trying to calm them down.

But they told her she was one of theirs and men protect their women.

But not all men. Which was why five years later she was still dateless and sexless.

And yet AJ and Pax were still camped out in her house, hadn't turned tail and run when she'd spilled her guts about that ugly night. Instead, they'd pulled her against them, not afraid to touch her or get close to her. They hadn't treated her like she was fragile—or damaged. They'd held her when she'd needed it most.

Even Joey was afraid to touch her most days. She wasn't the easiest to understand or get along with; she knew she ran hot and cold.

And still, AJ and Pax hadn't walked out yet.

But it was still early in . . . whatever it was going on between her and . . . them? She couldn't choose one or the other. She had a history with AJ, had been friends with him, had a teenage love affair with him. And he'd come back all grown-up and so very masculine and sure of himself. To see how he'd changed and grown was damn appealing. His stormy gray eyes had always mesmerized her, his coal black hair so thick and soft she could spend hours just kissing him and sinking her fingers into his hair. And now he had a man's body, held himself with confidence and pride and the knowledge that comes with having gone through what he had with his family, all the odds against him, and having survived it. She'd always admired his survival skills as a kid, and she did so even more now that she'd seen what he'd done with his life. The fact that they had unfinished business only added to the attraction between them. They'd only gotten started when he'd disappeared from her life. Teresa had always felt there should have been more between them. She'd wanted so much more with him.

Oh sure, she could have held a grudge at the way he dumped her that night all those years ago, but it was him being noble in the only way he knew how. At the time she couldn't see it, but years later she realized that had been his way to keep her safe. She knew what kind of trouble he'd gotten into after that. He'd wanted to distance her from what he was getting himself into. It had only made her miss him more.

Seeing him walk into the bar a few days ago had shocked her female senses into awareness for the first time in . . . years. It was a shock she'd needed, reminding her that she was still a woman—a woman with desires.

Pax was the unknown, someone new and exciting and oh so self-confident. He owned whatever room he occupied. And when he paid attention to you—whoa. He was the kind of man who could get a woman's libido soaring in a hurry because he had charisma, that slight touch of arrogance that wasn't too much, but just enough to be attractive. She found herself craving being near him, wanting to touch him, smell him, get close to him. There was something elementally sexy about the man, and she wanted more of whatever that special magic was he created in her body whenever he touched her.

Either one of these men could give her what she needed.

How was she going to choose? And if she did, would she finally be able to follow through?

"I'D LIKE TO KILL THE SONS OF BITCHES WHO DID THAT TO HER," CJ said, pacing the floor in Teresa's living room.

It had been hours since she'd gone to her room to sleep, hours since she'd revealed what had happened to her five years ago. And still, AJ couldn't calm the rage that boiled inside him.

"You and me both, AJ. And if we were still on the other side of the law and we had a chance to find them, we probably could do something to those guys."

AJ turned his gaze on Pax. "We're in a better position *now* to have something happen to them."

Pax's lips lifted. "Yeah, we have the connections now that we wouldn't have had before. But you know as well as I do that we can't do that."

AJ slumped into the chair. "I know. But it makes me feel better to think we can. I'd like to make the assholes suffer for what they did to her."

"So would I. But we'd have to find them first. And the chances of that are pretty slim."

AJ turned to Pax. "It had to be the Fists who did that to Teresa."

Pax nodded. "I thought the same thing. The guys dressed all in black, they wore condoms, didn't take off their helmets? And they just *happened* to come by when her bike broke down? What are the odds that was random?"

AJ didn't like it at all. "I don't think it was random. I think she was targeted. Like someone tried to send a message to Joey and the Thorns, and that message didn't get across to them."

"Or maybe it did, and Joey just didn't want Teresa to know."

"Shit," AJ said. "I need to talk to Joey."

"If he doesn't know about a connection to the Fists, are you sure you want to bring it up?"

AJ shrugged. "Either way, he needs to know, and we need to find out what he knows about that night. I don't like what happened to Teresa, and I really don't like that no one's ever paid for it. Someone needs to. The more we know, the better chance we have of finding the guys who did this to her."

"Man, this could fall outside of what we're allowed to do, legally."

AJ looked Pax straight in the eye. "Are you down with that?"

Pax didn't even flinch. "Hell yeah. I hate motherfuckers who hurt women. We need to find them and take them down."

"Good." AJ knew he could count on Pax. And in this they'd always been in agreement. No man took anything from a woman that she didn't give freely. There was no sex involved in an act like that. It was simple brutality and violation at that point.

He and Pax had their fun with women—plenty of fun with a lot of different women. And every single one of those women had been more than willing and always consented. That was one of their rules—no coercion. A woman was either into it or she wasn't. If she wasn't, then game off. There was no fun in having sex with a woman who didn't want to be there. AJ couldn't understand guys who got off on power trips like that. He didn't even want to analyze the whys of a man raping a woman. He only knew the guy should have his dick and balls cut off. There was nothing weaker than a man who forced his strength on a woman. Those were the true pussies in life. And AJ would like to make them all disappear by throwing them off a tall bridge somewhere.

Starting with the two who had hurt Teresa.

nine

a few days later they had nothing more to help Joey. Tests had concluded beyond a doubt that it was Larks's blood on Joey's clothes. The absence of a murder weapon hadn't seemed to dissuade the DA from filing murder charges against Joey. Witnesses had pointed to Joey doing the deed.

Teresa was devastated. Joey was resigned. This was unacceptable.

The only interesting find was in the autopsy report, which indicated that the knife blade used to stab Larks was atypical, had an unusually patterned edge with distinctive markings, as if it had been custom made. The coroner said the edges didn't match any standard knife edges in their database.

Which meant if they could find the guy who owned that knife and match it to the wound pattern on Larks's body, they would have their killer.

Teresa made the suggestion to Pax and AJ after she closed the bar that night. She'd finally been able to reopen the bar, and had

figured Pax and AJ would take off, head back to doing whatever
it was they did for the government. But they hadn't left. They'd
come with her to the bar and helped her and the girls clean it up.
Then whenever she went for updates on Joey's case, they'd hung
out at the police station with her, talked to Joey's lawyer, spent
some time huddled on their cell phones talking to their boss. And
when she opened the bar in the late afternoon, they'd go with her,
one on either side of her like two imposing bodyguards.

She had to admit she didn't mind that part at all. Even Heather
and Shelley were giving her raised brows and elbow nudges,
though she told them both nothing was going on with AJ and
Pax. They didn't believe her.

"I like those guys, Teresa," Heather said as they stood hip to
hip in the storeroom doing liquor inventory.

Teresa inhaled and let it out. "I like them, too."

"One tall, dark and handsome, the other tall, light and handsome. And both have eyes only for you. Goddamn, Teresa, it's
every woman's dream."

She ticked off the whiskey list. "Yeah, it is."

Heather put her clipboard down. "Okay, spill. What is it?"

Teresa turned to her and smiled. Heather was beautiful, popular and changed men as often as most women changed nail polish.
"You know what it is."

"You're gonna tell me again that you're not ready yet."

"I don't know. Maybe. I mean it's been five years. And these
guys . . . they make me feel, Heather. I haven't felt in so damn
long. And I want to. You know how much I really want to."

"Do they know?"

She nodded.

Heather's lips curled up. "And they're still here."

Teresa's smile matched Heather's. "Yes, they are."

"Most men wouldn't be. Many haven't been, as you well know," she added, wagging her finger at her. "None of the guys you've told have stuck around long enough to help you through it."

"I know. And they warm me in ways I can't even explain. More than physically. Their presence—the way they watch over me—"

"They care. They're protective. I can see it. They're nothing like those guys who hurt you."

"Logically I know that."

"At some point you're going to have to stop letting logic lead you and let a man touch you again. And I mean all the way touch you. You're going to have to have sex again. You have the need, don't you?"

She never talked about these things with anyone but Heather. "Of course I do. I get . . . urges, just like any other woman."

Heather crossed her arms. "Let me guess. You're taking care of those . . . urges, on your own, instead of letting a guy take care of them for you."

"Yes. But at least I can touch myself again. Sex is sexy to me again. At least I'm actually thinking about a man touching me again. That's progress, isn't it?"

"Well good for you. After five years you finally want sex again. Get going, Teresa. Otherwise, those assholes who hurt you win. You lose. You know damn well what they did to you wasn't at all about sex."

She shuddered a breath. "I know. You're right." Heather had never coddled her. That's why they were best friends. When she needed a good kick in the butt, she knew where to go. Heather had been there for her five years ago when her world had shattered. She'd held her, comforted her, let her cry for days, weeks, months, had held her hand when she didn't think she'd ever be whole again. And when the time had come for her to pick up the pieces and go on, Heather had been the one to shove a boot in her ass and make her start living again. She owed Heather everything.

"Look, Teresa. You have two hot men who want to take it slow and easy with you and help you get back in the real world. Honey, I'm surprised you aren't coming at the mere thought of it."

Teresa snorted out a laugh. "Believe me, my body is fully aware of them. It's a big step."

Heather laid a hand on her shoulder. "It's a big step that's been a long time coming. Do something about it. Let them help you get past this. If you trust them, they'll back off if it gets too intense." Heather peeked around the corner of the doorway, then looked at Teresa. "Besides, you could always start with doing them one at a time. Then graduate to both."

"Oh, God." Teresa leaned against the wall, the cool brick taking her rocketing temperature down. "One at a time would be more than enough, I think."

Heather's eyes went dark. "I'd do both of them in a New York minute."

"I'll bet you would." She envied Heather's ability to think about sex as just . . . sex. Teresa had to get that mind-set back. She *would* get it back. The rape wasn't going to define her for the rest of her life.

"You decide you want to dump them, let me know. I'll do whatever it takes to get a piece of both of them before they ride on out of town."

"Whore."

Heather laughed and picked up the clipboard, once again scanning the liquor boxes. "You say the sweetest things."

Traffic was light at the bar tonight, but it was about what Teresa expected. She had a few strangers pop in now and then, but her regulars had always been Joey and the rest of the Thorns, and with the start of Bike Week in Sturgis in a couple days, all the bikers had headed up north to South Dakota. Joey's guys hadn't wanted to go out of loyalty to him. Even though he was out on bail, he needed to stay put. But Joey had insisted the Thorns go have some fun. God knows someone should.

She paused in wiping up the bar. Of course. That's why they couldn't find the Fists. She dropped the rag in the sink and went to the table where AJ and Pax were nursing their beers and talking to Joey. She leaned over to talk to them.

"They're in Sturgis. That's why we couldn't find any of the Fists."

Pax arched a brow. "You sure?"

"No. But it makes sense. Our guys headed up there, didn't they?"

Joey nodded. "Russ and the others left at dawn."

"Do you usually go up there?" AJ asked.

"We go every year. Never miss it," Joey said.

"He's right," Teresa added. "This place is a ghost town during Sturgis Bike Rally week every August. All the biker clubs from the region head up there. I don't know why I didn't make the connection the other night." She took a glance at the clock. One hour until closing time. She was certain Heather and Shelley could run the bar for her. "We need to get on the road."

AJ raised a hand. "Wait a minute. Get on the road? What the hell are you talking about?"

"Sturgis. We need to go." She took a look around the bar, then swiveled back to them. "Or I need to go there. You can come along if you want, or not." She ran her fingers through her hair. "I'm going."

AJ exchanged looks with Pax, who shrugged and said, "I don't have a clue." Pax looked at Teresa. "What are you talking about, honey?"

"Don't you see? The guy who killed Larks has to be up there."

She decided to ignore their dubious looks.

"How do you figure?" Pax asked.

"The Fists went there. I'd wager this bar that's where he is. And I'm the only one who can identify him."

"No," AJ said.

"She has a point, AJ," Pax said.

Joey stood. "Oh hell no. No fucking way, Teresa."

"I agree with Joey," AJ said. "Let the cops handle it."

Teresa turned to AJ. "They don't even know who to look for. I do. I know he's there."

"Yeah, him and a half million other bikers," Pax said with a laugh.

"Needle in a haystack, Teresa," AJ added. "You don't seriously think you could find him up there."

"If the Fists are all up there, they'll hang as a group. They'll protect their own, including this guy."

"Providing he didn't turn against the Fists," Pax said.

"If he'd betrayed the Fists he'd be a dead man by now," Joey said. "Turning against one of your own club leaders requires swift and very public retaliation. If he killed Larks, the Fists would have taken him down right away. And we'd all know about it."

AJ nodded. "Joey's right. And if he didn't, if this was planned with the Fists full knowledge, then they all closed ranks around him."

"Which means he's with them. They're protecting him," Teresa said.

"In Sturgis, if they're all up there," Pax added.

"So maybe that's what did happen. But there's no guarantee," Joey said.

"Well maybe he did, and maybe he didn't. Either way, we have to help my brother. I can't do nothing when I might hold the key to his freedom."

"Hey." Joey laid his hand over hers. "I'm going to be fine. I didn't do this, and eventually the cops are going to figure that out. It's not your job to save me."

She palmed the top of the bar, her gaze clear and focused as she looked from AJ to Pax to her brother. "I know what I'm doing. And if the cops are here trying to find him, why can't we be up in Sturgis doing the same thing?"

"Do you really know what you're in for?" Pax asked "It'll be crazy up in Sturgis, honey. Crowded. Lots of bikers. Lots of men."

She sucked in a breath. For Joey, she'd do it. She had to. And she wasn't going to be afraid. She lifted her chin. "I can handle this. Let's go."

Pax slid his gaze to AJ, who shook his head.

"I don't like this."

That piqued Teresa's anger. "I'm going with or without you two."

AJ's gaze shot to hers. "That's not smart."

"I'll get some friends to go with me. I won't go alone. Russ and the other Thorns are up there, and I could meet up with them. But you're not stopping me."

"We'll go with you," Pax said, giving AJ a solid glare when AJ turned to him. "Won't we, AJ?"

AJ locked gazes with Pax, then finally shrugged. "I guess so."

Teresa turned to Joey. "I'm sorry you can't go with us. But can you hang around the bar and keep an eye on my girls?"

"You know I will. I still don't like this."

"I know you don't. But if our situations were reversed, you'd do it for me."

"Yeah, I would. But this is different."

She crossed her arms. "Don't get sexist on me. Besides, I have two of the best bodyguards around going with me. I'll be fine."

"I guess we're going to Sturgis, then," AJ said. "We'll leave first thing in the morning."

After Teresa closed up the bar, AJ sent her home with Pax. He detoured to Joey's apartment to talk to him.

Joey lived like a true bachelor: sparse furniture, beer cans and laundry strewn everywhere; not much in the fridge with the exception of beer. Joey grabbed a couple and handed one to AJ. They took seats on the worn-out sofa and chair in Joey's living room.

"I'm sorry you and Pax got mixed up in all of this. Really shitty timing for you guys."

AJ shrugged. "It's no big deal. I'm just glad we could be here for you. And for Teresa."

Joey took a couple slugs of beer, then wiped his mouth. "Man, you gotta keep an eye on her. I don't like this whole Sturgis thing."

AJ looked down at his beer, then back at up at Joey. "She told us about the rape."

Joey leaned forward, blew out a breath and looked at his shoes. "Damn."

"Now I want you to tell me the real story."

Joey's head shot up. "What real story?"

"It was a message from the Fists, wasn't it?"

Joey's brows slanted together in anger. "That's a lie. It was random."

"You trying to make me believe it, or make yourself? Don't bullshit me, my friend. We go too far back for that."

Joey laid his beer on the scarred table and stood, ran his fingers through his hair and walked to the front window, staring outside.

"We had just had a big showdown with the Fists the night before. Larks was laying down some serious pressure about us joining with him. He wanted to make inroads into our territory, needed the river to get access for his drug shipments."

"And the Thorns were blocking him."

"Hell yeah. This is our turf and he and his fucking drugs could shove it, which is what I told him. I told him he could stay the hell out of our territory or face the consequences. The Thorns were willing to go to war to protect what was ours."

"And?"

Joey blew out a breath. "Larks said we wouldn't win a war with them. We were too clean and the Fists fought dirty, and we might not like the consequences. Then they left. The next night, Teresa's bike broke down and she was raped."

AJ didn't say anything. He knew there was more Joey needed to say.

"There wasn't a goddamn thing wrong with her bike or her tires. I checked them myself all the time at the garage."

"Someone sabotaged her bike."

"Yes. She was set up to have a blowout and they were waiting for her."

"She was used as an example of what war with the Fists would be like. He wanted to show you what the casualties would be."

"They wore no colors, no patches and kept every part of their bodies covered. And when they raped her they never said a word. They knew Teresa would be able to identify them otherwise. But it was the Fists. I'd wager my soul on it."

"Retaliation?"

Joey had the decency to look ashamed. "We weren't sure, ya know? In my gut . . . yeah, it was the Fists. But retaliation would mean war."

"And you didn't want war." Not even on behalf of Teresa. AJ would have gone full throttle against the Fists if it had been his sister. But it wasn't his club and it wasn't his decision to make. Guilt pounded at him. If he'd been here, if he'd never left, things would have been different.

This would have never happened to her.

"Does she know it was the Fists who did the rape?"

The misery on his face gut punched AJ. "I don't know. We don't talk about it. She won't talk about it."

"You sure that's a good idea?"

"She had plenty of rape counseling. The Fists were all investigated, fingers were pointed at them. But there wasn't a scrap of DNA to identify anyone."

AJ leaned back and let out a breath. "This sucks, Joey."

"You're telling me? I've lived with this guilt for five years, that my sister had to suffer for something I did. How the hell do you think that feels?"

"She doesn't blame you."

"Of course she doesn't. That doesn't mean it wasn't my fault. I should have protected her better."

And if AJ hadn't turned tail and run out of town to escape the miserable existence of his life, a lot of things would have been different. And maybe he'd have still been here to protect Teresa. Guilt weighed heavily on him, too. "Teresa's a strong woman."

"She's doing okay. But I still hate leaving her alone. She likes living in our parents' house by herself, craves her independence, refuses to let the rape change who she is."

"Good for her."

"But it did change her, AJ. As much as she tries to pretend it didn't, it changed who she is. There's a light that used to shine in her eyes that isn't there. And her fear of men and relationships—"

"Yeah, I've caught a glimpse of that."

Joey's hands clenched into fists, and he turned away to face the window again, but not before AJ caught the tears brimming in his friend's eyes. "If I ever find out who did this to her, I'm going to rain down hurt on them like the fires of hell."

"I'll help you."

PAX WASN'T SURE WHY HE'D JUMPED ON THE IDEA OF TAK-ing Teresa to Sturgis, but she seemed determined to go and no way in hell was he going to let her go alone. AJ argued that it was a bad idea for her to go at all, but Pax figured she was going to be too stubborn to let someone else deal with it. It was important to her to find this guy and save her brother, and she wasn't patient enough to let the cops do it.

Though he couldn't blame her, since the local police seemed to think they already had their man and would probably be slow about gathering any additional evidence or suspects, even minus a murder weapon. That he didn't understand, but then he was always pretty thorough about everything, no stone left unturned and all that. How they thought they could convict Joey based on blood evidence on his clothes alone made no sense. Sure, there had been animosity between Joey and Larks, but that wasn't enough. And the Fists as eyewitnesses? Come on. The police needed to be hunting and hunting hard for the murder weapon. And if they weren't, then Pax agreed with Teresa—they'd go find the actual guy who did the deed, and hopefully he'd have the knife on him, especially if it was a one-of-a-kind. Guys who had knives custom made for them didn't ditch them in a Dumpster. Guys tended to be sentimental about their weaponry anyway, but especially one-of-a-kind weapons, which were definitely keepers.

They lucked out because General Lee had his own place in Sturgis. He usually went up there for the annual rally, but this year he was stuck on an assignment and couldn't make it. One phone call and Pax had secured the property for them, plus filled General Lee in on what was going on with Teresa and her brother. General Lee's only advice was to lie low and not blow their covers unless absolutely necessary. The entire Wild Riders organization operated under security and stealth. They didn't exactly flash their badges on a regular basis, and General Lee hadn't been happy AJ and Pax had done so in order to walk into a murder scene. Pax got that, understood the ramifications of too many people knowing about a secret organization that wasn't even supposed to exist. He promised the general they'd keep it low-key in Sturgis.

Which didn't mean they wouldn't be locked and loaded.

They packed up early that morning, the sun still nothing more than a glint of gray light over the horizon as they took off. Teresa climbed on the back of Pax's bike again. He liked having her back there, liked feeling her thighs sliding alongside his, the press of her breasts against his back when she leaned forward. AJ didn't say a word or look like he was unhappy about it. Then again, sharing a woman was normal for them, so jealousy had never been an issue before.

Sharing Teresa—a woman AJ had a past with—that might be something different.

But they weren't really sharing her, not after finding out what had happened to her. They were protecting her. That was it. That was all there was going to be. At least for now. Teresa was going to call all the shots, and that's the way it should be. She had to be in charge, at least of what she wanted as far as her body. As far as the investigation—Pax and AJ would have to take the lead on that since they had more experience, and he was afraid Teresa would go balls to the wall trying to clear her brother. There were better ways to get what you wanted.

The trip would have been nice if they'd taken it for any other reason, if they'd been able to take a slow and easy back-roads pace. But they weren't on vacation any longer, so they stuck to the interstate and got to the general's place late that same night. It was a grueling ride, but Teresa was a trooper about it, didn't complain once about her butt being sore or how long the ride was. They stopped plenty of times for gas, meals and drinks and to stretch their legs, but she seemed just as anxious to get there as Pax and AJ were. It probably helped that she swapped, periodically riding on AJ's bike, then back to Pax's, giving her ass a different seat to rest on.

Pax had to admit that the bike rally in Sturgis was one of his favorite places, so he didn't mind combining a bit of business with pleasure. It was the be-all, end-all of bike rallys. If you were a biker, this was the place you wanted to be, along with hundreds of thousands of other bikers. How they were going to find the Fists—and the guy who stabbed Joey—was another matter, but if Teresa was determined, he'd back her up.

TeReSa HeLD HeR BReaTH aS THeY WOUnD THROUGH ROaDS that made the bike turn nearly on its side. It was a good thing she trusted Pax to know what he was doing, but she still held on like she might be tossed off at every curve. She wasn't a novice at riding, but these were some steep curves, and she'd always had her own bike. Being on the back was a lot different than controlling your own destiny. When she wasn't fearing for her life, though, she was absorbing every inch of the breathtaking scenery as they cruised into the Black Hills of South Dakota. And she only caught a glimpse of the stunning beauty of the area as they cruised down the highway. Miles of majestic forest still awaited her, and she knew Mount Rushmore was nearby, as well as a rally filled with bikers and motorcycles of every kind. Despite being here for a genuine purpose, she couldn't help the rush of adrenaline.

Being on a bike again had been therapeutic, had forced her to face the trauma of that night at least in one way. The motorcycle hadn't caused the rape. She could ride without fear, and the itch to climb on her own bike again began to grow in earnest. Trouble was, she had sold her old bike. It was time to start thinking of getting a new one.

Progress. She liked that. It filled her with hope.

They drove up a long, single driveway, and Teresa held her breath as they climbed off. A light shone at the top of the yard, spotlighting the hill they stood on. At the top of the hill she saw . . . everything. Sloping hills, steep mountains, miles of trees, an entire landscape spread out before them. Behind them stood General Lee's house separated by private fencing and a big yard. The large cabin had a wraparound porch that looked as welcoming as anything she'd ever seen. It was wood-roofed and stone and rustic, with hanging pots swinging in the breeze. The porch light was on, and Teresa saw several Adirondack chairs with deep cushions, and could already imagine putting her feet up on the rail and watching what must be an incredible view from the porch. She couldn't wait till morning.

"We're staying here?"

AJ nodded. "Grange comes up here a lot on his time off. He likes the rides around the hills and into Wyoming."

"He must do a lot of traveling." She pointed to the RV parked under cover of the carport.

"He likes to see as much of the country as he can when he has downtime," AJ said.

She grabbed her bag and followed AJ up the front steps. He

slid his hand under one of the potted plants and pulled out a key, then opened the front door and turned on the lights.

THE INSIDE WAS JUST AS GOOD AS THE OUTSIDE. RUSTIC, BUT homey, with a huge L-shaped sofa, a cushy oversized ottoman set in front of it, a fireplace, wood flooring throughout and scattered area rugs. The place was huge, with three bedrooms plus two bathrooms. Much more room than Teresa had expected, enough to give her some distance from AJ and Pax, some time to think.

But did she really want that distance? Wasn't that what the last five years had been about—distancing herself from men? Maybe it was time to bridge the gap.

No. That wasn't why they were here. She had come here to find Larks's killer and clear her brother, and that's what she needed to concentrate on, not her personal hangups and finding a way through that particular mess.

"I put your stuff in the master bedroom," AJ said.

Teresa turned around. "Why?"

"Because you're the lady and you need the most room. Pax and I can crash anywhere."

"Hope there aren't bunk beds in those other two bedrooms," Pax said.

Teresa laughed at the visual of two men over six feet tall trying to squeeze into beds made for kids.

"I don't mind taking one of the smaller rooms."

Pax slung his arm around her. "I was kidding. AJ is right. We could take the floor if we needed to. We've slept outside before. It doesn't matter."

"They aren't bunk beds, dipshit," AJ said. "I already checked out the other two rooms. They're regular beds. Though Teresa has a nice king-sized bed."

Built for three?

The thought entered her head, unbidden, and stayed there as she went into the master bedroom and unpacked, then freshened up after the long ride. She couldn't seem to take her eyes off the bed. Big enough for her and Pax and AJ.

She felt the pull of desire as she imagined just what she could do with those men in her bed. Both of them.

Wasn't it time she took back control of her sex life? Wasn't it time she stopped being afraid of a man's touch? Wasn't it time she stopped letting those assholes who hurt her have power over her life?

Yes to all those questions. Hell yes. She was stronger than what had happened to her, physically and psychologically. It was time to put it to rest—not to forget, but to not let it lead her.

When she came out of the bedroom and into the living area, the sliding door was open. She stepped onto the back deck, her eyes widening at the sight of a sizeable hot tub and cushioned lounge chairs. The view from the back was just as good as the one from the front. There was a bit of a chill in the air tonight, and the thought of sliding into a steamy hot tub and watching the stars overhead appealed.

Pax and AJ were out there leaning against the wood railing.

"You bring your swimsuit?" AJ asked, his gaze shifting to the hot tub. They'd pulled the cover off and steam lifted off the top of the water.

She shook her head. "I didn't even think about it."

"Too bad," Pax said. "Nice night for a soak in the tub." Pax pushed off the railing and went back into the house. Teresa turned to AJ.

"I suppose you guys have swim trunks." She was already jealous, thinking how great a hot soak would feel on her tired muscles.

AJ laughed. "No. But if you want to get in there and relax your muscles from the ride, Pax and I can make ourselves scarce."

They'd do that, too. Would let her get in the hot tub all by herself. It was a lonely thought and didn't appeal to her at all. She wanted to share it with them. With both of them.

"How about we all get in and relax together?"

She refused to look away, wanted to see what was in his eyes, needed to know if it was going to be too much. She wasn't sure if what she suggested was a sexual invitation, or just an invitation to get in the hot tub and have some company.

AJ shrugged. "Fine with me. Why don't you get in. I'll go see if Pax wants to join us."

He left and she was out there alone. Plenty of privacy for her to strip. It was now or never.

She wanted this now. At least the hot tub part. She undressed and slid over the rim of the tub. The water was hot, but perfect. She found the button for the jets and turned them on. Bubbles obliterated the view of her body, and she leaned her head against the edge and stared up at the stars blanketing the night sky. They were so close they seemed about to fall down on her at any moment.

It was breathtaking out here, the air cool and crisp, which made the temperature of the water just right. Her muscles melted as the jets worked the soreness out of her back. She closed her eyes and drifted away, until a hand touched her face. She didn't flinch.

"You falling asleep in there?"

She smiled at AJ. "No. Just relaxing."

"How about a beer?"

She lifted her hand out of the water to take the can of beer from him, engaged by the steam rising off her arm. "Sure."

AJ popped open the top of his beer and sat on the edge of the hot tub. "Nice night."

"Yes it is. Where's Pax?"

"Inside, making us some snacks. Grange managed to call ahead and have the fridge fully stocked."

"Pax cooks?"

"Pax cooks. It's not steak, but it'll do for tonight. I was hungry."

Teresa turned around and saw Pax come out with a tray filled with . . . something. He set the tray down on the side bench attached to the hot tub.

"I made some finger foods. Easier to eat when you're all wet."

Chips and dips and sandwiches and vegetables, and suddenly Teresa was starving. She leaned over and started munching, and so did the guys. Before long, her beer was empty and AJ had replaced it with another from the cooler he'd brought onto the deck. Satiated, she sat back with her beer and smiled.

This couldn't get any better. Well, yeah, it could. Because Pax and AJ were fully clothed and sitting outside the hot tub. And she knew why. She appreciated them looking out for her and taking things slow and easy, but she refused to be afraid to be in a hot tub naked with two guys she knew weren't going to push her to do anything she wasn't ready for.

"Why don't you two get in here with me?"

AJ played with a lock of her hair. She'd put it up in a messy ponytail on top of her head before getting into the tub.

"Are you sure that's what you want?" he asked.

"I'm sure that's what I want." She scooted to the far side of the tub and waited, ignoring the racing of her pulse and the too-fast beating of her heart.

Pax looked to AJ. "I think I'll take this stuff inside. And I need to check in with Grange, let him know we're here. You go on ahead."

AJ nodded and turned to face the hot tub after Pax went inside. "You sure about this?"

She wasn't sure about anything where men were concerned. All she was sure about was that she wanted to be normal again, to have some fun. "Get in the hot tub, AJ."

His lips quirked, just like she remembered. "Yes, ma'am. You might want to avert your eyes, then, because I'm about to get naked."

Now it was her turn to lift her lips. "Why would I want to avert my eyes, then?"

His smile died, and what she saw on his face was pure hunger. But she still felt no threat from him. She knew AJ, trusted him, knew she was safe with him, even naked together in the hot tub. He was one of the most patient guys she'd ever known.

He pulled his shirt off, and Teresa sucked in a breath at the wide expanse of shoulders and chest. He'd matured so well in the years since she'd seen him last. Gone was the lean boy she'd known. He was muscled and broad, with a wide chest and flat stomach, a smattering of dark hair on both. He toed off his boots and pulled off his socks, then undid the belt buckle on his jeans and pulled the zipper down, letting them drop to the deck. Teresa's heart continued to beat faster, but it wasn't fear driving that beat, it was pure, unadulterated feminine appreciation for the man who stood in front of her clad only in tight boxer briefs that did nothing to hide his beautiful body.

He pushed the boxers off, and she got only a brief glimpse of his magnificent cock before he slid over the side of the hot tub and into the water.

"Goddamn. You didn't tell me it was going to be this hot. I'll probably never be able to give a woman children now."

She laughed. "It's not that hot, you wuss."

"It's hot enough. I'm sweating in here."

"Good God. I'll turn it down." She reached over to the controls and notched it down a few degrees. "Men are such babies."

"Hey, I can take a bullet. Just not a thousand-degree hot tub."

She rolled her eyes, and AJ laughed, stretching his legs out, his feet touching hers. He kept his gaze on hers, no doubt assuming one touch of his feet against hers and she was going to bolt and run like hell.

She couldn't blame him for that, considering how skittish she'd been with him and Pax. Yet he pulled his foot back, draped his sculpted arms over the sides of the hot tub, and leaned his head against it, effectively withdrawing from her. Yes, he was in the tub with her, but he wasn't *with* her.

"When will we head where all the other bikers are?"

"Tomorrow," he said, keeping his eyes closed and his head resting against the hot tub. "It'll give us a full day to check out the area, see where people are congregating and figure out the gang hangouts. Most people stay near the campgrounds or in the area in town where the vendors are. We'll go there first."

"Okay. And if we find the Fists?"

"You can look them over and see if you can spot the guy who stabbed Larks."

"And if I do?"

"We'll notify local authorities that he's a suspect in a murder in Missouri. They'll detain him."

"And if they don't?"

AJ smiled. "You ask a lot of questions."

"I like to know all the details so I can plan ahead."

He sat straight up. "You won't be able to plan ahead for something like this. Whatever happens, count on it being unpredictable. If we can even find the Fists . . . and your phantom killer."

"He's not a phantom. I saw him."

"I believe you. But there's only a small chance he's here."

"Oh, he's here all right. What a great place to hide out. The Fists . . . and this guy . . . have no idea what's going on with the investigation back home. For all they know someone has fingered him for Larks's murder, so they want to be as far away from that as possible."

He shrugged. "We'll see. Don't be disappointed if we don't find either him or the Fists here."

"And I'm going to say 'I told you so' when we find them both."

AJ laughed and stretched out his legs, brushing her feet again. He pulled back. Again.

Teresa frowned. "I'm not that fragile, AJ. You can touch me."

"I don't want to give you the impression I'm after something."

She cocked a brow. "So you're saying you don't find me attractive?"

He rolled his eyes. "I think you know better than that. You know I want you. I've always wanted you."

"You said you wanted me ten years ago, too. You used amazing restraint in walking away from me."

"More than you'll ever know. I didn't want to leave."

"But you did."

"I was a criminal. I knew where I was headed and I didn't want to take you with me."

"How . . . noble of you."

She sounded bitchy and knew it, but old hurts had arisen and she didn't know how to shove them back down where they belonged.

"I could have fucked you that night. Hell, it's what we both wanted."

"Instead, you let someone else take what you'd waited years to have. Did you ever wonder who was my first, AJ?"

The darkness hid his eyes, but she felt the tension clear across the hot tub. "All the time."

Maybe she wanted him to feel some of the misery she'd felt after he dumped her and left her wondering what it was that was lacking in her that caused him to walk away from something so good.

And what exactly was the point of dredging this up again? To hurt him? She'd succeeded. Or was she just trying to drive a wedge between them so he wouldn't get too close? God knew she was famous for that, using any excuse to keep men at arm's length.

Distance, always distance.

"I'm sorry I hurt you, Teresa. If there had been any other way to do it I would have. And I could have taken your virginity that night, but I already knew I was going to leave. And I wasn't going to take you with me. So which would have been worse?"

She shook her head. "I don't want to talk about the past anymore, AJ. I'm the one who's sorry. It was petty of me and I shouldn't have brought it up."

What had started out fun and light had turned deep and dark and miserable. She hated the damper she'd put on this evening, wished she could do something to lighten things up again.

AJ moved over to her side of the hot tub, occupying space on the same bench.

"I don't mind being held accountable for what I did to you. I deserve every bit of what you throw at me."

She tilted her head back to stare up into his dark eyes. "You did what you thought was right at the time. And I won't deny that it hurt, but the sensible part of me understands why you did it."

He touched her nose with the tip of his finger. "The sensible part of you isn't what I hurt."

"True enough. But we can't go back and change what is. We can only look forward."

He was close, but his body still didn't touch hers. The heat of the water and AJ being so close reminded her why they were in this hot tub in the first place.

Time to leave all things in the past behind and move toward an uncertain future, and the only way to do that was to let go.

She scooted closer to him until their thighs touched, acutely aware that neither of them were clothed. Her breath caught at the contact, but she was more interested in what was happening with his body under the water than she was in her own reaction to being this close to a naked man.

There was no violence in this situation, and what had happened to her before hadn't been about sex. The logical part of her mind knew this. It was time to get her body in line with what her mind knew. She wanted sex again, wanted to feel good and hot and have a man's hands and mouth all over her and not think about that time five years ago.

She half turned, dragging one leg up onto the bench so she faced AJ. "Where's Pax?"

AJ turned to her. "Inside."

"Why?"

"Because we don't want to overwhelm you."

She cocked a brow. "Did you flip a coin?"

"No."

"Oh. I see."

"What do you see?"

"Look, AJ. I know you like me. We go way back. Obviously you're the one stuck with babysitting the fractured woman."

He snorted out a laugh. "Is that how you see it?"

She looked away. AJ tipped her chin to face him.

"You're wrong." He let go of her. "Hey, Pax," he yelled. "Come on out here a second."

Teresa grabbed his arm. "What are you doing?"

"Pax!"

Pax showed up in the doorway. "What? There's a game on. Cleveland is up, bottom of the ninth and bases are loaded. This better be important."

"Teresa thinks I'm the one out here with her because I pulled the short straw."

She wanted to slide under the water until she drowned.

Pax shifted his gaze to her. "Is that what she thinks?"

"Yeah, that's what she thinks," AJ said.

Pax pushed off the wall and came over to the other side of the hot tub and kneeled down next to her. He slid his fingers to the nape of her neck and turned her head to face him. "Babe, you couldn't be more wrong about that."

He slid his mouth over hers and she gasped at the contact, the rush of heat, the unexpected flood of hunger that washed over her as his tongue invaded her mouth. This was no gentle kiss. It was need and desire and—oh dear God—he told her in that kiss that he wanted her. His fingers slid up into her hair to hold her steady, gently and yet with undeniable, masterful dominance, the kind a woman wants from a man when he's kissing her.

When he pulled away, Teresa was slack-jawed, out of breath, and could only stare into Pax's liquid chocolate eyes and wish he were naked and in the tub with her right now.

"I'm going to head to the store for a few things. I'll be back later."

He pushed off and left her with AJ.

ten

OH, GOD. AJ HAD BEEN WATCHING. TERESA WHIPPED HER HEAD around to find AJ studying her with a mixture of curiosity and desire in his eyes. She licked her lips, wanting to touch them with her fingers, but not wanting to give him the wrong idea. Her mouth tingled from Pax's kiss. Hell, her entire body tingled, from her nipples to her pussy, which had fired to life in such a major way.

There'd been no fear in that kiss, only wonder and joy and need.

She wanted more, but she was also confused as hell.

"You liked that kiss?" AJ said.

How was she supposed to answer that? Honestly, she supposed. "Yes."

AJ's lips curled upward. "Good."

She leaned back, studying him. "It doesn't bother you that I kissed him."

"Hell no. Watching you kiss Pax was hot."

"I don't know whether to be shocked or insulted or . . . something else entirely."

He reached out and smoothed his wet hand over her hair. "Why would you be insulted?"

"Most men are possessive and jealous, wouldn't want to see a woman they're . . . with . . . being touched or kissed by another man."

"Pax isn't just another man. If it were any other guy, then hell yeah I'd be pissed. He and I have been friends a long time. There's no jealousy between us."

"Why not?"

AJ shrugged. "There just isn't. What's mine is his. What's his is mine."

"You share your women all the time?"

"All the time."

"Why?"

"When we first joined the Wild Riders, he and I got close, became friends. We have similar tastes in women, so we found ourselves going after the same women all the time. And then we ended up with the same woman one night. And it worked out for us. Then it happened again, and it was something we both enjoyed, so why not?"

"And neither one of you gets jealous."

"No. Why would we?"

"Obviously you've never been in love."

AJ's eyes went stormy gray. "Yeah, I have."

Teresa looked away, then back at him. "That was a long time ago. We were kids then."

"We're not kids now."

"You don't love me now."

She expected him to look away, to change the subject.

"I'll always love you, Teresa. You were there for me when no one else was. You were the first—the only—girl I ever cared about.

But that whole love and permanence and forever thing? I realized a long time ago it's not for me. I can't offer that kind of lifestyle to a woman. My job takes me everywhere. I'd never be there for the kids. And I'm not going to ignore my wife and have my children end up resenting me. Children should feel wanted and appreciated and loved."

She swept her hand across his jaw. "You don't want to be lonely and cast aside like you were as a kid."

He lifted his gaze to hers, and she saw the pain that had been there when he was younger. "Something like that. I'd like to think I learned a thing or two from the mistakes my parents made."

"Your stepfather was an asshole and your mother was heartless."

AJ laughed. "Yeah, he was. As far as my mom, she was needy and depended on him for her sense of self. And he played on her weaknesses. I don't want to be like that."

"You're not."

He let out a soft laugh. "Don't be so sure. You haven't been around me in a while."

"Who you were then hasn't changed in here." She laid her hand on his chest and felt the strong, solid beat. "That night you and I . . . in the truck. On my birthday. Then, I didn't understand what you did."

"I'm sorry."

"No, I do understand now. It took me a while, and I was hurt that you left me. But I realized later that neither of us was ready for that step, and that you were the one who put a stop to it. I was full of dreams for you and me. I was full of forever. And that wasn't you."

"I had decided where I was going and it wasn't a place you wanted to be. I would have ruined you."

"I don't think you would have, but I understand you were con-fused back then."

"I was a criminal back then. I couldn't do that to you."

"Because you loved me that much."

"Because I loved you that much."

Her heart did a little flip, even though he'd said "love" in the past tense. "Most guys would have taken what I was offering without hesitation or even thinking how it would affect me. You had more honor at eighteen than your stepfather will ever have. So don't ever compare yourself to him again. You could never be him."

He went silent then, and Teresa wondered if he was thinking about what she'd said or about his past.

"I kept the necklace you gave me."

He arched a brow. "You did?"

"Yes."

"I'm surprised you didn't throw it away."

"It meant something to me. I might have been angry and hurt, but I still kept it. I keep it in my jewelry box."

He leaned his forehead against hers. "God, Teresa." He inhaled, let it out. "Thank you."

"For what?"

"For not hating me."

She laughed. "I couldn't hate you, AJ. I tried. But I couldn't."

AJ slid his hand along her neck. Teresa leaned back against the hot tub as his mouth met hers in a soft kiss that was so different from the one Pax had given her, but one that still curled her toes. Where Pax had been all hot fire and passion and demand, AJ was slow, torturous sensation, his lips barely touching hers at first, a light brush meant to tantalize, and did it ever. She lifted up to increase the contact, felt the curl of his lips in a smile as he pressed further against hers and upped the pressure just a bit more. And when his tongue slid between her teeth, again just the tip to tease her, she moaned against his lips and reached for his shoulders to pull his body closer.

She knew he held back, felt the tension in his muscles, and appreciated that he had such infinite patience with her, but now she wanted more.

"Touch me. Put your body against mine," she whispered against his mouth.

"You tell me when to stop," he said, and slid his arm around her waist to tug her flush against his body, his mouth fitting full to hers, his tongue diving in completely to sweep against hers in soft velvet strokes that made her tremble all over. And yet he still held her lightly in his grasp. She could push away easily and she knew he took care with her, didn't want her to feel pinned between him and the wall of the hot tub.

She wasn't even thinking about that, not when she could explore his mouth and his tongue and the touch of his body against hers. The hot tub suddenly seemed too . . . hot. She wanted out where she could explore him, look at him, touch him without the added heat of the water.

She pulled her lips from his. "It's too hot. Let's get out of here."

He leaned his face away, enough for her to see the heat blazing in his eyes. "I feel the need to remind you we're both naked."

She laughed. "I know. But I'm melting in here."

AJ hopped out of the tub, steam rising off his skin. He grabbed a thick white robe, not at all concerned about his nudity or his erection. Teresa wanted to stay where she was and just . . . look at him. But the heat in her body was steadily growing to dangerous levels, and if she continued to gape at AJ's body, she was going to have a meltdown. She stood and he held his hand out for her, helping her step out of the tub. Though his gaze roamed over her body, he held the robe while she slid into it.

"Aren't you cold?" she asked. She was warm in the robe. He was still naked, and it was definitely cool outside.

"Babe, I just got a look at your naked body. I'm anything but cold."

He tugged her closer and kissed her. Heat flared and swelled her breasts as he brought one arm around her back, drawing her against him. She stepped into the embrace, needing to feel his naked flesh against her naked flesh. It had been so long since she'd had that human contact of skin to skin, coupled with the passion that swelled inside her as AJ kissed her senseless.

They'd done damn near everything ten years ago, except they'd never been fully naked together. Oh, what she'd missed. The feel of his strong body against hers, the play of his muscles as she pressed her fingertips against his chest, the solid strength of him as he lifted her into his arms and carried her to her bedroom, as if she weighed nothing. And as he walked, he stared at her face, the intensity of his gaze a storm of rising passion. She shivered as he laid her on the bed and climbed on after her, pulling her against him.

"Cold?" he asked. "There's a blanket on the end of the bed."

"No. Not cold." She traced his jaw with her fingertips, in awe that she was lying next to a naked man in bed. This was light-years of progress. No shattering fear, no rush of adrenaline screaming at her to flee. It helped that it was AJ, someone she knew and trusted, someone she knew she could say "stop" to at any moment and he would; it would end, and he wouldn't be angry at her.

But she didn't want to stop, didn't want this to end. Not yet. She wanted AJ over her, on top of her, inside of her. She reached for his arm, pulling him toward her. He resisted, instead sliding his fingers in her hair, his fingertips moving around her scalp to the nape of her neck.

"You're even more beautiful now than you were ten years ago." One of his hands rested in her hair. He parted the robe and bared her body. She waited to tense up, but didn't. Instead, she enjoyed his frank appraisal of her as his gaze swept from her feet to her face and all the places in between.

"Do you remember when we used to make out in my car?"

She smiled at the memory. It was such an innocent time. "Yes. You had that old Chevy Camaro."

He shifted his movement, his hand sliding over her collarbone, his fingers resting on the swell of one breast. "With the too-small backseat."

It was hard to focus on his conversation with his fingers tapping across her breast. "I don't remember you complaining about the backseat then."

"I was too busy trying to cop a feel to complain about anything."

She giggled, and his palm slid over her breast. He let it rest there. "Like now?"

He arched a brow. "Like now. And just like then, I take each step slow and easy, waiting to see when you're going to knee me in the balls and push me away."

She laughed, her heart skipping a beat when he moved his palm over her nipple. It peaked against his hand, tightening with painful pleasure as he touched her with the barest tips of his fingers, floating over her nipples like a feather. It was maddening and wonderful to be worshipped like this, a slow and lazy dance to reintroduce her to sex.

But she wanted more, and she arched against his hand to let him know it, watching the stormy reaction in his eyes. His hand stayed steady, though, floating from her breasts to her ribs to her belly.

"I like this." He circled the piercing at her navel. "Sexy."

"I needed to take control over my body again after . . . after a while. That's why I got the tattoo and the piercing."

"I like them both." He flicked the dangling jewel at her belly, then laid his palm flat below it, his fingers resting right above her sex.

Teresa sucked in a breath at this slow dance of seduction. She was wet and needy, and it had been far too long since any man had touched her in the sweet, passionate way she needed to be touched. The only orgasms she'd had in the past five years had been self-induced, and she was damn tired of doing it herself. Her body was in full-on awareness of having AJ next to her, and she wanted more than she was able to vocalize.

But apparently AJ knew just what to do. And when he slid his hand lower to cup her sex, taking her mouth in a deep kiss at the same time, she gasped and rolled toward him, arching her hips to drive against his hand. He hissed against her mouth and she felt the restraint in his tightened muscles, knew it cost him to take this slow ride with her when he was probably used to throwing a woman down and fucking her senseless.

She'd like to be fucked senseless. But this was just what she needed right now, and she couldn't help but be seduced by the maddening way AJ slid his hand over her wet flesh, parting his fingers as they glided over her clit and down her pussy lips. He slipped his fingers inside her and used the heel of his hand to caress the tight nub, pumping and rubbing her until the sweet tension mounted and she lifted, rocking against his hand, arching ever closer to the hot, tingling pleasure.

She was already pathetically close to orgasm, but she wanted to wait, first because she didn't want to embarrass herself by coming almost immediately, and second because it felt so damn good to be touched like this she didn't want it to end too soon. She needed to soak this in, to experience every second and burn it into her memory.

If she allowed herself to think too much about it, she'd self-combust. A man was touching her again. It seemed like an eternity since that had happened. She had begun to think it never would, that she was frozen, would be unable to accept a man's touch ever again. But she could, and oh, it was good.

AJ slid his lips from her mouth to her neck, licking her, snaking a path to her collarbone and chest and leaving a trail of goose bumps. He put his mouth over her nipple, licking around the tightened bud with his tongue and finally capturing it, sucking it, each draw sending tingles of hot pleasure to her already scorching pussy. And while he sucked and licked at her nipples, he continued to fuck his fingers in and out of her pussy in this slow, leisurely manner, as if he had all the time in the world to play with her body.

She knew his touch, his mouth. It might have been ten years and they might both be different now, but some things she never forgot—her body never forgot. All these years and despite other men in her life, she could never erase the way his hands and mouth felt on her, the way he could take her to—right there—with seemingly little effort, and then dangle her over the edge and make her wait.

He'd always loved teasing her, said he enjoyed watching her face as he took her to the brink of orgasm. They'd waited so long for sex that those teasing moments between them had meant everything. But now, now she wanted to come, needed to have an orgasm by someone's hand other than her own—a man's hand.

She gritted her teeth and held on, dug her heels into the mattress and spread her legs to give him even more access to her.

"That's it," he said as he drove his fingers in deep. "Give it to me, Teresa."

His voice was dark pleasure that sank into her soul, winding her tight and making her spin out of control. She was selfish, she knew it; she wasn't touching him for any reason other than to use him as a lifeline. His hard cock lay against her leg and she should touch him, bring him as much pleasure as he was bringing her. She reached between them, searching, but he nudged her hand away and lifted his head.

"No. This time it's just you."

"But—"

"Later." He drove the heel of his hand against her clit and deepened his fingers inside her. A rush of heat exploded from within and she lifted.

"More."

Her word came out in a whisper, but her lips were tucked against his cheek and she knew he heard her.

"Faster?"

"Yes."

"Deeper?"

"Yes."

"Harder?"

Delicious sensation poured through her nerve endings. He mastered her body and she lost herself in his touch. "Oh, yeah. Please, AJ."

This time she couldn't hold back. She came with a cry, shuddering against him as she rocketed through her orgasm with an intensity that hit her like a crashing wave. It knocked her senseless, unexpected in both its intensity and the shattering emotion that roller-coastered through her as a result. She held on to AJ and rode it out until there was nothing left but pulses and his fingers dipping gentle and easy inside her.

She sagged against him, relaxed, spent and utterly amazed that she'd been able to do this. AJ had been so patient with her, taking her exactly where she'd needed to go, letting her set the pace until she found what she'd sought for such a long time.

This had been epic.

Take it easy, Teresa. It was just an orgasm, not world peace.

Yeah, definitely time to come down off this high. It had meant nothing—to anyone but her.

AJ kissed the top of her head and tucked her head against him. She listened to the beating of his heart—a little fast. She smiled knowing it hadn't been just her who'd been affected by all this. Her gaze skirted down his body, landing on his erection that hadn't yet subsided. She palmed his chest and charted her way down the sculpted planes of his torso, marveling at his flat, muscled abs. He must work out like a demon.

His cock lay rigid against his lower stomach. That was her target. She skimmed her fingers down . . .

And she spotted Pax leaning against the open doorway to her bedroom, arms crossed and smiling at her.

A million thoughts shot through her head at the moment. How long had he been there? What had he seen? What must he think? Was he mad—or hurt by her and AJ being together?

Teresa scrambled to sit up, grabbed the edges of the robe to cover herself. Pax's smile grew wider.

"A little late for that, honey," Pax said. "I've seen pretty much everything."

Her gaze shot to AJ, who shook his head and swept his legs over the side of the bed, running his fingers through his hair as he padded to the bathroom. "Voyeur. You could have said something."

Pax pushed off the wall and came into the room, then sat on the side of the bed AJ had just vacated. "Now, what fun would that have been? You two were busy. I was enjoying the view and didn't want to ruin things."

Teresa struggled to kick her brain cells into gear. "You . . . watched?"

"Yeah."

She didn't know whether to be embarrassed, angry or just plain turned on. Pax had watched them, had watched her. She processed that, what had happened between her and AJ, what Pax must have seen. Admittedly, the thought of him standing there watching it . . . okay, it excited her, but she was still mortified.

"Is that what you usually do with your women?"

"No. Usually I participate."

"Then why didn't you . . ."

He caressed her leg from her ankle to her knee. "Join in? Give it time, Teresa. There's no rush."

AJ came out of the bathroom a few seconds later, still naked, still seemingly unconcerned to find Pax there. Her gaze shifted between the two of them.

She didn't know what to say. "I'm . . . not used to this."

Pax's smile was a ghostly shadow, still there but almost wistful now. "Want me to leave?"

She reached out to grab his hand. "No. I just . . . don't know what to say about all this. I know what you two do . . . what you typically do . . . with women. I just don't know if I can be that woman."

AJ came over and sat on the end of the bed. "No one's asking you to be anything other than who you are."

She laughed. "I'm not sure I have any idea who that is."

Pax got up and Teresa raised her gaze to him.

"I have groceries to put away."

"Pax—"

But he was already out the door and down the hall. Teresa looked to AJ. "I hurt him."

"No, you didn't. He just knows you need space and he's giving that to you." AJ climbed onto the bed and sat next to her. "Neither of us expects a damn thing from you, Teresa. So don't go thinking you owe us anything."

"But the way you two are together . . . the sharing thing . . . I want to know more."

He stared at her for a few seconds before nodding. "You want to know something, ask me. Ask Pax. Either of us will tell you whatever you want to know. But who Pax and me are and what we do doesn't have to have anything to do with you. Or with me and you."

"But I thought—"

AJ stood. "I'm going to go take a shower. I'm beat from all that riding." He kissed her forehead. "You should get some rest."

"But—"

"We'll talk in the morning, babe."

He left the room and closed the door behind him, leaving her alone.

Two amazing, sexy, considerate men occupied this house with her. And she was spending the night alone in her bed. There was something elementally wrong about that.

eleven

PAX SLID THE EGGS AROUND THE PAN, WATCHING THEM FORM INTO perfect discs. Almost done. As they cooked, he grabbed his mug and gulped down the remains of his coffee, then poured another cup. The bacon was already done, the toast had just popped up and the hash browns were a nice golden brown.

"Morning."

He half turned and smiled at Teresa, and grabbed a mug for her. "Morning. Coffee?"

"I can get it."

"So can I. Sit down."

He poured her a cup and set it in front of her.

"Smells good. I just don't see you as the kind of person who cooks."

"Yeah? Why not?"

"Because you're this masculine powerhouse of a man. I'd expect to see you outside splitting logs with an axe."

He laughed. "Yeah, I heard that a lot from my dad when I was a kid."

"You always liked cooking?"

"When I was a kid, I dreamed about being a chef. I liked to play in the kitchen, liked to cook alongside my mom. My dad hated that. He called me a gay pussy and said no boy was supposed to be in the kitchen cooking unless he had no balls. But hey, it gave him another excuse to beat the shit out of me."

He slid the eggs from the pan to the plate. "How do you like your eggs, Teresa?"

She didn't answer, so he looked at her over his shoulder. He'd seen that horrified look before and wanted to kick himself for saying anything about his childhood.

Dumbass.

"Your dad beat you?"

"Yeah. How do you like your eggs?"

"Uhhh . . . scrambled."

He cracked three eggs into the pan, using his fork to stir the whites and yolks together.

"Why did your dad hit you?"

"No clue. Because he was angry a lot, I guess. My old man didn't need an excuse to grind on me or my mom. He seemed to take a lot of joy in the task. By the time I was thirteen, the beatings were daily and I was pretty much immune to them. By fifteen I was big enough that he wasn't messing with me much anymore unless I really pissed him off, but he was still hitting my mom on a regular basis. I tried to talk her into leaving him, but she said she loved him and he took good care of her." Pax laughed. "Yeah, he took care of her all right. He pounded on her so hard one night he almost killed her. I got in the middle of it and got my arm and some ribs broken. That's when the cops came. That's when they took me away from them. Because after all the beating he gave her and a week in the intensive care unit, she still wouldn't leave him."

"Oh my God. Oh, Pax." She was behind him in an instant, her arms wrapped around him, her body pressed against his back.

He didn't want this. Not this sympathy from her. He should have kept his mouth shut. He slid the eggs onto the plate and stood rigid. "Your breakfast is going to get cold."

"I don't care. Turn around and let me hold you."

He sucked in a breath, turned, and she moved into him. He had no choice but to wrap his arms around her while she did the same. She rubbed his back and damn if it didn't feel good to have her hold him.

"I'm so sorry, Pax. No one should have to go through what you did as a child. No one should have to carry those memories around. What your father did was unforgivable. And your mother failed to protect you. I'm sorry you didn't have people to care for you."

Pax sucked in a deep breath. He loved women, had vowed after watching his father beat the living hell out of his mother damn near every day of his young life that he would never do harm to one . . . ever. But he was also never going to love one, because love and relationships were just too scary, and while Pax wasn't afraid of anything, that was a place he wasn't strong enough to go.

Sex was fun as long as it was light and easy, and that's why it was always fun with AJ. A three-way was never a serious commitment. And that worked out just fine for him.

But having Teresa hold him, the press of her body against his, and knowing what she'd been through . . . this was different. Watching her with AJ last night had been a lesson in self-denial. His dick had been so damn hard he'd had to go into his room last night and jack off just imagining what he'd walked into—the way she'd looked with her legs parted, her sweet pussy pink and wet and open as AJ fucked her with his fingers, the scent of sex in the room, the way she'd whimpered and cried out as she surged against AJ's hand when she came.

Teresa was beautiful and desirable, and damn he wanted her. But she wasn't the typical woman he and AJ played with. And holding her like this felt way more than physical.

He pulled away and gave her a smile. "Let's eat."

But she didn't let go of him; instead she reached up with her hand and caressed his cheek and jaw, then wrapped her fingers around the nape of his neck, pulling his face down to hers.

Don't do this, man. Big mistake.

But it was already too late. His mouth was on hers, and the memories he'd brought up talking to her were too raw, too painful, and he needed to sink into something sweet. And Teresa was store window candy he knew he shouldn't have but damn if he didn't want it anyway. Her lips were warm and she tasted like cinnamon. He wanted to be easy with her, but he just couldn't. It wasn't in his nature to be slow and gentle like AJ. He tightened his hold on her and crushed his mouth to hers, inhaling her gasp and the following moan like they were the breath of life.

He waited for her to push him away, but she drew further into him, sliding her tongue against his, making his cock leap to life. He slid his hand up into her hair, the other snaking down to the small of her back, slipping into the waistband of her sweats so he could touch her bare skin. After watching her with AJ last night, he'd wanted to touch her, to taste her, and now that he was, the sensations were damn near overwhelming. That she wasn't pushing him away and running like hell shocked him. He knew he was all over her, pushing her against the kitchen table, trapping her.

Control it. Don't rush this.

But she made it difficult with her body soft and pliant against his, her mouth hungry and attacking, her hands sliding under his shirt to roam his chest and back. How was he supposed to read this? Teresa was AJ's girl. She was different than the other women they shared. Plus she'd been hurt by two men. He shouldn't be kissing her. He wanted to kiss her—and do so much more with her. She just felt sorry for him. This was sympathy, nothing more.

He was fucked up and confused and not the right man for her.

He finally broke the kiss, knew he had to or he wasn't going to stop. Breathless, he opened his eyes and looked down at her, at the way her raven hair looked wild and untamed as it framed her face, the way her eyes sparkled like emeralds, the way her mouth tempted him as she swept her tongue across her bottom lip.

She still had her hands under his shirt, her palms splayed across his back, her fingers dancing across his skin. He was on fire, his cock hard as steel and pressed against her. She had to know the effect she had on him.

"Thanks. I feel better now."

She frowned. "You think I kissed you to make you feel better?"

He pulled away from her. "Breakfast is getting cold. Let's eat."

"No. Let's not eat. You think that was a pity kiss?"

She balanced her hip on the end of the kitchen table, right where he'd taken a seat. She had a great ass, long legs, and damn she smelled good. And her hair all messed up gave him the impression of bed. He'd have liked to swoop her up and take her there and have her show him a little more pity. His dick wasn't going to ignore her for much longer. He took a scoopful of eggs onto his fork and swept them into his mouth.

"Pax."

"Your eggs are cold."

"I seriously don't care about that." She pushed the table back with her hip and straddled his lap, effectively cutting him off from his breakfast. Her hot body made contact with his aching dick and he couldn't help but put his hands on her hips, his fingers flexing against her soft flesh.

"Teresa . . ."

"When you kissed me in the hot tub last night, were you pitying me?"

He frowned. "Hell no."

"Just now, when I kissed you, it was because I wanted to. I have never in my life kissed a man because I felt pity for him. And I sure as hell have never kissed a man the way I just kissed you because I pitied him. And if you can't tell the difference, then you aren't half the man I thought you were."

She pushed off his lap, moved to the other side of the table and started eating her eggs.

Pax studied her for a few seconds.

"They're probably cold."

She waved the fork in his direction. "I told you I didn't care if they were cold. And they taste incredible. What did you put in these eggs, anyway? You would have made a great chef."

Her compliment shouldn't feel good. He was a badass biker with a history of theft and jail time, and if he hadn't had his ass rescued by General Lee he'd probably still be in prison. He didn't get all warm and gooey from a woman's compliment.

Usually.

"Thanks. And it's my secret egg-making recipe, so I can't tell you what's in them."

She snickered. "Oh, I see. Next time I'll just watch you."

"No, you won't. It's why I get up before everyone else. No one knows my secrets."

"I do now. At least some of them."

He lifted his gaze to hers, saw only warmth and compassion in her eyes. "Yeah, well, about that. I don't know why I spilled my guts to you. I never tell anyone about that."

"Does AJ know?"

"Yes. General Lee—he's our boss at the Wild Riders—made all of us talk to each other in detail about our pasts when we first signed up."

"Sounds painful."

"It was, but he was right. It brought us all closer, made us realize how alike we all were. That's how AJ and I got to be friends. What we went through was similar—both had fathers who hated us, mothers who weren't there for us when we really needed them. Plus we were the same age, shared the same interests. We started hanging out together and got tight."

"Easy enough to do when you share a similar trauma."

"Yeah. It was nice someone had my back for the first time in my life. And I know AJ always will. Just like I'll always be there to protect him. We've been best friends ever since."

"I'm glad AJ had someone like you."

"Well, it's not like I'm in love with him or anything," Pax said with a laugh.

"So your sharing in the bedroom doesn't include doing anything with each other."

Pax snorted. "Uh . . . no. We're fully hetero. We like to put our full attention on the women we're with, make them feel special."

"I can imagine they do."

Was that jealousy in her voice? Nah, couldn't be. "Haven't heard any of them complain."

"What if they fall in love with one of you, or both of you? Then what happens?"

He shrugged. "Hasn't happened yet. We don't let it happen."

"In other words, you don't stick around long enough for it to happen."

He owed it to her to be honest. "Yeah."

"Have you ever thought about long term, down the road, what if it does?"

"What if what does?"

AJ shuffled in barefoot, wearing unbuttoned jeans and no shirt, his hair mussed up from sleep. He stumbled to the coffeepot and grabbed a cup, filled it and grabbed a chair, then yawned.

"Morning, AJ."

He smiled at Teresa. "Morning. What are you two talking about?"

"She's asking what will happen if we fall in love with one of the women we fuck."

"Oh." AJ raised his brows. "That answer will require a lot more coffee than I've had. I bow out."

Teresa laughed. "Coward."

He raised his cup to her. "You got it."

After breakfast, they cleaned up and got dressed. They were going to ride into Sturgis and check things out in the daylight. Teresa put on her jacket and climbed on the back of Pax's bike. He liked feeling her behind him as they skirted the winding road toward the town.

Being on his Harley was the best part of any day. The chill in the air spiking against his face made him feel alive, and the Black Hills beckoned him. He wanted more time to explore the mountain roads.

But right now their target was lower ground and where all the action was—Sturgis.

TeReSa TOOK IT aLL In WITH awe aS THeY enTeReD main STReeT. How they could fit a half million bikers in a town normally populated by five or six thousand people was beyond her ability to understand.

"Wow," she said over Pax's shoulder. She'd always wanted to come to Bike Week, but had never found the time to make it. Now she saw what she'd been missing all these years. Wall-to-wall bikes and people crowded the sidewalks. Bikes were parked in the center of the street and at the curb as well as on the side streets. Thousands of them, in fact, more than she could ever hope to count. Shops were open and vendor tents were crammed in every available location. The smell of food cooking came from every corner, the loud beat of music pulsating from the open doors leading to the bars. Teresa scanned the vendor signs as they slowly rode by. Anything you wanted could be found here, from T-shirts to tattoos to bike accessories and biker clothes. And beer. Lots and lots of beer.

Though Main Street was only a few blocks long, it was packed with bikers, which made the street seem much bigger than it really was. Sturgis did a great job accommodating the masses that descended upon their tiny town every year.

They finally found an available parking place and climbed off. The sun was already beating on them and it was warmer down here, so they shed their jackets to walk around. Teresa noted immediately that AJ and Pax flanked her, one on either side as they made their way along the vendor booths.

Was it for protection or a show of possession? She wasn't sure, but she liked it. And judging from the envious looks she got from other women as they walked past, she should consider herself one lucky woman.

If only they knew what she *wasn't* doing with these guys.

Yeah . . . all those things she *should* be doing with them. She'd barely gotten started with AJ last night, and that had been all one-sided. As soon as she'd spotted Pax, she'd frozen up.

But what should she have done? Invited him to join in? What might have happened then?

That thought stayed with her as she scanned the crowd, looking for the Fists. As much as she'd have liked to visit every vendor tent and shop on every block, she knew that's not what they'd come here for. She turned her attention instead to the bikers, who were just as interesting to watch as all the vendors and scenery. They came in all shapes, sizes and colors, and various states of dress . . . and undress.

Teresa's eyes nearly bugged out of her head when she saw what some of the women wore. Or rather, didn't wear. Some wore jeans and skimpy bikini tops, or ass-bearing shorts. Some wore no tops at all, just brightly colored Xs pasted over their nipples. Teresa was beginning to wonder if she'd stumbled into an outdoor strip club by mistake.

"Seriously?" she mumbled out loud as a woman walked by in shorts that bared the bottom half of her ass cheeks, and no top on, her boobs jiggling as she strutted across the street. "Don't women fathom that it's sexier to leave something to the imagination?"

AJ laughed. "It's a free-for-all here. Some women like to let it all hang out while they're in Sturgis."

"Obviously."

She glanced at both the guys to see if they were ogling the half-naked chicks that seemed to surround them. Surprisingly . . . they weren't. Like her, they focused their attention on the bikers, no doubt doing what she was doing—scouting for the Fists.

"I can't believe you two are passing up all this naked female flesh."

Pax slid his arm around her waist. "Why do we need to look at other women when we're with you?"

She tilted her head back to stare up at him, thinking he was making a joke. He wore sunglasses, so she couldn't see his eyes, but he wasn't smiling. Was he serious?

He was. Wow. She had no snappy comeback for that kind of testament.

"Well. Thank you."

AJ draped his arm around her shoulder. "Besides, there's no better looking woman here than the one between us right now. Even fully clothed."

She looked to AJ. "Yeah, I'll bet you say that to all the girls."

"No. Just you."

Dammit. If they kept this up, she was going to get serious about these two. No wonder they had no trouble wrangling women. Devastatingly good-looking and charming, too. How could any woman resist?

How could *she* resist?

After walking the entire Main Street, Teresa's feet were tired and she decided all the bikers looked exactly the same. They'd begun to blend together in this mile-long blur of black leather and white T-shirts. And it was hot outside. She needed a drink. There were too damn many people in this place, and crowds and heat didn't mix well.

"This is getting us nowhere," she said, stopping in the middle of a crowded sidewalk.

"You look tired and thirsty," AJ said. "Let's go in one of the bars for a drink."

She nearly collapsed against him in gratitude. "Great idea."

The first bar they hit was a giant hot spot on the corner, already packed despite it being just shy of noon. Being a bar owner, Teresa knew that when it was time to party, bikers liked to drink no matter what time of day it was. They pushed through the doors and were blasted by raucous rock music and a pack of people that made Teresa envious.

Now she was beginning to feel at home. Cool air-conditioning greeted them, and they wound their way through the thick crowd,

Pax leading the way. He grabbed her hand and pulled her along, AJ laying his hand at the small of her back as he took up the rear.

She was really starting to like being sandwiched between two tall, muscular men. Her own personal bodyguards. And more.

They rustled up seats at the bar and ordered drinks. Teresa wanted soda and AJ and Pax ordered beers. She soaked up the atmosphere in the huge saloon, always on the lookout for new ways to spice up her own bar.

This place was chaotic and jam-packed. Sure, they had a captive audience with it being Bike Week, but still, she liked the way it was run. The décor was vintage, right down to the scratched and worn surface of the bar top and the smell of sawdust, beer and sweat. But it was lively, the music was roaring, and even better than that, there were three bars servicing patrons. And on top of the bars were women dancing. They wore skimpy bra tops with shorter shorts and leather chaps under them, or little miniskirts with bikinis underneath. All the girls were clean and damn good-looking, which led Teresa to believe the owners knew exactly what they were doing. Put enough bars in here to fulfill the customers' needs, put good-looking women on top to dance and draw in customers, and while the customers were ogling the women, keep the alcohol flowing with plenty of bartenders.

The music was loud, there were pool tables and video games, and even a mechanical bull. There was also a limited menu—burgers, hot dogs and sandwiches—not too much to bog down the waitstaff, but enough so your patrons wouldn't go somewhere else when they got hungry. Teresa could hear the cash registers *ka-ching*ing away. Her senses were on overload, and she figured she could park her butt on this bar stool, stay all day and never get bored looking at the people.

Even better was the prime location in the center of Main Street and right on a corner. She imagined a lot of people came here, and admittedly she was jealous. She loved her little bar and it got plenty of business, especially from bikers, but to have something major like this would be a dream come true.

They lingered for a while and watched people come and go, until AJ suggested they take a ride and look for the Fists.

Teresa was reluctant to leave the comfortable air-conditioned bar, but she knew they had to find the guy they'd come here looking for. She could almost forget they had an actual reason for being here and use this trip for research on how to make her bar business better.

They climbed on the bikes, and this time she rode with AJ, not wanting either of them to think she was favoring one over the other. She had no idea why she thought about that, or even if either Pax or AJ gave it a thought, but it mattered to her. Besides, she liked switching off.

And didn't that thought get her mind whirling with all kinds of interesting ideas?

They took the slow ride down Main Street again, and Teresa kept a sharp gaze down every side street, along both sidewalks, searching for any sign of the Fists' telltale insignias on leather.

Nothing.

Even the open roads leading into the Black Hills were filled with bikers in both directions. They were everywhere—in town and riding the hills. Her head spun trying to track the bikers flying by. How were they ever going to find the Fists?

"Where are we going?" she asked AJ.

"To the main campground."

Teresa knew about the big campground. It was where everyone camped out and partied for the duration of the bike rally. Plus there were also live concerts every night, as well as bike exhibitions of all kinds, from stunt bikers to hill climbers to burnouts. And all the food and drink you could handle, just like on Main Street.

The campground was what used to be nothing more than a pasture, grown into a venue that now took in millions in revenue every year. Teresa had read about it, heard stories about the no-holds-barred partying that went on there. She was excited and curious as they rode underneath the infamous sign. RVs and tents stretched for miles along the dirt and grass fields, as far as Teresa could see. It was just as crowded with people here as down on Main Street.

Once they found a place to park, they climbed off, paid their entry fees so they could come and go at will from the campground and concert arenas, and started wandering around.

If there was decadence on Main Street, it was tripled here. There were no rules except to have fun, get down and dirty, and party. Loud music, the roar of thundering motorcycles kicking up dust clouds, and the cheering of crowds permeated the air. Teresa didn't know which way to look, because there was something to gape at in each direction.

And again, bikers everywhere. It would take forever to wind their way between the RVs and tents to look for the Fists. They concentrated instead on the main arena where the entertainment and food were located.

"How would you ever expect to find someone you were look-ing for?" she asked, exasperated as they walked around, seemingly in circles. Spending hours on her feet was taxing, the heat had grown to be unbearable, the crowds were packing in like sardines, and all she wanted to do was jump in the swimming hole where people were enjoying cooling off on this blistering hot afternoon.

"Needle in a haystack, babe," Pax said. "No one said this was going to be easy."

"I think we warned you about this," AJ added.

She blew hair out of her face, sweat trickling between her breasts. She had too many clothes on; she was hot, tired and sweaty.

And cranky. "I know. There's got to be a better way. We're getting nowhere doing it like this. For all we know they could have been here while we were down on Main Street, and now they're down on Main Street while we're here."

AJ nodded. "Could be."

"Come on," Pax said, linking his fingers with hers. "Let's go for a ride in the hills where it's cooler."

She groaned in relief. "That sounds like a slice of heaven."

The ride cleared her head and cooled her body down until she could breathe again. She leaned back and simply enjoyed the beauty of the Black Hills—the way the road wound one way then the other, the tall trees that loomed above them, the scent of pine and earth, the imposing rock formations that had stood the test of time and the elements and now showed off their majestic beauty as they zipped by.

She could live here. Easily. Oh, she'd miss her brother and all her friends, but this place was beautiful. So green and untouched. Other than it being packed full of bikers for a couple weeks out of the year, there was a raw and untamed part she longed for, a solitude and fresh start where no one knew her and her history. This place was new, and the scent of something clean and unmarred refreshed her spirit. Maybe she'd lived in the city too long. Maybe it was time to consider making some changes to her life.

Several changes.

She felt renewed as she sucked in great gulps of pure oxygen, the pungent smell of the earth invigorating her.

For the past five years she'd let the world slip by, had stayed where she was safe, had closed the rest of the world out and not let anyone in that could potentially hurt her.

She used to be the kind of person who took chances, who loved adventure, who could take off at the drop of a hat, climb on her bike and go where the wind took her.

After the rape she'd sold her bike, rarely went anywhere but work or to her house—a carefully mapped out journey that she knew was safe. Her circle of friends had become her trusted network of people she'd known her whole life. No one new entered the picture, not without being vetted by Joey or her best friends.

She was always afraid. She hated being afraid.

She'd stopped living. She'd let the bad guys win. They still controlled her life. They still touched her. Maybe not physically, but they still lived inside her, eating away at her very soul, at who she used to be.

How could she have let that happen?

It had to stop. It had to stop now. She had a right to live, to be happy and wild and adventurous like she used to be. The rape hadn't changed her—she had changed herself. She refused to do it. Not anymore. Five years was damn long enough.

The old Teresa was coming back.

Starting now.

TWELVE

SOMETHING HAD GOTTEN INTO TERESA, AND AJ COULDN'T FIGURE out what the hell it was.

But there was a difference. Something raw and angry, a telltale edge about her that hadn't been there before.

The weather had shifted from cool to hot, and maybe that made her cranky, though he didn't think it had been just the weather. After they got back from the ride in the hills, she announced she wanted to go to the Harley dealership and buy a new bike.

She'd bought a Harley. Just. Like. That.

He knew she loved to ride, had loved having her own bike before she'd been attacked. He didn't presume to understand all the psychological shit she'd gone through after, other than that she'd told him she'd gotten rid of her bike and hadn't ridden since.

Then, suddenly, she wanted her own bike again.

As a rider, AJ understood that riding on the back of someone else's bike was nothing like being at the controls of your own. And once you had your own bike, typically you never wanted to ride behind someone else again.

But he understood why Teresa associated riding with what had happened to her.

"Are you sure this is what you want?"

She nodded, her jaw set in a determined line. "This is definitely what I want, what I need."

AJ looked to Pax, who shrugged as Teresa finished signing the papers on her new Harley, a sweet Softail Rocker C in a hot red color she'd chosen for herself. Not too small, not too big, just perfect for her height and leg length. She'd just whipped out her checkbook and paid for it, said she had plenty of money and it was damn time she started riding again.

Once everything was signed, sealed and delivered, she climbed aboard her bike. AJ had to admit she looked damn sexy.

"Honey, that bike fits you like it slid out of the factory with your name on it," Pax said, walking around Teresa's new bike.

She slid her palm over the handlebars and grinned. "She purrs. Damn, it feels good to straddle a bike again. It's been too long." She lifted her gaze to Pax and AJ. "Let's ride."

They did, taking a tour of the Black Hills again, this time on another route that would give Teresa a chance to test her bike along the steep curves of a winding mountain road. AJ was out in front at first, but then he drifted back and let Teresa take the lead. He figured after all this time not riding, she'd want a full face of mountain air and the chance to run along the switchbacks.

Besides, he liked watching her braid flipping behind her back as the wind blew it, and the way her body seemed at one with the bike on the curves. She hadn't forgotten how to ride. No real rider ever did, no matter how long they'd been without a bike.

She led them up the hills, from one peak across another. It grew colder up here, and as AJ pulled up alongside Teresa, her cheeks were red. Her gaze drifted to his and she had a wide grin on her face. She goosed the throttle and tore off ahead of him.

Yeah, it was in her blood again. He knew the feeling.

She finally brought them back down, ending up on Main Street.

It was dark now, and the party was going full swing on the street and in the bars. They parked and Teresa's face was flush from the cold, her cheeks bright cherries as she sported a wide grin.

"Feel good?" Pax asked.

She stretched, putting her hands on her back, then grinned. "It was amazing. I can't believe I waited so long to get a bike again."

"It's about time, then, isn't it?" AJ slung his arm around her shoulders. Pax took up position on her other side.

"Yeah. It's about time I started doing a lot of things," she said, her gaze skirting over both of them. "Let's go back to that saloon we were in earlier today."

She already knew where to go and led the way, Pax and AJ behind her.

"Something jazzed her up," Pax said.

"Yeah. Don't know what it is, but she's happy about something."

"I like the change in her."

AJ nodded. "Me, too."

The bar was even more crowded at night than it was during the day. Pax moved in front of Teresa so he could be the lead when they wedged their way in. They found a corner, which was going to be the best they could do until a table or spot at the bar opened up.

"I'll go get us some beers," AJ said.

"I want to dance." Teresa turned to Pax. "Come on."

AJ laughed. "Lucky you. I'm fetching the beers."

"Shit." Pax followed Teresa out on what was definitely not a roomy dance floor. A group of sweaty bodies crammed together like cattle in a pen wasn't his idea of a good time. But Teresa wanted to dance—so they were going to dance.

She somehow found an inch or two of open space and raised her arms over her head, moving her hips to the beat of the music. Pax did his best to get his feet moving, but all he was really interested in doing was watching Teresa. He'd seen her dance in her bar that first night. Watching the way she moved her body, the way she got lost in the music—man, that really got to him. He could sit back and watch that all night. She did the same thing now, only she was dancing with him—for him. Her hips locked with his and she wound her arms around his neck, sliding her body from side to side. He gripped her hips and held on, his gaze roaming every square inch of her exposed flesh as she undulated against him. Denim against denim, her breasts brushed his chest as she hung on to his shoulders and dipped her head back.

Yeah, he had to admit that even though he hated dancing, having Teresa's body rocking against his wasn't a hardship at all. He slid his arm around her waist and brought her flush against him, took her hand in his and decided it was his turn to lead. He gave a gentle push and twirled her around, then drew her back in, capturing her waist and sliding his hand along her hip. She grinned, then laughed as she caught on to his movements. Then they were moving in unison, her body one with his. She turned in his arms, presenting her back to him, her ass sliding and shimmying across his crotch.

It was just like sex—without the fucking.

Getting a hard-on in the middle of a crowded dance floor was a bad idea, but a man could only handle so much torture, and Teresa rubbing her butt back and forth across straining denim was doing a number on him. He gritted his teeth, grabbed her hips and whipped her around to face him, taking her arm and placing it around his neck.

"You're doing a little dirty dancing here," he said, rocking his pelvis against hers.

She arched a brow. "You complaining?"

"Hell no. But you're going to be embarrassed when you have to walk out of this crowd and your partner has a hard-on."

She shimmied in, pressing closer to said hard-on. "I'm not embarrassed at all. As long as you don't use it on anyone else."

He sucked in a deep breath and tried to remember to keep things light and easy with Teresa. He backed off a little, but she only moved in again, raised her leg and draped it over his hip to rock against him.

"I'm tired of being treated like I'm fragile, Pax. Don't back away."

"I'm trying to respect where you've been and what you went through, Teresa."

"I appreciate that. Now I just want to be treated like I'm a normal woman." She moved in, wrapped both arms around his neck. "A normal woman you might want to take to bed."

He pulled her tighter against him. "You know that's exactly what I want to do. But you also know the deal."

She tilted her head back, her green eyes sparkling under the lights of the dance floor. "Yes, I know the deal."

A deal he knew she wasn't ready for. Yet. Pax lifted his gaze to the fringes of the dance floor. "AJ's scored us a table. Let's go have a drink."

He took her hand and led her off the floor and toward the table. Okay, so maybe he'd chickened out, but the way she looked at him—the way she made him feel—he wasn't sure if *he* was ready for that. And he was damn sure she wasn't ready for him and AJ, no matter what she said.

"Who'd you have to kill to get this table?" Teresa asked as she took a seat and the beer AJ slid her way.

AJ grinned. "I can be charming if I need to be."

Pax snorted, and AJ slanted a dirty look in his direction.

"Okay, so I might have muscled a couple of puny guys who thought they could take the table."

"That's what I thought." Teresa put her feet up on AJ's lap and took a long swallow from the bottle of beer. "It's hot out there on the dance floor."

"Yeah, you looked pretty hot when you were out there," AJ said. "For a minute I thought you and Pax were going to get down and dirty right there in front of everyone."

She laughed. "The thought had crossed my mind. But Pax is too much of a gentleman."

Now it was AJ's turn to snort out a laugh. "I don't think I've ever heard Pax referred to as a gentleman."

Pax looked affronted. "Hey. I'm not without chivalrous qualities."

"Please. I've seen you in public with women. I know what you're capable of."

"Really," Teresa said. "Do tell."

"I don't think you want to hear those stories," AJ said.

"I do. Tell me."

AJ shrugged. "Okay. There was that time in Louisville with that cocktail waitress . . ."

Pax frowned, then nodded. "Oh yeah. Fucked her against the wall outside the bar while she was on her break. And don't forget the two girls in Milwaukee."

AJ laughed. "Oh yeah. The one who did me under the table in the back of the restaurant."

Teresa's eyes widened. "Under the table?"

"Yeah," AJ said. "That was a memorable night. I nearly choked on my steak."

"You sure do meet interesting women."

"We tend to hang out with women who like to have a good time, who enjoy partying and pleasure," Pax said.

"With no expectation of love and commitment, of course," Teresa added.

"Of course. It's all just fun and games," AJ said.

"Until someone falls in love with one of you. Or both of you."

AJ picked up Teresa's hand, slid his fingers in hers. "Now, who would go and do a dumb thing like that?"

TERESA SCANNED PAX AND AJ, HER PULSE POUNDING DOUBLE time. Who indeed? Her body swelled with heat and need, the desire to take on both these men and prove to herself she was still a sexual being.

And maybe that was just libido conjured up by the dancing. Besides, she wasn't here to satisfy her own carnal desires. She was here with a job to do.

"Any sign of the Fists?"

AJ shook his head. "Not yet."

She sighed and took a long swallow of beer. "Chasing around looking for them seems like a colossal waste of time."

"Agreed," Pax said. "If they're here—and that's a big if—we need to plant ourselves somewhere and wait to see if they show up."

AJ nodded. "Which means either here on Main Street or up at the campground. Those are the two hot spots. If the Fists are here, they'll hit one of those two places."

Teresa looked around. "How popular is this place?"

"You don't come to Sturgis without stopping in here at least once," Pax said. "Most people come in several times. It's legendary."

That's what she thought. Which gave her an idea.

"Any idea who owns or runs this place?"

AJ leaned over her shoulder and pointed. "Steve Flyton. Heavy-set dude over in the corner bar."

"I'll be right back."

"We'll go with you."

She turned and placed a hand on each of their chests. "Then we'll lose these prime seats and I like it here. I'm going over to talk to Steve."

"About?" AJ asked.

Teresa lifted her lips. "About a job."

Pax's brow lifted. "Why?"

"Because if this is the place to be, what better spot to watch for the Fists? Rather than looking for them, let them come to us. Besides, you guys can be out riding and I can be here working."

AJ shook his head. "Don't like that idea. You'd be left unguarded."

She rolled her eyes. "I hardly need a bodyguard."

"I agree with AJ. If the Fists do come in here and the guy who killed Larks spots you and happens to know you saw him do the deed, you're in trouble."

Okay, so they had a point. "Fine. First things first, let me see if I can wrangle a bartending job out of Steve. Then we'll work on the rest."

She waited while they considered it.

"It's not a bad idea," Pax said. "We won't find them riding around in circles."

AJ shrugged. "Go for it."

Now they were getting somewhere. Excited, she rose and

maneuvered her way through the crowd toward where the mostly balding guy with the rather scraggly brown and gray beard leaned against the edge of the bar. He wore a Flying Heads Saloon T-shirt big enough to cover his ample belly and jeans that balanced precariously low on his hips, and he grinned like he'd just won the lottery when she came up to him.

"Well, hi there, darlin'."

She introduced herself. "Love your place here. I own a bar in Missouri. I'm jealous of how popular yours is."

"Yeah, we do pretty well here during the bike rally. We try to keep the beer flowing and the women dancing."

"You have customers waiting for drinks. You need more help behind the bar."

He turned and frowned. "Yeah. Some of the kids who work here would rather be partying than working. That means sometimes they don't show up when they're supposed to."

"Need some hands?"

He arched two very bushy eyebrows. "You offering?"

"I am."

He scratched his beard and studied her. "If you own a bar, I assume you know what the hell you're doing."

"I do."

"I need people to work nights. That's when I have a hard time staffing."

"No problem. I'm not here to party."

"Okay then. Go see that pretty brunette behind the far corner bar. That's my wife, Sandy. She'll get you set up and she'll probably kiss you with gratitude." He motioned and got Sandy's attention, then pointed to Teresa.

Teresa laughed and shook Steve's hand. "Thanks a lot."

Sandy looked ragged and tired, and she was so grateful to have Teresa on board she did kiss her cheek, especially since Teresa required little to no training. She was ready to go to work that night, and Sandy wanted nothing more than an hour's break to put her swollen feet up on a chair and rest. So Teresa got right to work.

Bartending there was easy since most people either wanted beer or shots or soda, so she didn't have to make any fancy drinks. She popped the beers fast and she already knew what the hell she was doing, so her tip jar took money almost as quickly as she took beer orders. The crowd pressed in on her, obviously sensing she was filling orders and filling them fast. But still, she managed to hold her own and at the same time keep an eye on everyone she served. So far, none of the Fists had come in. But she figured this was a prime spot. She had every confidence she was going to see them here and it was only a matter of time.

By the time the bar closed at midnight and everyone shuffled out, Teresa was tired but exhilarated. At least now they had a plan. She finished cleaning up the bar.

"You did good tonight."

Teresa smiled at Sandy, who was tall and thin and tattooed nearly all over. She wore her salt-and-pepper hair stick short, showcasing a row of piercings in and outside each ear.

"Thanks. I like bartending. I'm not much for standing around and doing nothing, so this gives me something to do."

"Aren't you here on vacation?"

"Well, yes. But I bought a new bike while I was here. Now I have to pay for it. So you saved my life giving me a job."

Sandy laughed. "I know how that is. Always something pretty out there we have to spend our money on."

Teresa folded the rag and laid it on the bar. "Isn't that the truth? I'll be paying for this bike until I die."

"Well, I'm glad you got the bike, and we got you. You did good and we're glad to have you working with us. See you tomorrow night?"

"You bet."

AJ and Pax came toward them.

"Bar's closed, guys. You'll need to leave."

Teresa scratched her nose. "Oh. They're . . . with me."

Sandy's brows lifted. "Both of them?"

Teresa tingled as Pax and AJ flanked her. "Yes." She introduced the guys to Sandy. They shook her hand.

Sandy looked over AJ and Pax, then nodded. "Oh, to be young again." She shifted her gaze to Teresa. "You are one lucky woman. Enjoy these two." Sandy walked away, muttering something about youth and stamina.

Pax slid his arm around Teresa's waist. "You ready to go? You worked hard tonight."

"Not really. It was fun. Did you two spot anyone familiar?"

"No," AJ said.

Teresa sighed. "They're here. I know they are."

AJ held the door open for her. "It's still early. Give it time."

There were concerts and all-night parties going on, but Teresa was done. She wanted to go back to the house and collapse. When they got there, Pax started up the grill, saying he was hungry.

"It's after midnight, Pax," she said, flopping onto one of the chairs outside.

"I don't care. I need food." He turned, spatula in hand. "You want a burger or not?"

Her stomach grumbled loudly, making her realize how long it had been since they'd eaten. She laughed. "I guess that's your answer." She stood. "I'll go make a salad."

While she fixed a salad and Pax grilled the burgers, AJ set the table. The whole scene was so . . . domestic. She could imagine doing this every night for these guys.

For two men.

But that wasn't likely to happen. First, the guys worked for the government, often on assignment God knows where, so they weren't going to have nine-to-five jobs in the same town where she lived. And for that matter, she didn't have a regular job, either. She worked nights at the bar, not getting home until after two in the morning. So her whole dream of domesticity just fizzled into the ether.

The second thing was, living with two men wasn't exactly the slice of suburban bliss she'd had in mind when she dreamed of her happily ever after. Then again, nothing about her life had turned out like she'd imagined back then. So why should this be any different? Besides, who was talking about forever and commitments anyway? At this point she'd just like to be able to have decent sex without breaking out in hives or tensing to the point of wanting to throw up.

Her moment with AJ had been perfect. But it had been just a tease, a glimpse into what she could have. AJ touching her, Pax watching. Now she wanted more. A lot more. She wanted to follow up all the way to the big finish. She was a young single woman in the prime of her life. She was self-sufficient and independent, with a great job. She should be having awesome sex right now.

She just didn't want to start something with either of them that she wasn't sure she'd be able to take all the way. The problem was that until things got started, she didn't know what she could finish and what she couldn't.

Would they even be willing to take that step with her, not knowing if she could go through with it? She thought about that while they sat in the kitchen and ate. Teresa stole glances at them while they were busy eating. They were so different in appearance, and yet so similar in so many ways. So utterly different from the men who'd hurt her, and even from the guys she'd tried to be with after. That's what she had to wrap her mind around.

They didn't pressure her; they had no expectations of a sexual relationship. Even though the three of them were holed up in this house—such an intimate environment—she could be just a friend to them and it would be okay. Yet they'd still protect her as if there was a bond between them. She'd seen plenty of that today as they stood knee-deep in thick crowds and she noticed how both of them surrounded her. It was unspoken, but it was there.

She didn't understand why, but their lack of expectation made her appreciate them so much more. It made her want to give back some of what they'd given to her.

After dinner, they grabbed drinks and sat outside. The night was clear, the smell of the hills wrapping around her senses. She loved being out here where it was cool at night and the stars glittered like diamonds in the black sky. She rested on the cushioned chaise lounge, laid her beer on the table next to her and raised her arms over her head, completely relaxed as she gazed up at the sky.

"You're kind of quiet tonight, honey."

She pulled her gaze away from the stars and onto Pax. "I know. Sorry. Been thinking."

"About what?" AJ asked.

"You guys."

They were sitting in chairs on either side of the chaise, facing her. Pax leaned forward and rested his arms on his knees. "Yeah? What are you thinking about?"

"How nice it is to be here with both of you. How you don't expect anything from me. How different it is to have exceptional men like you in my life. I'm very grateful."

Pax looked down for a second, then back at her, obviously uncomfortable. "You make us sound like heroes, Teresa. We're not."

"We're just men," AJ added. "We're not perfect."

"Oh, I know that. I have no illusions, believe me. She leaned forward, straddling the chaise. "I just want you to know how much I like being here with both of you."

"We like being here with you, too," Pax said.

She swallowed, her heart thrumming a fast beat. "I was hoping . . . it could be more than that."

Pax looked at her. So did AJ. Neither said anything.

Pax stood. "You don't ever have to be afraid with us, Teresa."

She frowned. "Where are you going?"

"To bed." He leaned over, kissed the top of her head. "Good night."

She stared at him as he walked away, then turned to AJ. "I don't get it. I say I want to get closer, and he walks away."

AJ picked up her hand. "I think he sees you as belonging to me. Because of our past. He doesn't want to step all over that."

"A long time ago we did belong to each other."

"We did."

"Until you left."

He looked away. "I had to, Teresa. You know that."

"I do." She squeezed his hand. "When you love someone, you think nothing can stand in the way of that."

He went silent, his eyes meeting hers and staying there. She was lost in the dark gray depths that seemed to hold so many secrets. She felt like she was so close to something monumental, that all she had to do was reach out and it would be hers.

But then AJ stood, leaned over and kissed her cheek. "It's late. You should get some sleep since you're the only one employed around here." He straightened, winked. "Good night, Teresa."

And just like that, she was alone out on the terrace.

She'd been determined to step back into the game of sex tonight. With AJ or Pax or possibly even both of them. But the night she'd planned had evaporated. Again. They'd left her. And she had no idea why.

THIRTEEN

TERESA PACED HER BEDROOM, UNABLE TO SLEEP. SHE SHOW-ered, dried her hair and tried to lie down, only to drift off for an hour and wake up again. She'd had a long day. Why wasn't she exhausted?

Unfinished business. Both her mind and body knew this and wouldn't let her rest. AJ and Pax had left her and she damn well wanted to know why. She couldn't have made her intentions more clear.

So why didn't they take her up on her offer? What did she have to do—strip naked and throw herself on them?

She appreciated them being careful with her, but she didn't want that. Not now. She wanted sex. The hot, dirty, throw-her-against-the-wall-and-fuck-her-until-she-screamed kind of sex. They were being too solicitous. They were treating her like a sister. Or worse yet, like the other guys she'd tried to date after the rape. They were backing away. And she knew that's not what they wanted any more than it's what she wanted.

It was pissing her off.

Tired of pacing a rut in the bedroom carpet, she flung open her bedroom door and marched down the hall and into the living room. Moonlight called to her from the terrace. Some fresh air might do her good. She was tired of the dark and her own thoughts. She opened the door and stepped outside, the blast of chilly air knocking her senses into full awareness.

Okay, cold out here. She went back in and grabbed the blanket from the back of the sofa, then stepped out and slid onto the chaise, throwing the blanket over her bare legs.

Another clear night. Just her and the stars again. Millions of them, all watching over her. At least they didn't up and leave her alone when she needed them most.

And wasn't she just cranky as hell. What exactly were her expectations of Pax and AJ, anyway? They'd been there for her since the moment they'd arrived in her hometown and hadn't left her side once. Just because they didn't behave exactly as she expected them to didn't mean they didn't care. If anything, they probably cared too much.

And that was the problem. It was the wrong kind of caring.

She had only herself to blame for this dilemma. She'd poured out her heart and blabbed about the rape.

Now both of them were afraid to touch her. They'd probably expected her to go off the deep end the first time she saw a penis again.

She was over it already. She wanted sex.

"Can't sleep?"

She turned to find Pax leaning against the doorway. Bare chested, he wore only his jeans, the button undone as if he'd hastily tossed them on.

He looked delicious and utterly edible, which didn't improve her mood at all. She shifted her gaze to the darkness beyond the terrace.

"No, I can't sleep."

"Want some company?"

She shrugged, then heard the scrape of one of the chairs as he pulled it next to hers.

"Something bothering you?"

"No." *Yes.*

"Want to talk about it?"

Talking was the last thing she wanted to do. She didn't answer.

"Teresa."

She let out a big sigh, then turned to him. "I don't understand you two."

His brows lifted. "Us two, meaning me and AJ?"

"Yes."

"What don't you understand?"

"Why you don't want to have sex with me."

Okay, way to blurt it out, Teresa. Pax stared at her like she'd grown two heads.

"You think we don't want to have sex with you."

"What else am I supposed to think? I was throwing out some definite signals earlier. And then you both left me out here."

"We're just trying to be careful with you."

"I'm tired of men being careful around me, like I'm some kind of precious cargo that has to be handled with care. I'm not going to break, goddammit. I need someone to touch me, to treat me like I'm a normal woman."

He stood. "Teresa—"

She raised her hand, already well aware of the excuses and apologies she'd heard countless times before. She'd thought Pax and AJ were different. They weren't. "Never mind. I don't need to hear whatever it is you're about to say. I've been down this road before. I tell guys I've been raped and they walk on eggshells around me. No man knows how to handle a damaged woman."

"You aren't damaged."

"Spare me." She kicked off the blanket and stood. "I'm going to bed."

Pax was up and in front of her before she took another step. "That's enough."

She laid her hand on his chest. "Exactly. It's enough. I've had enough of men not being able to look me in the eye, afraid to touch me, treating me like I have leprosy or VD just because I was raped. It wasn't my fault those guys took something from me that I didn't offer."

Pax frowned. "No. It wasn't your fault."

"Then why do I feel like five years later I'm still paying for it?" She moved to skirt around him, but he latched on to her wrist and pulled her against him.

"Don't walk away."

"Let me go."

Instead, he pulled her against him. "No."

"I said let me go."

He snaked an arm around her waist and drew her closer to him. Her breasts hit his chest and the air whooshed out of her lungs.

"I want you, Teresa. I've wanted you since the first night I met you. Now you tell me what you want. Straight up."

She caught a glimpse of the raging passion in his eyes, thought about telling him to go to hell, but it would have been a lie. "You know what I want."

"I need to hear it."

"Kiss me."

His eyes had gone dark, dangerous, hungry. "Why?"

"Because I want you. I want to be naked with you. I want you to touch me, to make love to me, to treat me like a woman instead of something broken."

He slipped his hand behind her neck and brought her mouth to his.

An explosion of heat slammed her body at the first touch of his lips against hers. As before when he kissed her, he wasn't gentle. She didn't expect him to be, didn't want him to be. Pent-up passion and maybe more than a little frustration had taken control and she needed a man like Pax—a man who would take her without being afraid she would crumble.

She wasn't going to crumble. She wanted to be held and touched and kissed by a man who wouldn't treat her like she was fragile, or damaged, who wasn't too afraid of her past to help her bury it.

She threaded her fingers through his hair and rose up on her tiptoes to press her body against his. His heat burned through her thin T-shirt, his jeans scraping her bare legs as she lifted against him. Too many barriers. She wanted to feel his skin. She reached between them to draw the zipper down on his jeans.

Pax inhaled sharply. "Not yet, babe," he said, then swept her into his arms and carried her inside. She thought he'd take her to her bedroom, or his, but he sat her on the sofa. He leaned over to switch on the small table lamp, bathing them both in soft light.

"I want to see you." He swept her hair from her face with his fingers and kissed her again, surging up to press his chest against her breasts.

She was pinned between the sofa and his body, loving the pressure of him against her. She wrapped her legs around his thighs, arched her body against him, felt the hard evidence of his cock that told her how much he wanted her. A shot of need knifed through her, moistened her, made her ache as she awoke to sensations she thought she'd never feel again.

He fanned his fingers into her hair and held her head as he kissed her with a hard passion, his tongue sliding in to capture and stroke against hers. She moaned as sensation skittered through her body, shocked at how utterly alive she felt at this moment. Tears pricked her eyes and she forced them back, not wanting to give Pax the wrong idea. She wasn't upset, wasn't unhappy. This was glorious, like a rebirth. Sexual desire surged through her and she welcomed it with open arms. Pax touched her with his mouth, his hands, his body, and all she could think of was what would come next—not what had come before, all those years ago.

He swept his hand down her cheek, her neck, over her breasts, lingering there to tease and taunt her nipples through the fabric of her T-shirt. He lifted just enough to watch her, his eyes focused on her as he rolled his palm over her nipples. She sucked her bottom lip between her teeth and allowed herself to feel. After all these years, she was giving herself permission to feel again.

It felt so damn good she wanted to cry. But crying would only distract her—and Pax—from this moment, and she wasn't going to let anything derail what was happening.

Pax moved to the floor. On his knees, he positioned himself between her legs and rested his hands on her thighs.

A woman could get lost in eyes like his—penetrating her, coaxing her into revealing her secrets—especially the way he zeroed in on her face, on her eyes, as if she was the only woman for him.

She knew it wasn't true, but for this moment in time, she was his woman. She reached for his hand and rested hers there. He twined his fingers with hers and raised her hand to his mouth, kissing her fingers, taking the tips into his mouth to suck. Sensation throbbed in her pussy and she swallowed, hard, trying for calm but feeling her heart pound.

He let go out of her hand and reached under her T-shirt for her panties, slid them down her legs and off. He lifted her shirt, baring her pussy.

"Spread for me, honey," he whispered.

She did, and he cupped his hands under her butt, then put his mouth on her sex.

Moist heat enveloped her clit as he captured it with his tongue and lips. She felt like dying right there on the spot. It was so good, so hot, she was flooded with indescribable sensation and couldn't lie still. She lifted against his mouth and he hummed against her clit, which only served to skyrocket the pleasured agony even further.

She had been touched so rarely like this. Having AJ last night and Pax tonight was something she couldn't have fathomed. It was hot and wicked, and all she could think was how damn lucky she was to have two men who worshipped her body, who took her to the edge of reason.

She wasn't going to last long. And being able to watch what he did to her was so intimate, so erotic, especially when he stopped to look at her, as if asking if this was what she wanted.

Hell yes this was what she wanted.

The man stole her breath away.

This is what she'd been waiting for all these years. Nothing was going to stop the runaway train now.

Not even AJ, who stepped out from his bedroom wearing only a pair of boxers, his hair rumpled from sleep. This time, Teresa refused to be shocked or embarrassed. She wouldn't cringe or try to move away from Pax. This was their life, and if she wanted to be part of it, she was going to have to get over either of them stumbling into whatever she was doing with the other.

AJ didn't seem surprised at all to see Teresa naked from the waist down or Pax with his mouth on her pussy. He came around to the back of the sofa and laid his hands on her shoulders. He bent and pressed a soft kiss to her ear and stayed there.

"Feel good?" he asked.

She sucked in a breath as Pax stabbed his tongue inside her pussy. "Yes."

AJ rubbed her shoulders, keeping his touch benign, just watching her and her reaction to what Pax was doing. She knew why.

She reached for his hands and drew them down, over her breasts, needing his touch on her as much as she needed Pax's mouth.

"You sure about this?" he asked.

Pax stopped, looked up at her.

She looked at Pax while she spoke to AJ. "Yes. I'm sure. Touch me, AJ."

Pax smiled and bent over her sex again, taking a long, slow lick, watching her as he did. She shuddered.

AJ kneaded her breasts, toying lazily with her nipples while Pax continued to work her sex, seemingly in no hurry to take her over the edge now. She lifted against him and he pushed her back down, licked her pussy lips, teasing her.

Teresa swallowed, her throat gone dry as she tried to hold on while Pax sucked her pussy and AJ played with her breasts. When AJ lifted her T-shirt over her head, she didn't object, in fact she needed to feel his hands on her nipples.

AJ came around to sit beside her on the sofa and pressed a soft kiss to her lips, sliding his fingers in her hair to hold her head while he pleasured her lips and tongue with his own until she was lost in the sensation of his mouth, of Pax's mouth, of the incredible things they did to her. When AJ broke the kiss, she looked at him and he smiled, then leaned down to fit one of her nipples into his mouth, cupping his hand around her breast to tease the bud with his tongue, licking around it, then sucking it until she gasped for breath at the dual sensations of having her nipple and her pussy sucked.

This wasn't her. She didn't have sex with two men. Two men had held her down and raped her five years ago.

But maybe this *was* her. Maybe she'd been waiting for these two men all these years to help her obliterate the pain of the past. Because she wasn't thinking about that night anymore. And every time she'd tried to be with a man since the attack, it had come rushing back to her—the fear, the trauma, every vivid horrible detail, until she had been forced to push them away. Not the fault of those men—hers.

But not tonight, not with Pax and AJ. She couldn't conjure up the horror of that night if she tried. All she felt was languid pleasure, the desire to experience more, to touch them, to get them naked and lick them all over. These men were so different than the men who had done terrible things to her, things that were about power and pain and not about sex.

This was about sex. Glorious, wonderful, feels-so-damn-good-please-don't-stop sex. They were worshipping her body, not hurting it. No images of that night assaulted her. She was in this moment, with these men only.

And she knew, instinctively, that with one word they would stop.

But oh, she so didn't want to stop.

"I want to touch you," she said, though she had no idea which of them she said it to. And it wasn't like she made a move to do anything about it. Pax had her pressed to the sofa with his hands on her thighs while his magical tongue continued to lap over her pussy, and AJ's dark head was bent over her breasts. She felt boneless, drifting on a cloud of sensual bliss.

"Let's do this for you first, Teresa," AJ whispered against her ear. "We have all the time in the world. Relax and enjoy it."

She sighed and fell into the pleasure.

"That's it." AJ shifted, moving behind her to cup her breasts in his hands. She lay against his hard chest while Pax adjusted to the shift by rising up and lifting her butt again, then licking against her thighs.

"Watch Pax eat you," AJ said, rolling her nipples between his fingers. "We want to hear how it makes you feel."

Electric shocks of pleasure shot from her nipples to her pussy, and she moaned, wriggling against AJ. She felt his erection against her butt, and she imagined what would happen next, anticipating it and yet loving this moment, too. How would it feel to have Pax lick her pussy while AJ was fucking her? Her stomach did somersaults at the thought.

AJ tilted her head to grasp her chin with his hand and plow her mouth with a kiss that stole her breath, sliding his tongue between her lips to wrestle with hers. She whimpered as Pax slid a finger inside her pussy. AJ deepened his kiss and skimmed the pads of his thumbs over her nipples.

Pressure built and she couldn't hold back.

"AJ," she whispered against his lips.

"Yeah?"

"I need to come."

"We want you to come, honey. Relax and let go."

Pax tucked two fingers inside her pussy and sucked on her clit, planting his hot, wet mouth over her like a suction.

"Come for us, Teresa." AJ licked her neck, pushed her hair away from the nape and nibbled there, then bit her, sinking his teeth gently into the soft flesh of her nape.

She shuddered, the sensation sending tingles and goose bumps and the hottest pleasure she'd ever felt skittering down her spine.

"Oh, God," she said, trembling at the delicious pain. She fell, her orgasm hitting with an intensity that would have knocked her over if she'd been upright. An explosion of sweet sensation catapulted her, making her shudder and cry out as Pax took her over the edge. AJ held her, kissing her neck and her shoulder until the spasms trickled to aftershocks that still left her shaking.

And then Pax was there, his face aligned with hers. He cupped her face and pressed his lips to hers. She threw her arms around him and kissed him back with full fervor, tasting what he'd done to her.

While she kissed Pax, AJ stroked her back and slid his fingers in her hair.

She felt worshipped.

This wasn't at all what she'd expected. It had been so much better.

And they had only just begun.

FOURTEEN

THERE WAS GENUINE PASSION AND SOMETHING JUST SO SWEET about the way Teresa kissed him. Pax felt emotions he'd never felt before. Things that didn't have anything to do with sex at all.

Which made him determined to keep this just about sex, and nothing more.

"So what are the rules about all this?" Teresa asked, her expression one of curiosity and just a tinge of wariness.

Pax smiled at her, liking that she was new to all this. "There are no rules. We just do what feels good . . . what feels right . . . for everyone."

"Which means if something doesn't feel good or right, you say no," AJ added, shifting her so she sat sideways on his lap. "And we stop. You understand?"

Teresa's lips lifted. "I understand. But I trust both of you."

Pax felt a tightness in his chest that had never been there before, a sense of responsibility to do this right for her. "You tell us what you want."

Her lips curled in a smile. "Since I'm the only one without any clothes on. Having you both naked would be a great start."

Pax laughed and stood. "I think we can fix that easily enough." His jeans were already unzipped, his cock stone hard. Tasting her had been heaven. Her pussy was sweet and tart, and he'd thought about nothing but sliding inside her and fucking her until she came. He wanted to see her face when she let go, wanted to know that those men who had hurt her were erased from her memory. He wanted to give her new memories. Good ones.

He let his jeans fall to the floor, liking that she watched, that she looked at his cock, then at his face and smiled. It made him want to bury himself deep inside her so he could surround himself with that warmth that always seemed to be missing in his life.

She's not going to make you whole, man. No woman can do that. No woman has yet, no woman ever will.

He knew that. But just for a little while, he could sink inside her and hold on to something sweet and feel like maybe he deserved a woman like her. Even if it was a fantasy. Even if it wasn't permanent.

Because nothing ever was.

"You are so beautiful," she said, moving in to him, laying her hand on his chest.

His heart pounded, as if this was the first time for him. But it sure as hell wasn't the first time. Not with a woman, not with him and AJ and a woman. But it felt like it was just him and Teresa and no one else existed as she rose up and pressed her lips to his. And goddamn if it wasn't the most perfect kiss—soft and sweet, as she tested his mouth with just a little pressure, her breath warming his lips, the tip of her tongue teasing his.

Restraint wasn't in his nature, but for Teresa, he would resist crushing her against him and doing what came naturally. He'd let her play, just hold her loose and easy and not scare the living shit out of her by throwing her down and burying himself inside her. But damn, he wanted to. He really wanted to.

And when she stepped back and smiled up at him, her face flushed, her eyes glassy, he could only imagine how overwhelming this must be for her. After what she'd been through, after not having sex in so long. AJ and him must be too damn much.

"You want to be alone with just AJ, you say so and I'll back out," he said.

She frowned, cocked her head to the side and slid her fingers in his, gripping hard. "Pax, I want to be with you."

He sucked in a breath, kind of shocked at the relief he felt at her answer. "Okay."

She swept her hand across his cheek, something he couldn't define in her expression. All he knew was it made his gut hurt to see it there. Then she turned to AJ.

AJ STOOD BACK AND WAITED WHILE TERESA WAS WITH PAX. HE didn't want to overwhelm her by standing too close and smothering her. Besides, this gave him a great view of her mighty fine ass, the tattoo on her lower back only adding to the sexiness of her body.

When she turned to face him, she quirked her lips. "Get naked."

He grinned and dropped his boxers, his erection jutting up to bob against his stomach. Her eyes widened and she lifted her gaze to his face, then licked her lips.

Damn.

It had been a long time, and they'd been kids back then, not adults. He'd wanted to make love to her back then, but knew if he did he'd never be able to walk away from her. And staying just hadn't been an option for him. He'd wanted no ties, and Teresa was a huge tie.

He wasn't sure he'd be able to walk away from her now, but

nothing short of the end of the world was going to stop him from making love to her tonight. He drew her into his arms. The silky feel of her naked flesh against him made him draw in a breath.

"Finally," he said, smoothing her hair away from her face. "I've waited a long time for this."

She tilted her head back and smiled. "Me, too."

"Pax and I will take good care of you. You don't have anything to be afraid of."

"I'm not afraid. Not of the two of you. I just don't know what to do."

Pax come up behind her and nodded to AJ. "You call the shots, babe. You tell us what you want, and don't want," Pax said.

She shuddered against AJ, then half turned so she could look at both of them. "Let's go stretch out on that big bed in my room. I've never had the opportunity to play with two men."

They let her lead them into her room. AJ watched her hips sway back and forth as they walked the hallway and she opened the door to her room. She pulled the curtains and moonlight streamed in across her king-sized bed, then she turned to them.

"Is this enough light or do you need more?"

"Whatever you want, Teresa," AJ said.

She seemed to consider it for a moment, then moved to the nightstand and switched on the small light there. "I want to see both of you a little better. This is a first for me and I don't want to miss a thing."

AJ sucked in a breath. Neither did he.

TERESA WONDERED IF IT WAS POSSIBLE TO BE EXCITED AND scared shitless at the same time. She supposed it was possible, because she felt both. Here she was, in her bedroom with two testosterone-laden men, and she had no earthly idea what she was supposed to do with them. She was sure it showed, too, because AJ came up beside her and wrapped his arms around her.

"There are no rules to this, Teresa. No written set of instructions that say you have to get from point A to point B in a certain way."

Pax came over and sat on the bed, taking her hands in his. "We just do what feels good, what feels natural to everyone. Whatever you like, we like."

"You make it sound so simple."

"It is," he said, pushing onto the bed and leaning on his elbows. "I can tell there's something you want to do. What is it?"

She shuddered, then half turned to AJ. He smiled and nodded. "Go ahead."

She crawled onto the bed and came up beside Pax, then turned to AJ and held out her hand, inviting him to join them. "Come on."

AJ climbed on the bed and positioned himself opposite her, lying on his side with one hand propping up his head. He swept her hair over her shoulder and let his fingers trickle down her spine. She shivered and inhaled. One man touching her, the other looking at her like he wanted to eat her alive.

"You're in charge here, Teresa," AJ said. "You have the power."

Her eyes drifted closed for a second as she realized what that meant, what AJ was telling her. They weren't going to demand anything of her or take over what was happening. It wasn't like that night five years ago. She would call the shots. She understood what this meant, what they were doing for her.

She shifted and sat on her heels, content for the moment to stare down at these two incredible men.

"I'm like a kid in a candy store," she said. "Right now I just want to window-shop. And then I want everything."

Pax laid his palm on her thigh, the heat of his hand searing her flesh. "Look all you want. We aren't going anywhere."

They were both tan, with powerful bodies. AJ and Pax had lean, natural muscles she found incredibly appealing. She reached out to touch Pax's chest, a solid brick wall. He laced his hands behind his head and watched her. Then she shifted her gaze to AJ.

"Go ahead. Touch him. I don't get jealous, Teresa. Anything you do to Pax is going to turn me on, so quit worrying."

She leaned over Pax, her hair falling forward to tickle his face. He laughed and she did, too. And when he gathered her hair in his hand and held it for her, her smile died and she bent to lightly brush her lips against his. He tightened his grip on her hair, drawing her closer, his groans making her wet, making her bold.

"Kiss me, Teresa."

She did, pressing her mouth against his. He took possession like she knew he would, wrapping his arm around her, sealing his lips to hers, his tongue claiming hers like there was a battle to be won. She surrendered gladly and fell against him, powerless against the sensations of hunger and need Pax drew out of her with one kiss. She found his nipples and slid the pads of her thumbs over them, wondering if he'd like what she liked. The sounds he made against her mouth told her he did.

She could get lost in his kiss.

Shaken, she pulled away and turned to AJ. He had been watching, his eyes darkening to a midnight storm. She pushed him onto his back and leaned over him. It was a heady experience going from one man right to the next, knowing that—at least for tonight—both of them belonged to her. AJ cupped her face and brought her mouth to his, teasing nips and licks against her lips that left her breathless with anticipation of the next. And when she thought she couldn't take any more, he took her mouth in a deep, soulful kiss that made butterflies dance in her belly, made her wet and needy and ready to climb on top of him and slide his cock inside her until the ache exploded into an orgasm. It was so different from the way Pax kissed her, and it was patently obvious she was never going to mistake one for the other.

She wondered if fucking them would be this different, too.

The thought made her tingle all over.

She sat up to catch her breath, overwhelmed from the sensations pinging through her. She took a moment to stare at both men, who seemed content to lie on their backs and let her do just that. What it must cost them to restrain themselves like that.

She danced her fingers over their chests and abs. Neither of them even flinched as she dipped farther south. Then she paused and realized they were hers to do with as she wanted, a fact that hadn't yet sunk in.

She knew what she wanted to do, so why was she so hesitant?

"Go ahead," AJ said. "Do it."

She reached out and skimmed her fingers over the base of his cock, wound her hand around it, measuring the heat and thickness of him.

"That feels good, Teresa."

It was a heady feeling to be able to give him pleasure. She turned to Pax, so different than AJ in just about every way. And he was watching as she stroked AJ's cock, imagining, she thought, how it would feel when she touched him. She didn't want him to wait—she couldn't wait—she skimmed her hand over his shaft, too, lifted it, stroked it, loving the sound of his sharp intake of breath.

"Damn" was all he said, and he lifted against her hand, pushing his cock against the tight fist she'd made.

Two cocks in her hands, two men in her bed. And she was still so far outside her element she had no idea what to do.

She shifted onto her knees, both her hands still filled with cock. She liked being in charge. Touching them, feeling the velvet texture of their shafts as she stroked them in unison, seeing the strained looks on their faces. She pulled up to the crest, slid down, then back up again, swirling her thumb over the soft heads, was a heady experience. She was in the position of power now, of giving them pleasure, and she wanted to give them so much more.

She let go of AJ and bent over Pax's cock, tilted her head so he could watch. He swept her hair to the side and held it while she let her tongue snake out to slide slow and easy over the crest. It beaded with milky fluid and she lapped it onto her tongue, then placed her mouth over the tip of his cock, taking it gently between her lips inch by inch.

And she watched him while she did, needed to see his face, just as he'd watched her while he'd given her such incredible pleasure.

This time, AJ didn't just lie there. He shifted and came up behind her, cupping her sex and smoothing his fingers over her pussy. Delicious sensation flowed through her like a molten river of lava as he began to move his hand back and forth, teasing her clit and pussy lips, sliding his fingers inside to wet them and taking them back to roll over her clit until the pleasure she received mixed with the pleasure she gave.

She wanted more, widening her legs, and in doing so she strad-dled Pax, her breasts lying on his thighs as she grasped his shaft in her hand. He slid a pillow under his head so he could be half-upright, watching her as he lifted, sliding his cock between her lips while AJ moved in and did magical things to her pussy and clit with his tongue.

She broke away from Pax only long enough to see what AJ was doing. Her body was on fire, throbbing from his tongue and his fingers and oh, God, what was he doing to her?

"I want to see, AJ."

"Here." Pax slid out from underneath her. "Now flip over onto your back and you can see."

She turned over and AJ put his mouth on her again, deliberately taking his time to lick the length of her, adding his fingers to torture her even further. She gripped Pax's cock and began to stroke as AJ continued to lick her. And when Pax bent and took a long, slow lick across her nipple, she slid her fingers into his hair and held him there, her gaze flitting between his tongue at her breast and AJ's mouth on her pussy.

The magic of what they were doing was too much, taking her where she had no hope of holding back. She fell into climax, aware of the tight grip she had on Pax's cock. As he sucked hard on her nipple, he didn't seem to care when she cried out, and AJ pumped his fingers harder inside her, licking her over and over again until she was shaking and needed more than just hands and mouths on her.

"Fuck me," she said, lifting against AJ. She'd had enough of foreplay, this endless, sweet torture that drove her to the brink of madness. She wanted his cock inside her and she was damn well going to demand it if she had to.

AJ got up and left the room only long enough to return with a box of condoms. He slid one on in a hurry and was back between her legs, parting them. Teresa watched in anticipation, rolling her hand over Pax's cock, looking up at him, warmed as he smiled down at her and smoothed her hair away from her face.

AJ held on to her knees. "You ready?"

"Yes. Fuck me now."

He slid his cock inside her, inch by inch, letting her get used to the feel of him. She was so wet already, but it had been a long time. Her pussy gripped and sheathed him as he buried himself all the way inside her. As she pulsed around him, AJ's eyes closed and he tilted his head back.

"Ahh, you feel good, Teresa."

A rush of pleasure and heat flowed from her, and she lifted

against him, shuddering at the sensation, at the knowledge that this was so right, that being with these men felt so perfect. She glanced up at Pax and gently tugged at his shaft to bring him to her.

He leaned forward and she took him in her mouth. She had to have him inside her, too, had to taste him while AJ fucked her. She swirled her tongue around the crest of his cock head and slid him inside her mouth, the heat and thickness of him as he rocked against her tongue only intensifying what she already felt being fucked by AJ.

"When you suck Pax, your pussy gets wet, Teresa. Did you know that? It squeezes me and spills your hot cream all over me."

She did know. She felt the quivers, the moisture as AJ withdrew and thrust inside her again. He was so tender and careful with her, so restrained as he moved within her. She loved that gentle side of him when he looked anything but a gentle man. That's what had always attracted her to him—the incongruous nature of wild versus tame, that he could rein in those impulses, that he had that kind of control. She saw that same control now as he moved inside her, the taut muscles of his upper body straining as he held back, moved gently against her. She wondered what he'd be like unleashed, all that power directed at her.

Pax pulled his cock from between her lips and put his mouth there, kissing her, his hands roaming over her breasts.

"I want to hear you breathe, listen to the sounds you make while AJ makes you come," he said. "And after he comes, I'm going to fuck you."

She shuddered at the dark promise in his words, at the way he looked at her like he wanted to possess her, devour her, own her. He skimmed his palm possessively over her breasts and down her belly, slid his fingers over her clit and began to move them against her as AJ fucked her.

Her breath caught as she looked at Pax, the storm blowing hot and furious in his dark eyes. He bent and kissed her, never once stopping the movement of his hand at her clit, rubbing her in tandem to AJ's thrusts. The sensations were overwhelming. She grasped Pax's arms and held on. She was drowning, unable to control what was happening to her. Only this time it wasn't at all like five years ago—this was incredible, a maelstrom of sensation that threatened to steal her sanity.

"Let go," Pax said, murmuring against her lips before he kissed his way to her jaw and neck. "Let loose, Teresa. I want to feel you squirm and cry when you come."

She wanted to come, could feel it rising with every touch from Pax's hand, with every movement of AJ's cock inside her. She rocked her head from side to side as the sensations assaulted her, one on top of the other. AJ held on to her legs, lifting her as he drove deeper. Pax slipped an arm around her and held her up.

"Watch, Teresa. Watch what we're doing to you."

This was so painfully intimate she wasn't sure she could, but as she did, she glanced at both of them. They were hers. She was theirs. A bond forming that couldn't be broken. She would never do this with anyone but them.

Pax dipped and took her mouth in a kiss that ravaged her from the inside out, his tongue diving in and taking possession of hers, driving the last of the ghosts away as he cradled her to him and rocked his fingers against her clit. She cried out against his mouth as her orgasm hit her a split second later. Pax let her go and AJ came down on top of her, kissing her as her climax shuddered through her. He swept his hand underneath her to lift her, then shuddered with her as he came, his fingers digging into her buttocks as he ground against her.

Spent, shaking, she held on to AJ while Pax stroked her hair. AJ lifted, smiled down at her and kissed her, then withdrew.

She should be satisfied, but she wasn't. Not yet. She turned to Pax and held her arms out for him.

"Are you sure you're not too tired for this?"

She shook her head. "I'm not tired. And we aren't going to be finished until you're inside me."

Pax sucked in a breath and nodded, went to get a condom. A moment later he was there next to her, lying on his side. He lifted her leg and draped it over his hip.

"I've wanted to fuck you from the first second I laid eyes on you at the bar."

Teresa swallowed and wove her fingers into his hair, remembering that first night, how meeting him had given her that first jolt into her reawakened sexuality. "Ditto."

He slid into her, nice and easy, and as much as AJ had held back, she knew Pax held back even more. When she moved against him, his jaw clenched. She caressed the spot where he held that tension and felt it relax.

"I'm not going to break," she said, smiling at Pax. AJ moved in behind her to cup her breast and kiss her neck.

"I know that," Pax said, stilling. "You're stronger than any woman I've ever known. A survivor." He rested his hand on her thigh and surged against her, making her gasp. "But you're not ready for all we have to offer. Not yet. So let's just take it slow and easy tonight."

"You tempt me," she said, kissing Pax and laying her hand over AJ's, helping him caress her nipple. "I want to know everything about the two of you."

Pax thrust. "You will. Plenty of time for that."

She groaned and tilted her head back against AJ, turning so he could kiss her. "I never thought it could be this good."

"It gets better," AJ whispered against her mouth. "A lot better."

Pax shuttled his hips, rocking against her clit, awakening her desire to fever pitch once again.

And it got better? "I'm not sure I'll survive more than this."

"You can take more than you think." Pax tightened his grip on her leg, lifting her so they could both see where they were connected. He pulled out, then pushed in with more force this time. "You were made for us, Teresa."

She believed it. The three of them fit perfectly in so many ways.

How could they take her to the limit so quickly again? She was so close, on the ragged edge and ready to take the leap. It was so good that tears pricked her eyes. This was all too much—too much pleasure, too much emotion. She wasn't ready for all of it yet. But she couldn't stop it any more than she could stop from climaxing as Pax quickened his pace and began to drive his cock harder inside her. Her orgasm came from deep within, and she held on to both her men as she rode out the wave that burst from every nerve ending and seemed to go on forever. Pax tightened against her, making eye contact with her as he went over the edge, and she'd never seen anything so amazing as this man when he came inside her. It was so raw, so true and brutally honest it shook her to her core. She wasn't sure any man had ever let her see so deeply inside him. She wondered if Pax had even been aware of it, because he closed his eyes and pulled her against him while they both rode out the aftereffects.

She didn't want to let go of this pleasure.

She didn't want to let go of any of this.

But eventually they disengaged and AJ and Pax led her into the giant bathroom, where they all shared a shower. They soaped her up and washed her body tenderly, then rinsed and dried her off and helped her into bed.

She thought they'd leave her, but she was wrong. They fit her in the middle of her giant bed, and Pax climbed in on one side of her, AJ on the other. AJ turned off the lamp, and the three of them nestled together in the darkness of the room, the shades closed against the filtering gray light.

It was nearly dawn and Teresa was exhausted, yet sleep eluded her. She was nestled in bed with two men, and had just had sex for the first time since the rape. Really great sex, where the memories of that horrible act had been erased by something incredibly beautiful.

It had been a phenomenal night. Her entire life had just changed. Her mind was filled with possibilities and thoughts and what ifs.

She closed her eyes and let sleep take her.

FIFTEEN

TERESA WOKE TO PINPRICKS OF BRIGHT SUNLIGHT BREAKING through the shade as it fluttered back and forth from the overhead fan. She blinked and opened her eyes fully to see glimpses of a very bright day outside.

She tilted her head back to glance at the clock on the nightstand.

Noon. Wow. She was about to jump out of bed, but a steely arm imprisoned her. She skimmed the arm with her fingers, smiling as she recognized the hand.

Pax. She slid back under the covers and wriggled against him, backing into one sizeable erection.

"It's part of the territory, darlin'," he whispered as he nuzzled her neck, planting kisses against her nape until she broke out in delicious goose bumps.

"Is that right?"

"Yeah. Happens every morning I wake up against a beautiful ass like yours."

"Huh. So you're saying I'm not special?"

He smoothed his hand over the curve of her hip and slipped his shaft between her thighs. "Oh, I'd say you're pretty damn special."

Desire sparked hot as languid sleep faded instantly. She reached behind her to cup his neck. "Why don't you show me how much?"

"Grab a condom and I will."

She did and handed it to him. He had it on in a matter of seconds, the heat of his body once again flush against her back. He shifted her, aligning her pussy so he could slip inside her with one careful thrust.

"You always wake up wet?"

"Only when a hot cock like yours is pressed against my ass."

"So you're saying I'm not special?"

She laughed. "I'd say your cock is very special to me right now."

He kissed her back, sweeping her hair away to nibble at her neck, lightly biting her.

"Oh, I like that." Tingles spread down her spine. She moaned as he thrust deeper and cupped her sex to rub her clit.

"What do you like? The biting or the rubbing?"

"Both."

Desire flashed hot and fast as he moved within her, cupping one breast in his hand to play with her nipple. She reached down to rub her clit as he rocked inside her with a slow, easy rhythm that built the tension in a hurry. He knew just how and where to stroke to give her maximum pleasure. Caressing the throbbing bud only added to the need to go off. She tightened, holding still, feeling him thicken inside her as he took her right to the edge.

"I'm going to come, Teresa. Come with me."

She increased the movements of her fingers over her clit. She was slick, wet, and she slid her fingers down to feel where they were joined.

"Ah, Christ. I like you touching me." The sound of his voice, so husky with need, the way his cock grew rigid as he thrust deep inside her, brought her climax shuddering through her. Pax gripped her hip and tightened his hold on her, pushing into her with one hard thrust, then burying his face against her neck as he came.

Panting, he kissed her neck and shoulder.

After Teresa caught her breath, she said, "I like waking up like this."

Pax drew her around to face him, planting one seriously hot kiss on her. "Me, too."

She gazed up at eyes that a woman could spend all day admiring. "You keep looking at me like that, we'll never get out of this bed."

He grinned. "Is that a bad thing?"

"You two going to spend the entire day in bed? I'm hungry."

Teresa's head shot up to see AJ. "Where've you been?"

"While you two were sleeping like the dead, I took a ride down to Main Street to see what was going on."

"Anything?" she asked, sitting up.

"No Fists, if that's what you're asking. Now, get up, Pax. I'm starving to death."

Pax rolled over and got out of bed to head to the bathroom, shaking his head at AJ as he walked by. "What, are you incapable of fixing breakfast?"

AJ climbed onto the bed and kissed Teresa, drawing her against him. "You're the chef," he said to Pax. "I'm just the recipient of your masterpieces. I made coffee. Isn't that good enough?"

"Yeah, yeah," Pax said from the bathroom. He came out and leaned against the doorway. "I think I want eggs, bacon and pancakes this morning." He looked over to the shades. "Or should I say, this afternoon. How do y'all feel about that?"

Teresa's stomach growled. "I think I'm starving. I'll get dressed and come help you."

"Not if I convince her to stay in bed with me," AJ said, drawing her head to his chest.

Pax laughed. "I'll go start breakfast."

He left the room and AJ rolled over on top of Teresa, kissing her until she lost her train of thought. Is this what it would be like to share a life with these men? One making love to her and then other taking his place?

As AJ worshipped her mouth with his lips and tongue, she thought that wouldn't be a bad thing at all. She'd never felt so cared for.

"Come on," he said, rolling off the bed and holding his hand out. "Time to get up and get something to eat."

She let him help her up. "I'll get dressed and meet you in the kitchen."

AFTER BREAKFAST—OR BRUNCH—THEY ALL SAT OUTSIDE AND drank coffee. Teresa studied Pax and AJ, who seemed to always get along so well. She wondered how each of them felt about her being alone with the other. AJ hadn't seemed surprised or upset to find her in bed with Pax this morning, and it had been quite obvious what the two of them had been doing. Yet AJ didn't seem jealous.

She didn't know whether she should be offended by that or relieved.

"Uh-oh," Pax said.

"What?" AJ asked.

"She's thinking. I can tell."

"How can you tell?" Teresa asked.

Pax dipped his finger between her brows. "You get this little crinkle right here when you're deep in thought."

She'd dated a lot of guys in her lifetime and not one had ever noticed that. "Is that so?"

"Yeah. So what's got you thinking?"

"Actually, I was pondering some things about you two."

"Oh shit." AJ looked to Pax, then back at her. "What did we do?"

Teresa laughed. "It's not bad. I'm just . . . curious."

"About?"

"This threesome thing."

AJ leaned over, wrapped his fingers around the back of her neck and drew her close for a kiss. She shuddered out a breath when he let her go.

"I would have thought last night might have answered at least a few of your questions."

"Oh, it did," she said, picking up her coffee and taking a sip. "A few, anyway."

"But not all," Pax said. "So ask."

Teresa looked to AJ and swallowed hard. This needed to be said, the questions had to be asked because she had to know where things stood. "Pax and I had just had sex when you walked into the bedroom."

AJ nodded. "Yeah. So?"

"Didn't that bother you?"

"No. Why should it? Pax walked in on you and me having some fun before. It didn't bother Pax."

"Nope," Pax said. "It doesn't work that way, Teresa. We're not territorial."

She pursed her lips, not wanting to say what thought had popped into her head. It was stupid, really.

"You think it doesn't bother us because we don't care."

Her gaze slid to Pax, wondering how he'd gotten so good at mind reading. "Yes."

"It's not like that at all. We don't treat women like something we own. We want them to have a good time when they're with us. If we didn't care, we'd fuck 'em and forget 'em. We don't do that. When we're with a woman we want her to feel special."

AJ leaned over and took her hand. "And we don't want to fuck you and forget you, Teresa. Did you feel used?"

"No. I guess I just worry about how to . . . divide my time."

AJ laughed. "Don't worry about that. Pax and I aren't jealous of each other. Whether you're with both of us or one at a time, we can handle it."

"It should always be your choice to make," Pax said.

"Somehow, for a woman, that all seems a little too good to be true. What do you guys get out of it?" she asked.

Pax and AJ answered almost simultaneously. "You."

THE BAR WAS SLAMMING BUSY THAT NIGHT. TERESA BARELY HAD time to breathe between filling drink orders, which made Steve and Sandy deliriously happy. Even Steve had to get behind one of the bars tonight, and though he filled drink orders, he wasn't wowing the crowd with his looks or his body. That is until he tried showing some skin, rolling his T-shirt up over his ample belly and tying it underneath his sizeable man boobs, which damn near made Teresa choke she was laughing so hard, as were most of the customers, who promptly filled up Steve's tip jar. But Sandy warned him: If he tried to get up on the bar and wiggle his ass, she was going home.

Fortunately, Steve declined and let the dancers handle that aspect of drawing in the customers. And Teresa was happy, because the loud music and sexy girls dancing on the bar, as well as the nonstop flowing beer and great food, meant a huge draw of customers streaming in and out and the possibility of the Fists coming in. And if the Fists came in, there was a chance the guy who killed Larks would be among them.

It was time for her team to get a break. She had to clear her brother. And she had finally convinced AJ and Pax to get out there and roam around on their bikes while she worked the bar.

Spreading out was the best way to hunt for the Fists, rather than all of them holed up in one spot. She had this place covered, and it was biker central, with her situated at the main bar, next to the front doors. If the Fists came in, she was going to see them. Pax and AJ had gone out riding and said they were going to split up, one heading up to the concert area at the campground, the other one milling about down on the main drag and wherever else groups of bikers were hanging out. Teresa felt confident they had all the bases covered.

And the Fists were here in Sturgis, she knew it, she had a gut feeling about it, and her gut feelings were never wrong.

In the meantime, she was enjoying the music as well as the throng of bikers clamoring for another beer. The clientele was patient and friendly and out for a good time. She had a prime spot and the tip jar was full.

"Teresa!"

She flipped around and saw Russ, Joey's best friend and VP of the Thorns. She grinned. "Hey, Russ."

"What are you doing here?"

"Working."

"I see that. I didn't know you were coming to Sturgis for the rally."

She leaned across the bar to whisper at him. "Well, I'm here to find the guy who stabbed Larks so I can clear Joey."

Russ arched a brow. "By yourself?"

"No. I have a couple friends with me."

"Find the guy yet?"

She shook her head. "I haven't even spotted the Fists yet. Have you?"

"No. But there are a lot of bikers here. And we're camping nearly a hundred miles away. So we've been mostly riding and seeing the sights. This is our first trip into the main drag."

"It's awesome here, isn't it?"

"Yeah, it is." He grabbed the beer Teresa offered and took a long swallow. "So how did you get this gig?"

"They were shorthanded and I have the experience. This place is a prime location, so I figured it would be a good spot to stay put and see if the Fists show up."

"Great idea. We'll keep our eyes open and I'll call you if I spot them."

"Thanks, Russ."

He moved off to join the other Thorns, who waved at her after Russ pointed in her direction. After about a half hour they all took off. It made her feel good to know Joey's guys were all here, too. Between them and AJ and Pax, she felt safe.

"So what are you doing when you get off work tonight?"

A tall, good-looking biker leaned over the bar while she fetched him a beer. "Going home with my guys," she said with a smile as she handed him his change.

His brows raised. "Guys? As in plural?"

She winked. "Guys as in plural."

He looked her up and down, smiled and nodded as he walked away. She served another customer, and a decided warmth spread through her belly.

Yeah. Her two guys. It had felt good saying it. Even if they really weren't hers, not for the long term anyway. But while she was here, they definitely belonged to her, so she intended to own that fantasy for as long as she could.

Funny how easily she'd adapted to the lifestyle. One night of hot sex with two men and she was all in. But who wouldn't be after being with Pax and AJ? She'd never felt more completely loved and valued as she had been last night.

And there was that warm, giddy feeling again. Though they weren't here right now, she could feel their presence, could smell each of them, so unique even in their individual scents, which went beyond soap and shampoo into something more earthy and elemental. She craved their touch, their kisses, the way she felt when she was around them.

She wanted more. More of them, more of that magic they'd wound around her last night. She knew they'd held back, and next time she didn't want them to.

Next time. Her flesh heated at the thought of next time, her pussy dampening as she conjured up visuals of what they'd do to her. So much potential, an endless variety of scenarios and positions.

And thinking about sex with AJ and Pax was not helping to keep her mind on her job, or giving her a keen eye to watch all the bikers filing in and out. She forced her attention into filling drink requests, grabbing a tall glass of water for herself, hoping it would quench the heat she'd conjured up with her fantasies.

Yeah, that damn had sure burst, hadn't it? For someone who'd been repressed for so long, one night of great sex had sure sprung open the well of her imagination.

She'd been so lost in thoughts of AJ and Pax she almost missed him. But a flash of something familiar on the back of a guy's vest caught her eye. She served up a few more beers to patrons hanging at the bar, her gaze following a biker who quickly blended into the thick crowd.

Dammit. Had she imagined seeing the Fists logo on that vest?

She tried to train her vision on where she'd last seen him, but he'd been swallowed up by the throng of people and she had customers clamoring for drinks. So she turned her attention back to the bar, and that's when she saw them come through the front door.

Fists. A dozen of them at least, pushing through with a group of other bikers, their insignias easy to spot on the backs of their leather vests.

They were here! Her heart climbed up into her throat and her palms began to sweat as she struggled to fill drink orders and keep her eye on the group of Fists at the same time.

They didn't stop at her bar, which was probably a good thing because she didn't want to risk being recognized. It was also a bad thing because they'd moved clear to the other side of the room, where there was an exit door. What if they just came in and left right away?

She leaned over and whispered to Claudia, the woman tending bar next to her, "I'll be back in a sec."

Claudia nodded and didn't even look up from her task of popping the tops off four bottles of beer. Teresa bowed up from behind the bar as unobtrusively as possible and made a circle around the dance floor. She knew the Fists—they wouldn't be out on the dance floor. They'd be belly up where the beer and whiskey were plentiful, so she wound her way to the bar at the back of the club. No sign of them there, so she had to fight her way through the crowd to reach the bar located opposite the one she worked and near the other door.

That's when she spotted them, all huddled together like a group of cattle, throwing back shots like they were dying of thirst, and following those up by guzzling down their beers.

She stayed in the background and studied their faces, tattoos and necks. Dammit, none of them was the guy she was looking for. But wherever the Fists were, she knew he'd be close by. He had to be.

So when they started to head out the door, panic set in. She waited until the last one was out and the door closed, then rushed to the bar where Sandy was working.

"I have an emergency. I need to head out."

"One of your fellas?" Sandy asked, clearly concerned.

Teresa hated lying to her, but she nodded. "Yeah."

Sandy laid her hand on top of Teresa's. "I hope he's okay. You go on. We'll manage."

Guilt slammed into her stomach, but she pushed it aside, sprang through the door and headed for her bike. Fortunately she had a good spot, and she climbed on, jumped on the throttle and headed out into the street in search of the Fists. They could still be on foot, or maybe they'd wandered into another bar. In this crowd of bikers she might not—

There they were, pulling out from one of the side streets and heading out of town. Grateful to have spotted them, she inhaled a deep breath and willed herself to relax. Now all she had to do was lay back a little, let a few bikers get between them and her, see if they picked up more Fists and figure out where they were going. She thanked the half million bikers at this event because it made it easier for her to blend in as she followed.

After about twenty minutes of heading up into the hills, the Fists pulled into what looked like a small, well-hidden campground in the middle of forest. Teresa stayed back at the entrance since you had to pay to enter. Instead, she rode just ahead, where she pulled into a lot—more of a scenic overview, really—that overlooked the camping area and the hills. She climbed off her bike and wandered around, trying to look like a tourist, even took out her cell phone and pretended to be taking night shots—of what, she had no idea since her cell would take crappy shots at night, but the overview was well lit and the craggy rocks rising up on the other side were spectacular for photos, so it would appear like she had a good reason for being there. And she wasn't alone, lots of other people were enjoying the view despite the late hour. She meandered over to the edge of the lot and peered down at the campsite.

Unfortunately, it was dark and she couldn't see a damn thing other than a few campfires and some lanterns. She had no way of knowing where the Fists had set up camp or even if they were actually camped there.

She blew out a breath of frustration and resigned herself to the fact she was going to have to call in reinforcements. Pax and AJ weren't going to be happy that she hadn't stayed put at the bar, but what was she supposed to have done? Let the Fists walk out of there and chance never figuring out where they'd gone?

She punched in AJ's number.

"WHAT THE HELL DO YOU MEAN, SHE ISN'T IN THERE?" PAX SHOT a glare at AJ as he exited the bar and rounded toward his bike.

"She's not at the bar. The owner said she took off because one of us had an emergency of some sort."

Pax crossed his arms. "That makes no fucking sense. So why the hell *did* she leave the bar?"

AJ shook his head. "No clue. Her bike isn't parked where she left it when we were here earlier, so she's obviously taken off."

"Son of a bitch."

AJ knew exactly how Pax felt. He was worried about Teresa. She should have known better than to leave by herself. And what reason could she have had for doing that? "You don't suppose the Fists found her and hauled her out of there, do you?" he asked.

"No. She'd have put up a fight in front of a lot of witnesses. There's no way she'd have let that happen without causing enough of a fuss that others would have put a stop to it."

AJ nodded. "You're right. So why else would she leave?"

His phone vibrated and he pulled it out of his chaps, relieved when he saw Teresa's number come up. "Where the hell are you?"

"I knew you were going to be mad at me. I found the Fists."

He wasn't mad. He was relieved she was okay. "Where are you? Where are they?"

She told him what had happened and her location.

"Don't move, and for God's sake, don't attempt to contact them until we get there."

AJ closed the phone and shoved it back into his jacket pocket.

"What?" Pax asked. "She okay?"

"Yeah. She's fine. A dozen or so Fists showed up in the bar. When they left, she followed them to a campground about thirty minutes from here."

"Oh."

"That's all you have to say is *oh*?"

"Well, I don't really like her going off on her own, but it was a smart move on her part."

AJ dragged his hands through his hair. "I don't like it. What if the guy who killed Larks spotted her?"

"Obviously he didn't, so give her some credit for thinking on her feet."

"And going off by herself is what got her . . . hurt . . . before."

Pax climbed onto his bike and turned to look at AJ. "What do you want to do, man? Build a bubble around her or put a bodyguard on her who'll be with her forever? You have to let her have her independence."

"Independence is fine. This is different. She should have called us."

"They'd have been gone by the time we got here. And we'd have lost a chance to find them. And Teresa isn't stupid. She isn't going to walk into a trap."

AJ sighed. "I know. I just . . . worry about her."

"So do I, but if you start pushing her into a corner and telling her the world isn't safe, all you're going to do is scare her. And then everything we've tried to do for her these past few days will be for nothing, because she'll never get over what those assholes did to her. Women get raped in their own homes when their doors and windows are locked tight, AJ. What happened to Teresa had nothing to do with circumstance or location and you and I both know it. It was a calculated move by the Fists to get Joey's attention and make him cave. It doesn't mean she can never ride anywhere alone anymore. You have to give her some space."

AJ stared at him for a few seconds. "You're right. I do. But I won't stop worrying about her."

"I know, man. I know." Pax started up his bike. "Now let's go find her."

It was a long ride and it gave AJ entirely too much time to think about things, especially things related to Teresa. Like why he was so protective of her. Yeah, he understood he maybe felt responsible for what had happened to her five years ago. If he'd stayed put, if he hadn't left, things might have been different. They might have stayed together, and he might have been with her that night. Maybe she would have never had to go through that trauma.

And maybe the universe just didn't work that way. But he couldn't help feeling like he needed to be by her side now. Whether that had anything to do with him abruptly leaving all those years ago, he had no idea. All he knew was he craved being near her right now. And right now was pretty much where AJ's world existed.

They pulled into the lot and found Teresa's bike tucked behind a motor home. She wasn't near her bike though, so they had to hunt for her in the dark. AJ's phone buzzed with a text message from Teresa that said she was near the ledge on the northeast side of the lot, by the trees leading down to the campground. He signaled Pax and they moved toward the front of the lot, spotting Teresa crouched down in the dirt.

She was safe. That's all that mattered.

For now.

sixteen

Teresa was glad to see the guys. It was cold and dark and she wasn't afraid to admit—at least to herself—that she preferred their company to skulking alone in the darkness.

"See them?" AJ asked as he got in position next to her, Pax next to him.

Fighting back another shiver, she shook her head. "Too damn dark to see other than random shapes and campfires. I hear lots of partying going on, but I didn't want to go into the campgrounds and risk being recognized."

"Good call."

"I'll get the binoculars," Pax said, pushing off and heading for his bike.

"Tell me those are night vision," Teresa said to AJ, watching Pax disappear into the darkness.

"You know about night vision stuff?"

She rolled her eyes. "I know some things. I do read and watch crime shows."

AJ snickered. "Not quite the same thing as what you see on TV and read in books, but yeah, they're night vision."

Pax returned a few minutes later and nestled into a crouch next to Teresa.

"I saw them drive down the main dirt road and dip over a hill. I didn't see them turn so maybe they stayed straight on."

Pax nodded, adjusting the binoculars to the left where the entrance to the grounds was. He swept them slowly over the camp. Teresa waited, biting her lower lip, not wanting to disrupt him, but oh she really wanted to take a look.

"Here." Pax handed them to her.

She grinned, surprised. "Really?"

He showed her how to work them. "It might take your eyes a few seconds to adjust to them, but then you'll be able to see like it's daylight."

She looked through them. Pax was right. At first, everything was fuzzy, but after a while she adjusted.

Wow. It was easy to distinguish what was what in the campground. She couldn't see someone's eye color, but she could identify people easily enough.

"Look south, all the way to the edge, beyond that thick group of trees. The Fists are there, separated off by themselves."

She followed Pax's instructions, moving the binoculars slowly so she wouldn't lose her bearings. There, beyond a cluster of tents where people had gathered to be together, were the Fists, settled by themselves at the far corner of the campground, cut off from the main group by a line of trees.

She handed off the binoculars to AJ and turned to Pax. "Gives them plenty of privacy, doesn't it?"

Pax nodded, frowning. "Also makes it damned impossible to go riding in there to check them out."

"Because there'd be no reason to go that far in. They're at the end, the facilities are midway. No one would have any reason to breach their campground."

"That sucks," AJ said.

"Yeah," Teresa said, wrinkling her nose as she pondered a solution. "So now what?"

"Maybe one of us stays here to keep watch. I assume you didn't spot your guy?"

She shook her head. "Well, no. But that doesn't mean he isn't there."

She waited for Pax and AJ to doubt her, to tell her they'd tried, but they'd located the Fists, the guy she claimed had killed Larks wasn't among them, and it was time to pack it up and head home.

"They could be hiding him. There's a motor home tucked in behind their tents," Pax said.

"Really? I didn't see that."

He handed her the binoculars. "Look again. It's butted up against a group of bushes. Hard to see because all the tents are set up in front of it, but it's there."

She did look, straining her eyes like she was trying to find what was different about two pictures that looked exactly alike. Then she spotted it. "I see it now. Wow, I totally missed that the first time."

"They're hiding it," Pax said.

"For a reason, obviously."

"What reason?" Teresa asked AJ.

AJ shrugged. "Don't know. But we're going to have to find out."

"How are we going to do that?"

AJ grinned at Teresa. "We need Grange's RV."

THEY'D GOTTEN LUCKY WHEN THEY SHOWED UP AT THE ENTRANCE to the campground. There were a few spaces available, and one just happened to be on the southeast side, behind the Fists. The owner of the campsite said it wasn't an ideal spot because it was remote and a good walk to the facilities, but to them it was perfect. A wall of trees and bushes separated them from the Fists, so they wouldn't be able to see them from their campsite, but the three of them could damn sure hike through that thicket and spy on them.

Their second round of luck was the RV Grange owned. Pax had gone back to the house to grab the RV and trailer his bike behind it. They looked just like a bunch of travelers, now, not out of place at all.

Teresa thrilled at the thought as they set up camp, then went inside the RV. Spacious, but one bedroom, and that was pretty tiny.

"No way are all three of us going to fit in there." Two people, yes. Three, and considering two of those persons were sizeable males? She didn't think so.

Pax gave her a lopsided grin. "You can sleep in there. AJ and I will sleep on the couches."

She put her hands on her hips. "I'm not sleeping in that bed without you."

"Then I guess we'll be snuggling."

Despite the chill coming in from the open windows and the goose bumps on her skin, the look Pax gave her and the thought of sharing the tiny bed with both of them heated her from the inside out. "I like snuggling."

AJ came up behind her and wrapped his arms around her. "Much as Pax and I would like nothing more than spending the rest of the night warming you up, we need to get to work."

He pressed a kiss to the side of her neck, then released her. She zipped up her jacket to ward off the chill and turned to him. "What do we need to do?"

"Get close enough to the Fists' encampment to get a glimpse of who's there."

"And see if the guy who killed Larks is camped out there?"

AJ nodded.

"Which means I get to go with you."

"We're not about to leave you here by yourself," Pax said. "And you're the only one who knows what this guy looks like, so yeah, you're going with us."

Excitement shot through her at the thought of skulking through the woods in search of the bad guy. Okay, maybe she watched too much television. But it still felt good to be included in something that had the potential to be dangerous. The old adrenaline junkie inside her awakened and jumped up and down, eager to get started.

"So what do we do?"

AJ glanced at his phone. "It's almost one-thirty. They might be in bed for the night, but maybe not. I say we head over now."

"Do we want them asleep or awake?" she asked.

"Awake. I want to know who's out there. If they're all in tents or in that RV, we're not going to get a chance to check them out."

"What if they're all asleep?"

"Then we'll be back there in the morning to scope things out."

She nodded and let AJ and Pax take the lead.

Pax took her hand, his gaze direct. "Be careful of every step you take. Walk where we walk, especially when we get close to their camp. One snap of a branch of crunch of a leaf under your boots will alert them to us."

"Okay."

"It's not going to be easy, because it's going to be dark in there. We'll move slow and stay close so you can follow easier."

"You can trust me. I'll be careful."

He palmed her neck and brushed his lips against hers, then smiled. "I know you will."

She shuddered at the warmth of his kiss; she always felt enveloped by something she couldn't put words to when either Pax or AJ touched her or kissed her. She wanted time to think about that, to sort it out, but now wasn't that time.

They headed toward the thick trees that separated them from the Fists. AJ went in first and Teresa followed, with Pax taking the rear. True to her word, she was attentive, mirroring AJ's every careful move. The woodsy floor was littered with twigs and leaves and just about anything and everything that made noise if you stepped on it. Teresa cringed each time their boots made a crunch or snapping sound. It was late enough that most of the camps had quieted down for the night—but not all the camps, fortunately. And those raucous sounds carried, thankfully, masking whatever missteps the three of them took as they made their way through the woods.

The first thing Teresa saw was a faint light, then she heard the low sounds of voices. AJ held his hand up and she stopped, Pax coming up next to her.

They crept toward the entrance of the Fists' camp, staying low and out of sight. AJ led them to the north, where they had a clear view but were still hidden within the shelter of trees and bushes.

Now Teresa could see the Fists' campfire. There were six of them sitting in a circle around the fire, drinking beer, smoking and talking. The wind picked up and smoke blanketed the circle, partially obscuring her ability to identify them. She waited, her heart pounding, for the wind to shift.

Now. She leaned forward and blinked, wishing it were daylight so she could see better, but hoping the campfire would provide enough light. Two of the guys were bald. She scanned their faces and necks, but she knew without a doubt that neither was the guy who killed Larks. Disappointment sank into her stomach. She turned to AJ and shook her head.

Pax gently tugged on her arm to lead her back toward their own camp. Teresa shook her head and pointed toward the RV.

"Can't. Too dark and too many people. Later," AJ whispered against her ear.

Still, she resisted, her gaze lingering on the darkened RV. What if he was in there? They were so close.

But Pax pulled on the sleeve of her jacket again, and she knew he was right. There was no way they could get in there with those guys hanging around outside. Better to try again in daylight.

They did the slow creep back through the woods, and Teresa tried not to think of bugs falling into her hair or snakes slithering across her boots. She kept her eyes trained on AJ's back until they were clear of the foliage. She ran her fingers through her hair— just in case—before entering the RV.

It was warmer in there, so she shed her jacket and pulled off her boots. It wasn't a huge RV, but there was enough room for the three of them to stretch out on the two cushioned sofas that sat parallel to each other. AJ had grabbed beers for him and Pax, while Teresa only wanted water. That whole escapade had made her throat go bone dry.

"So now what?" she asked.

"Now we'll work in shifts so we can keep an eye on who comes out of that RV," Pax said. "The only way to do an accurate count of who's really staying at that camp is to keep constant watch over it."

"So we're going to take turns?"

AJ shook his head. "Not 'we,' honey. Pax and me."

She crossed her arms. "That's not right. I'm perfectly capable of hanging out in the woods and watching a campsite."

"You're not a trained agent," Pax said. "AJ and I are. So don't even think about arguing with us."

"Pax is right," AJ said. "There's no way we're going to put you in danger. We can handle ourselves."

Teresa couldn't believe this. "I have a gun and know how to use it."

AJ picked up her hand. "And what if they hear you and you have a dozen guys come crashing into the woods after you? You gonna shoot all of them?"

Irritation piqued within her. "That's the worst-case scenario."

Pax nodded. "Exactly. Which is something you should always be prepared for when you're going on surveillance."

Dammit. She hated not being part of this. "You can't identify the guy. I can."

"I think we have a pretty good idea which one he isn't. And you gave a damn good description of his appearance and neck tattoos. If we spot him, we'll notify you and you can ID him."

She glared at AJ and blew out a long, frustrated sigh. "Fine. But I don't like not contributing."

AJ squeezed her hand. "Honey, without you we couldn't do this. You're the biggest contributor."

Somehow that didn't make her feel better.

seventeen

AJ had taken the first shift, leaving Pax to stay with Teresa. Not that he minded being alone with her. They'd both taken a shower—unfortunately not at the same time, since the shower was nothing more than a small box. Since then Teresa had been watching him and not saying much at all.

She was wound up tight and pacing the confines of the RV. Pax sat at the table and watched her walk past, her arms snugged tight under her breasts, her head down. She took the steps slow, but the tension rolled off of her in waves.

Finally, he'd had enough. He stood and blocked her path. "Babe, you need to calm down."

Her head shot up. "I'm fine."

"She says through gritted teeth." He offered a teasing smile she didn't return. Okay, he'd just have to try and figure out what was wrong. Maybe she was worried about AJ being out there.

"AJ's fine."

"I'm not worried about AJ."

"Then why don't you tell me what's got you so bent out of shape?"

"I should be out there, too. I should be able to participate. This isn't fair."

He laid his hands on her shoulders, let his fingers press in. Yeah, her muscles were tight as boulders. "No, it's not fair. But it is what it is and you have to accept it."

She shrugged his hands off and backed away. "I don't feel useful."

He took a few steps forward, refusing to let her walk away from him. "I don't know how much more useful you can be. You're the key to getting your brother released from this murder charge. You just can't be the one hiding out in the woods."

She tilted her head back to meet his gaze, and Pax was lost in the sadness he saw there. "I need to do more."

He slid his knuckles across her cheek, mesmerized by the softness of her skin. "Why?"

"Because Joey has always been there for me."

"And you're bending over backward for him. So why isn't that enough?"

She looked away, brushed past him to take up pacing again. "I don't know. I just have to . . . do this myself."

He frowned. "Why? Why can't you let AJ and me handle this part?"

She stopped. He heard her sigh. "I can't explain it. You wouldn't understand."

"Try me."

She turned. "I don't want to owe you."

Stunned, he could only stare at her. "What? You think you owe us for helping you?"

"I don't know. I'm just not happy about this." She sat on the sofa and pulled her knees to her chest. "I want to do things by myself. For myself and for Joey. I didn't want to bring you and AJ into this. I feel like all of this . . ." She lifted her head. "What does it mean, anyway?"

He had no idea what she was talking about. She was talking in circles. "What does what mean, honey? I'm not following you."

"This. You, me and AJ. We've somehow fallen into this . . . relationship. If it's even a relationship. It doesn't make sense. I'm feeling things and I don't want to feel them. How the hell am I supposed to handle what's going on with the three of us? How do you guys handle it? Or maybe you just don't. It's probably fun and games and sex, and you don't feel a damn thing. But I do, goddammit. And what the hell am I supposed to do about that when the two of you pack up and leave?"

Oh. Now he understood. He sat next to her. "Why do we have to understand it?"

She shrugged. "I don't know. It makes me feel strange."

"Uncomfortable?"

She lifted her gaze to his. "Honestly? Sometimes."

"In what way?"

"Like right now. AJ's out there in the cold by himself and you and me are here in this warm RV alone together."

Ah. Things were starting to make sense. "And you want to fuck me."

Her head shot up, her gaze making direct contact with his. "I didn't say that."

"You didn't have to. AJ's out there and you want me and that makes you feel guilty."

She looked at him, then gave a quick nod. "Okay, fine. Yes."

He dragged her onto his lap, eliciting a surprised gasp from her. But when she tried to wriggle away, he held tight. "Don't ever apologize for wanting either of us, whether we're together or alone."

"But—"

"No buts. AJ and I are adults. We know you want both of us. I can one hundred percent bet you that AJ assumes we're fucking right now."

Her brows lifted. "You sure about that?"

"Yes. And I can also bet you that when it's my turn to go out there he's going to crawl into bed with you and fuck you."

He saw the flare of heat in her eyes, knew she was imagining that scene. "And that doesn't bother you."

"No. Why should it? It's not like you don't want me or that you want him more than me. I'll have my time with you. And even if you did want him more than you wanted me, that's your choice to make, Teresa. We don't control how you feel or who you want. That's your decision. Free will, you know. You have a right to want what you want . . . and who you want."

Her body was pliant and warm against his. "I don't understand the two of you. This makes no sense. Men are territorial and possessive."

"Quit trying to label AJ and me like most men. We aren't wired that way."

"I just think—"

He slid his hand under her hair, cupped the nape of her neck, and drew her lips to his. "Stop thinking so much."

He kissed her and she melted against him. Yeah, that's what he wanted, and he knew it's what Teresa wanted, too. She just needed to stop denying herself what her body craved, needed to stop trying to figure out what the three of them meant to one another. If Pax tried too hard to think about what it meant, he'd drive himself crazy. So he chose not to think about it at all, not to think about anything but how it felt at the moment when he held Teresa in his arms. It was the only thing that mattered.

He slid his arm down her back. Her body was warm and he sought bare skin wherever he could find it—the spot where her tank top dipped inward, revealing her shoulder blades. He slid his hand inside there and she shuddered against him.

He pulled his lips from hers. "You cold?"

She leaned away and smiled at him. "No. I like the way you touch me." She grasped his hand and laid it over one breast. She wasn't wearing a bra, and her nipple hardened against his palm. His cock, already half hard, went to full erection at the feel of the bud stiffening against his hand. But that wasn't enough, because he wanted to see her, touch her skin, taste her. He lifted her shirt and bared her breasts, brought her sweet flesh to his mouth to put his lips around her nipple. She gasped and tightened against him, arching upward and wriggling her butt, which made his dick go crazy.

He liked that she let loose with him, that she went a little wild when he sucked her nipples.

"Pax."

He really liked her whispering his name and the way she slid her fingers into his hair. He let go of one nipple and moved to the other, capturing the bud and sucking gently, folding his fingers around her breast to feed. She whimpered, and her cries of pleasure were the sweetest sounds.

She was relaxed against him, abandoned fully in what he was doing to her, just what he'd wanted for her—for them. He let his fingers dance down her flat belly, tucked them under her sweats, surprised and really damn happy to find she didn't have panties on.

He lifted his head and watched her face as he cupped her sex. It was damp with arousal and he used that moisture to swirl over her clit, then dip his fingers inside her.

"You're wet."

Her eyes opened and she stared up at him with such desire it hurt.

"I want you."

He tucked his fingers in farther, using his thumb to roll over her clit. Her lips parted and she let out a soft moan as her body responded by squeezing his fingers and spilling wet desire all over his hand.

"I like that, Pax. Do it some more."

Whatever reservations she'd had about what had happened to her five years ago seemed to be gone, at least for now. She was fully involved in this—in him, and though he didn't normally do a woman without AJ being there with him to keep things light, easy and fun, there was something about Teresa that made him want to dive in and possess her, make her his.

In the far recesses of his mind he knew he was stepping into dangerous territory, a place that went beyond physical pleasure to something much deeper, but he couldn't hold back now, not when this beautiful woman gave him everything he'd ever wanted—and more. He wanted to make her come, and he wanted it just for himself.

"Come for me, Teresa. Let me feel it."

He drove the heel of his palm against her sex and quickened the motions of his fingers. Her movements and the sounds she made told him he'd hit the right spot, and he kept his motions right there, watching her face tighten as she inched closer to her orgasm.

She gripped his arm and held him there. "Pax."

"Yeah, baby."

"I'm going to come."

He increased the pressure just enough, and she tilted her head back and let out a soft cry that made his balls quiver as she came, writhing against him. He drew her up and pressed his mouth to hers, taking in every shudder and gasp until she finally settled with soft, panting whispers against his lips.

He deepened the kiss, letting his tongue wrap around hers, stroke it, lick it until her after-climax lull ramped up hot and fast again. She shifted, straddled his lap and rocked her pussy against his hard cock.

"This would be a lot more fun if we were naked."

She hopped off and dropped her sweats to the floor. "Get your cock out so I can climb on it. I'll be right back."

By the time he had his jeans unzipped and his cock out, she was back with a condom packet in hand. This time, she tore the packet and rolled the condom on him, her fingers shaky as she finished the job.

"You in a hurry?" he asked, holding on to her hips as she settled herself over him again.

"I might be."

He tried not to be, didn't want this to be over fast. His balls were already swollen into tight knots and he was ready to explode inside her. He took a deep breath as she held on to his shaft and eased herself onto him. He gripped her hips, remembering to ease his hold on her so he wouldn't hurt her, but damn he wanted to take her and take her hard. It was a good thing she was on top and could control the pace. His hunger for her increased every time he was with her, and he didn't dare unleash everything he had on her.

Instead, he leaned his head back and let her lift up and slide down on his cock, gritting his teeth as the sensation damn near overpowered him. She was wet, her pussy juices coating his condom-clad shaft as she rose and fell in a soft, natural rhythm. He smoothed his hands over her hips and across her ribs toward her breasts, focusing on keeping things easy and light as he cupped the globes in his hands and swept his thumbs over her nipples, lifting his gaze to her face when she gasped.

She laid her palm against the wall and rocked back and forth, dragging her pussy against him, her breasts swaying with the rhythm she set. She leaned forward, brushed her nipples across his chest as she kissed him. Pax just held on and let her set the pace. He had to admit he enjoyed her moving and swaying over him while he just sat there and felt her squeeze his cock with her pussy, even if it wasn't in his nature to let a woman do all the work. He liked being a more active participant, and okay, he liked taking control, but if this was what Teresa wanted, he wanted to give it to her. And it freed his hands to skim the sides of her ribs, to sweep over her breasts and play with her nipples. She moaned when he rolled them between his fingers. He increased the pressure just a little and she let out a soft cry, tilted her head back and arched her breasts at him.

She fell forward against his chest, then ground against his cock, digging her nails into his shoulders. He gripped her hips and helped her now.

"You like it rougher," she said, her face only an inch from his.

"Yes."

She wriggled against him and his balls throbbed. "Show me how hard."

"Teresa . . ."

"I want all of you, Pax. And you're holding back, thinking I'll be afraid." She skimmed her fingertip across his bottom lip. "You don't scare me."

His fingers pressed into her hips. "You don't know that."

Her lips curled. "Try me."

It took every ounce of willpower he had not to show her everything he had. "Teresa, there's a dark side of me."

She sucked in a quick breath. "That excites me. It means you're passionate, something I've always known about you. Why are you holding that passion back from me?"

It was hard to have this discussion when his dick was inside her soft, wet pussy, when all he wanted to do was keep fucking her until he released the tension building up inside him. "Let's not do this now."

"Oh, let's definitely do this now." Her soft smile curled into one of wicked intent. "Show me what you've got."

A muscle ticked in his cheek. "Be careful what you wish for."

"Or I might get it? Give it to me, Pax. I want all you've got."

He snaked his arm around her waist and shot upright, holding her as he made his way to the hallway. He slammed her back against the wall, his hands sliding down to grab her by the ass. He planted his mouth over hers and let her see what was really inside him. All the passion, all the need, everything he'd never given to a woman before, he gave to Teresa.

He thrust hard with his cock and his tongue, forcing both deep inside her, punishing her for wanting what he knew would drive her away from him. But he couldn't help himself. She'd asked and he'd wanted to give this to her, to show her who he really was, what he was capable of, even if it destroyed what they'd just started.

He pounded against her, hard, harder, then sank down to the floor where he spread her legs and slid between them, lifting her knees to her chest so he could thrust deeper inside her, once again taking her mouth in a brutal kiss.

It was only then he became dimly aware that she was kissing him back with equal force, that her fingers tangled in his hair, that she scored her nails down his arm—and not in protest. He lifted his head and looked down at her, shocked to see the glittering pleasure in her eyes, the softness of a smile on her face.

"More," she whispered, cupping his neck to bring his lips to hers again.

The floodgates burst. He reared back and powered inside her, burying himself deep. He drew her legs down and spread them, his fingers pressed to her inner thighs so he could keep her open, so he could watch his cock sliding in and out of her, taking it slow and easy now, giving her a chance to catch her breath.

But she arched her hips to draw him inside.

"Don't stop, Pax. Let me feel you."

Panting, he dropped down on top of her, her breasts crushed against his chest. He slipped one hand under her butt and dragged the other through her hair, tangling his fingers in the softness of it, pulling on it to draw her head back so he could kiss her mouth and slide his tongue across her neck while at the same time pushing her butt up to tighten their connection.

"You want all of me? You got it," he said, anger and passion fusing as he tunneled hard inside her, his orgasm like a storm raging inside him. He could feel it in the tightening of his balls, the quivering of his cock as he pushed with relentless force inside Teresa. And still she wouldn't back down, raking her nails down his back, biting at his lips and refusing to yield, taking everything he had to give and demanding more, until he dug into the carpet and pushed them both forward with the force of his thrusts.

He found the crevice between her buttocks, moist with her pussy juices, and rocked his finger back and forth over her anus. Teresa moaned, lifting her gaze to his.

"Yes. Do it."

He slid his finger inside her and finger fucked her ass as he continued to thrust inside her pussy with hard strokes.

"You like being double fucked?"

"Yes."

"I'm going to fuck your ass soon, Teresa. You ready for that?"

Her gaze met his, and her lips moist from licking them, she said, "Yes. Fuck me there."

He shoved his finger deeper inside the hole, feeling it grip tight while her pussy convulsed around him. His cock twitched and he pulled back, not ready to shoot inside her just yet. Instead, he pulled out. "Get on your knees."

She rolled over and pulled herself up. Pax shoved his cock inside her pussy again, and Teresa screamed in pleasure, tossing her head back and pushing against him. He parted her butt cheeks. "I can see your ass now," he said, sliding his finger back and forth over the puckered hole. "So tight, so hot. You want me to fuck you there?"

"Yes."

He slid his finger inside, burying it all the way, fucking her in both places. She threw her head back, all that beautiful hair spilling over her shoulders.

"Nobody takes this ass but me, Teresa. It's mine." He pulled his finger out and back in again, fucking her in rhythm to the strokes he gave her pussy. "Mine."

"Yours," she said. "Now fuck me hard and make me come."

She reached between her legs to rub her clit and shattered, her pussy gripping his cock and taking him with her as she pushed back against him, squeezing everything he had. His orgasm roared out of him, blinding him, making him dizzy until he glued himself to her back and held on, wrapping his arm around her and kissing her damp neck.

And when they both could breathe again, he lifted her and squeezed them both into the tiny box of a shower. They laughed as they maneuvered for room, but neither of them minded the intimacy as they soaped up and rinsed off. After they dried, they fell onto the bed and Pax pulled the blanket over them.

Teresa snuggled against him and Pax closed his eyes, not sure when he'd ever felt more content.

Even the warning bells clanging in his head, trying to remind him not to get close, couldn't keep him from wrapping his arm around her to snug her closer as he drifted off to sleep.

eighteen

Teresa woke to the smell of bacon, one of her favorite things. Well, that and coffee. She stretched, smiling at the soreness of her muscles that had been oh so beautifully used last night by Pax. She rolled over and frowned, realizing it was daylight pouring in through the tiny window.

She slid out of bed and threw on her clothes, opened the bedroom door to see AJ cooking breakfast. She went over to him and put her arms around him.

"Morning."

He kissed the top of her head. "Morning. Didn't mean to wake you."

She moved to the coffeepot to pour a cup. "You didn't. The smell of bacon and coffee did. Can I help?"

"Yeah, you can make some eggs if you want."

When breakfast was ready, they sat at the table with their plates and coffee.

"Did you come to bed?"

He nodded over a sip of coffee. "Yeah. You were out of it. Pax must have really worn you out."

"I guess so. Sorry."

He frowned. "For what?"

"You and I didn't get to—"

He laughed. "No one's keeping score, Teresa. Just because you had sex with Pax last night doesn't mean I was going to jump you as soon as I came to the trailer. It doesn't work that way."

She flipped her hair behind her ears and scraped up eggs onto her fork. "I guess I just need to learn the rules."

"The rules are whatever we want them to be. Now, me? I'm not big on rules."

"Aren't you in the wrong profession then?"

He laughed. "Sometimes it seems that way."

They ate in silence until their plates were empty. Teresa washed the dishes and AJ dried them and put them away. She couldn't help but think this might have been their life if things had been different. She let out a laugh.

"What's so funny?"

"I was just thinking about you and me doing dishes together. How this might have been us if we had stayed together all those years ago."

"Might have been. But I don't think so. I wasn't really the domestic type back then."

She turned and leaned against the counter. "Oh, and you are now?"

"I'm older now."

"Which means?"

He shrugged. "I don't know. Maybe I'm more settled."

She wasn't buying it, refused to even consider that AJ was the white picket fence and wife and kids type. "Please. You're no more settled now than you were ten years ago. Look at your job. You probably don't spend more time in one place than whatever it takes to complete an assignment. Then you move on."

"That's my job."

"No, AJ, that's your life. And that life no more suits a family now than it did back when you had wanderlust and a desire for adventure."

And it would never fit her. Not any more now than it did ten years ago.

He took a seat at the table and looked up at her. "What do you want me to tell you, Teresa? How many more times do you want me to apologize for leaving you all those years ago? I know how our lives might have been different. Maybe I'd have been able to clean up my act and we could have gotten married. We might have had a couple kids." He smiled wistfully. "I know you wanted kids."

She palmed her stomach, the pain unbearable. "We used to talk about that."

"Yeah, we did. We had a lot of plans for the future."

She went over and kneeled in front of him. "We were kids. We didn't know what we were talking about. They were dreams, AJ."

"Dreams I crushed when I decided to leave."

The look on his face before he turned away—the regret, the sadness. Wow. She'd had no idea. "You carry a lot of guilt about that, don't you?"

He shrugged. "I feel bad for leaving you. A lot of things might have been different."

"Maybe. Maybe not. We'll never know. You live the life you're meant to live, given the circumstances. You can't change what is."

He smoothed his hand over her hair. "Are you always so forgiving?"

She smiled. "Not to everyone. Some people I will never forgive for what they did. But you and me? We were young and had big dreams and no sense of what the real world was like, AJ. It's time to move on from it. We're adults now."

"With different dreams?"

"With different realities. We're not the same people anymore."

"Magnanimous and forgiving. So maybe we should start over."

She averted her gaze. "Can't do that. Too much history between us. You know too much about me, not just about the past, but what happened while you were gone. I have no secrets left to hide."

He swept his palm across her cheek. "You're the only one who knows my real name."

"Really. Really? You know what 'AJ' stands for? You gotta tell me."

Pax stood in the open doorway of the RV, grinning.

"Why, yes, I do. It's A—"

AJ clamped his hand over Teresa's mouth and threw her to the floor. She laughed uncontrollably as Pax rushed over to pry AJ's fingers away.

"Oh, come on, man," Pax said, dropping down on the floor and wrestling with AJ. "Let her tell me. The Wild Riders have been wanting to know what 'AJ' means for years now."

Free of the two of them, who were now rolling on the floor like kids, Teresa sat up and leaned against the wall, hiccupping from laughing so hard. "Oh, AJ, this might cost you."

He grabbed her by the ankles and tugged her between them. "You think so? I can keep you silent."

But Pax pulled her against him and tickled her ribs. "And I have ways of making you talk."

Before long she was out of breath and shrieking with laughter, crying for mercy and begging to be let up. They let her go and she fixed them all cups of coffee while the guys—or boys, rather—picked themselves up off the floor and made it to the table.

"What's going on at the Fists' camp?" AJ asked.

"They're locked down tight. Stayed up almost all night. A couple others came out of the RV and they partied hard, smoked some weed and emptied a keg of beer. I'd say we have a couple hours' reprieve at least while they all sleep it off."

Before Teresa could ask, Pax said, "Didn't see your guy."

She refused to be disappointed, instead focused on the RV. He had to be there. "Okay. So now what?"

"We'll head over and keep an eye on them in a little while. I'm going to grab a nap. Teresa kept me up all night."

"Hey." She laughed. Pax drew her into his arms and brushed his lips over hers as he walked by. There went that slow warmth spreading over her. She laid her hand on his chest. "Sleep well."

"I won't sleep at all because you won't be with me. But I'll try."

He shut the door behind him and AJ said, "He's lying. He'll be dead as soon as his head hits the pillow."

She smiled. "He deserves to. Long night. For you, too."

"I got some sleep," AJ said, coming up and putting his arms around her. "Wrapped around a beautiful woman."

She snorted. "Yeah, a comatose woman."

"That's okay. I'm patient."

She arched a brow and slid her hand between them to palm his cock. "How patient?"

His cock began to harden as she rubbed back and forth across the denim.

"You keep doing that and you'll see my patience disappear."

"Let's see how fast." She pressed in deeper, his cock harder now, and AJ pushed her backward until the back of her knees hit the sofa.

"So, not patient at all, are you?"

"Neither are you." He slid his finger down the front of her shirt, let it linger between her breasts. "You want me to fuck you?"

Quivers of anticipation hardened her nipples and made her pussy wet, driven higher by the hard cock pushing against her hand. She dropped to her knees and reached for the button on his jeans. "Oh, I think we'll definitely get there. But first I want your cock in my mouth."

He hissed out a curse as she drew his zipper down and jerked his jeans over his hips, freeing his cock. She slid her cool fingers over his hot flesh and brought it to her lips, tilting her head back to stare up at him as she slid her tongue over the crest.

"Teresa." He leaned over to grab her hair and wind it around his hand, holding it while she took his shaft in her mouth, her tongue riding the ridged length of him as she brought him inside.

She reached underneath to cradle his ball sac in her hands, squeezing gently as she popped his cock out of her mouth to lick around the tip and down the shaft.

"You make me crazy when you do that."

She smiled up at him and stroked him with both hands, then rolled her tongue around the crest. He groaned and pushed his cock over her tongue and into her mouth. She pressed her lips over his shaft, giving him suction, taking him deeper, watching his face contort with grimaces of pleasure.

His pleasure heightened hers. His hard cock in her mouth made her ache to have him inside her.

He pulled out and drew her up, putting his mouth on hers in a kiss that seared her senses. He wrapped his arms around her and lifted her, pushing her onto the sofa.

"I need to fuck you, now," he said, reaching into the pocket of his jeans for a condom. He put it on and pulled her pants and panties off, stopping only long enough to slide his fingers over her sex.

She shuddered at the contact, held her arms out for him and he came to her, kissing her again. She loved the way his lips fit to hers, the softness in them, the way he took his time in kissing her. She found gentleness in AJ's kisses, always had, could float away to senselessness in the way his mouth moved over hers, his tongue lazily playing with her tongue, as if he had an entire day to do nothing but kiss her. Even in the heat of passion as they were now, he waited to fuck her, took his time to tease her lips, lick at her tongue, and brush his mouth against hers until her entire body swelled with heat and need and she whimpered, hungry to feel him inside her.

Finally, he moved up against her and fit his cock at the entrance to her pussy, rubbing his shaft against her clit. Tension and desire sparked. She reached for his arms, gripped him and lifted against him.

His gaze met hers as he slid inside her—so intimate, so perfect as he pushed in and buried himself all the way. She reached up to slide her palm against his cheek as he began to move within her, hot passion and soaring tenderness combining to make her ache with emotions she didn't dare name.

Not now, not when this should be all about sex and fun and fulfilling a physical need. AJ couldn't give her what she wanted anywhere else, but here, in this moment, with his body connected to hers, he was everything she needed.

She lifted against him, asking him without words to give her more. He cupped a hand under her and brought her closer, rolling his hips to drive his flesh across her clit. Sensation flowed outward, bundling into a tight knot of pleasure. She rode it with intent, grasping his shoulders and arching again, needing to come with him inside her, needing to splinter around his shaft, to feel as if they were part of each other, forever connected at least here.

"AJ," she whispered, cupping the back of his neck and pulling him down to press her lips to his as he lifted his hips and plunged into her with more fervor. She felt him thicken inside her, growing

impossibly hard as he withdrew and thrust deeper. It was a lan-
guorous ride to heaven, one that made her toes curl and her skin
break out in chills because he was taking her right to that point
where reason fled and pleasurable insanity awaited. And when she
was right there, she broke the kiss to look into his eyes—and came,
her lips parting to let out her cries. Now she couldn't hold back,
trembling as the intensity of her climax took over.

AJ tightened his grip on her, his gaze still focused on her as he
came, too, the lines around his eyes crinkling as he grimaced and
dug his fingers into her hips. He shuddered with her as they rode
out this wild storm together, then fell together in a heap against
the sofa.

Panting, sweaty, Teresa stroked AJ's back, her limbs utterly
limp, her heart utterly content.

He kissed her neck and murmured her name, and she sighed,
her heart swelling and bursting with love for him.

Damn. She still loved him. She'd tried so hard to keep it from
happening, but she couldn't hold it back; she knew it was point-
less, but what could she do? She was still in love with AJ, and knew
he eventually would leave her.

Again.

THE TREK THROUGH THE WOODS WAS MUCH EASIER IN THE
daylight. After Pax got up, the three of them headed back to the
Fists' camp. It was nearly noon and yet no one had stirred. Their
bikes were all still parked there, so no one had taken off yet. But
Teresa had learned one thing.

Surveillance was boring, full of bugs and made her legs cramp.
After two hours the guys sent her back to the RV and told her
they'd call her as soon as the group started to pour out of their
RV. She agreed that was a great idea, because crouching down in

the woods while mosquitoes and God only knew what else bit her was definitely not her cup of tea.

Not that she was all girly. She didn't mind getting dirty and would gladly stay out there to watch—when there was actually something to look at.

She had no idea how Pax and AJ did that for a living. It was mind numbing. Maybe the exciting parts of the job made up for the surveillance part.

She yawned. And maybe if she'd gotten more sleep last night she wouldn't have been falling asleep in the woods. Back sitting alone in the RV she was even more sleepy, and she didn't want to be napping and groggy in case AJ and Pax needed her in a hurry. She needed to get outside. Fresh air would wake her up.

She'd washed a few things, so she went out to hang them on the line they'd put up for her. She liked the woodsy outdoors, the smell of trees and earth—as long as she didn't have to kneel in it for hours. The sun was high overhead and it was a warm day, so she grabbed a lawn chair and took a seat, letting the sun heat her body and the breeze slide over her.

She closed her eyes and thought about everything that had changed in the space of a few days. Her life had undergone an epic change, and she had AJ and Pax to thank for that. With the help of their infinite patience she'd taken the phenomenal step into sex again.

But she had to be honest with herself. It had gone far beyond sex.

And that she didn't want to delve too deeply into, because she didn't want to put any kind of damper on the fun and closeness she shared with them right now. It was best to keep things light.

So far she hadn't done a very good job of keeping things light. She'd already realized she had never stopped loving AJ. And Pax did things to her heart that made it clench. She was toppling right on the edge with him and could fall so easily. But she also knew trying to think of anything remotely permanent with these two men was going to go nowhere but down a road of misery and heart-break, so she had to tuck these feelings she had for both of them deep inside and remember that once this trip was over, they had their jobs to go back to and they'd both be leaving. She was only a pit stop for them. She was only fun and sex. And temporary.

And what was so wrong about having some light, temporary sex? She sure as hell wasn't ready to step into some kind of long-term commitment, and AJ and Pax were the wrong men for that anyway.

At least she felt normal again, and that was a huge step in the right direction. She was going to have to be satisfied with that for now. She played over in her mind what she'd done with AJ and Pax, smiling at how far she'd come. And, oh, she was so grateful to them for their patience with her in getting her back to some semblance of normalcy again. And maybe she was confusing grati-tude with love. That's probably what it was. They'd been the first men she'd had sex with since the rape, and she was grateful they'd held her hands and walked her through it. And when they left her, there'd be other men down the road, until someday she found the man of her dreams.

If such a man existed.

But right now she was having a great time with Pax and AJ, and that was damn good enough.

So maybe it was time to stop overthinking the hell out of every-thing and stop thinking about love.

The heat from the sun relaxed her and she let her eyes drift closed, that familiar tiredness washing over her. She had almost fallen asleep when the sound of a cracking twig shot her straight up in the chair. Alert, she looked toward the woods where AJ and Pax were, expecting to see one or both of them returning. She waited almost five minutes and didn't see them, then decided it was probably a woodland creature or a bird or something that had made the noise. Or maybe just her imagination.

But then she heard it again, and realized it hadn't come from the direction where AJ and Pax were. It was on the other side of the woods.

Her pulse kicked up and she inhaled deeply through her nose. *Stay calm.* It was probably nothing.

She rose from her chair and looked around, using her hand to shield her eyes from the sun. Their RV was at the bottom of the hill, completely cut off from the other campers. No one had any business down this way. There were no showers or facilities down here. And besides, there was nothing on the other side of those woods as far as she knew—except more woods.

Maybe it was a wolf. No, wolves were nocturnal and it was broad daylight.

Okay, Teresa. Don't panic. Time to go inside and lock the door and wait for Pax and AJ. It's probably just an animal.

The back of her neck prickling with unease, she took a leisurely walk toward the RV, hoping to avoid alerting anyone to the fact that she was scared out of her mind.

And that's when something hit. No explosion of noise, but something slammed into the ground in front of her and sprayed dirt up against her legs. She wasn't stupid. That was a bullet, coming from a gun with a silencer or something because she hadn't heard the telltale pop.

Now it was time to panic. She ran like hell for the RV, which fortunately was only a few feet away and blocked whoever was shooting at her. She threw open the door, jumped in, jerked it closed and locked it, her knees weak and her body shaking.

Her phone. Where was her goddamn phone? She had to call AJ or Pax. She was breathing so fast she made herself dizzy. Okay, time to force her breathing into a normal rhythm or she was going to hyperventilate and pass out. But then the door handle rattled and she whipped around and stared at it, deciding to screw finding the phone. Where the hell was her gun?

She ran to her bag and threw all the clothes out of it, fumbling for her gun. Clip was in and she cocked it, her body drenched in sweat now as she made her way back to the front of the RV. Another shot pinged through the window and she hit the floor as glass shattered around her.

Stupid. Windows, idiot. He can see you.

Her phone! She spotted it on the counter and shimmied over on her belly, taking the chance to inch up and grab for it. Another shot, another shattered window. With fumbling, shaky, sweaty fingers, she dialed AJ. He picked up and whispered a quick, "What?"

"Someone's shooting at me!"

That was all she had time to say because the door handle rattled again, this time harder. Another shot, this time at the door handle. She crawled toward the door and braced her back on the front of one sofa, her feet on the other, and took aim at the door.

As soon as whoever it was got through that door, she was going to shoot him.

Or die trying. Because she was never going to be a victim again.

nineteen

AJ HAD NEVER RUN SO HARD IN HIS GODDAMN LIFE. BY THE
time they breached the clearing, dread had hit his stomach. Shattered glass littered the ground, bullet holes tattooed the RV, and
the door handle hung lopsided. His gun was already out and so
was Pax's, pointed as they approached with caution. They'd torn
through the woods not caring what kind of noise they made in
their effort to reach Teresa.

AJ got to the door first and pulled it open, then held up his
hand as he saw Teresa on the floor just inside with a gun aimed at
the entrance.

"Teresa, it's us. Don't shoot!"

She dropped the weapon as he flew through the door and
grabbed her up into his arms.

"I was outside and someone was out there," she said, stuttering
out her words. Her body was drenched in sweat and she was shaking like a leaf. "I started to go in and a shot hit the dirt in front

of my feet. No noise. He used a silencer. Then he hit the RV and tried to get in."

"I'll check the perimeter," Pax said, rocketing down the stairs and outside.

All AJ wanted to do was sit on the floor and hold her until she wasn't scared anymore, but instead he pulled her out at arm's length so he could see her face. "Are you hurt?"

"No."

AJ drew her against him and held her tight, feeling his own heart jackhammer against her chest. "It's okay. We're here now. You can let go."

She did, her body relaxing, and she fell against him and sobbed. AJ held her and stroked her back and her hair, thanking God she hadn't been shot. He didn't know what he'd do if he lost her.

Pax came in and AJ turned around. "Clear?"

"Yeah." Pax motioned to Teresa.

"She's okay. Scared, not injured."

Pax nodded and holstered his gun, then came over and put his arms around her, too. She cried harder and AJ just let her, knowing she needed this. When she was finally cried out, they sat her on the sofa, and he and Pax flanked her.

"Whoever it was is gone," Pax said. "Picked up shell casings. Looks like a forty-caliber."

Teresa wiped her eyes and nose and filled them in on everything she'd heard and seen and the location of the shooter. "I don't understand what he was after."

"It's pretty clear," Pax said, his face grim. "He was after you."

She looked up at him, her eyes wide. "Me? Why?"

AJ turned her to face him. "Because you can identify the guy who really killed Larks."

She sniffed, blew her nose. "Okay. That's a good thing, right?

RIDING THE NIGHT   239

That means he's here. They know I know. That's got to be why someone's trying to kill me. That means we're getting close."

AJ shook his head. No panic about someone trying to kill her. No hysterical demands to get her the hell out of there. She was putting puzzle pieces together instead. What an amazing woman.

"I think the most important thing is to keep you safe."

She turned tear-filled eyes to AJ. "You two will do that. I have every faith in you."

Yeah, because they'd done such a great job of that just now. AJ exchanged a glance with Pax, who nodded. They'd fucked up and left Teresa alone. That wasn't going to happen again.

"Let's get this cleaned up and get you back."

"But what about the Fists?"

"The Fists aren't who were worried about right now," Pax said. "You're our first priority."

They cleaned up the RV and took it back to the house. AJ called General Lee to let him know what had happened to Teresa, and to his RV. Grange was way more concerned about Teresa's safety and didn't care at all about his RV getting shot up, which was pretty much what AJ had expected him to say.

Pax had walked the grounds around the RV and collected bullet shell casings. They also took pictures around the scene and scoped out the area for footprints or anything else the shooter might have left behind, but as dry as it had been around there, the ground didn't yield anything—or the shooter had done a damn good job covering his tracks. They weren't going to alert the local police about the shooting for various reasons, mainly because they wanted to keep their identities on the down low, but also because they didn't want the local cops in on in this. The fewer people involved, the better, and AJ and Pax could handle the investigation.

There were no prints on the shell casings, which didn't surprise

AJ. Whoever went into the woods to shoot at Teresa knew to cover all his bases. Someone knew what he was doing, which meant he'd gone into this with intent.

After they'd gotten back to the house, Teresa went into her room to unpack and take what she notified them would be a very long, very hot shower. AJ figured she just needed some time alone to process and unwind.

Pax was outside grilling steaks. AJ brought two beers out and set one on the table next to the grill. Pax lifted the bottle in salute. "Thanks."

"So what do you think?"

Pax took a long swallow and set the beer down, then flipped the steaks over and closed the grill lid. "I think if whoever was shooting at Teresa had wanted her dead, she'd be dead."

"Agreed. He was trying to scare her."

"And us, trying to get us to take her and go."

Pax nodded and picked up the bottle, turning it over and over in his hands. "Someone knew how to handle that weapon, and Teresa isn't trained to dodge bullets. The chair she was sitting in was at least twenty yards from the door."

"He'd have gotten her on the first shot. She was a sitting duck from his vantage point."

"Yup."

"Which means we're close—or she's close—to figuring out something."

Pax frowned. "But why not kill her? Why just scare her away? I mean, wouldn't that solve the problem of her possibly identifying who killed Larks?"

AJ shrugged. "Maybe. But scaring the hell out of her and getting her to run is a lot less messy than a dead body. A dead body brings in the cops. This was an easier solution because it would have gotten her—and us—to back off."

"You've got a point there." Pax lifted the grill lid and flipped the steaks. "The question is, what do we do about it? Do we protect her, take her out of this, or do we stay and see it through?"

"We stay and see it through, of course. I'm not going to be shot at only to turn tail and run."

AJ's gaze shifted to the doorway where Teresa stood. She wore gray sweatpants and a white tank top that hugged her breasts. He wanted to kiss her, make love to her, hold her close and keep her safe so nothing bad would ever happen to her again. But he also knew he couldn't lock her away from bad things forever. "It's dangerous for you here."

"Whoever it was shot at me to scare me, didn't he? He could have killed me if that's what his intent was."

Pax scooped the steaks onto a plate. "Figured that out during your long, hot shower?"

She took the plate from him. "As a matter of fact, I did. Nothing like a hot shower and a good cry to clear your head."

Pax kissed her forehead. "Feel better now?"

She tilted her head back and smiled at him. "Yes. Now let's eat. I'm hungry."

AJ shook his head. She'd been shot at today and she still managed to have an appetite. There was no doubt the woman had inner strength even she wasn't aware of.

She went inside and AJ and Pax followed. While they ate dinner, they strategized what steps to take next.

"Like you said, if this guy wanted me dead, I would be, right?" She waved a forkful of salad at both of them.

AJ looked to Pax, who turned to Teresa and nodded. "Yeah. Your chair was too far away for you to get to safety. Anyone with a half-decent aim could have taken you down in one or two tries."

She pursed her lips and nodded. "I should have realized that right away. Maybe I'd have had my wits about me then."

"I think in your situation any one of us would have thought the same thing—that someone was trying to kill you. You did the right thing."

"This pisses me off. I don't like being threatened."

"Which means you don't want us to take you home," Pax said.

"Oh, hell no. We came here to find the guy who killed Larks. Obviously we're close to doing that, and someone tried to scare the shit out of me today so we'd go away."

"Honey, you were threatened today to scare you off," Pax said. "Next time it might be the real thing. You understand what I'm saying?"

She lifted her chin. "I know that. I'm still not leaving. They're not going to make me afraid again. I won't hide anymore and I won't be a victim anymore."

"Pax and I will make sure you're not left alone again."

She turned her gaze on AJ. "You can't protect me twenty-four hours a day, AJ."

"For as long as we're with you, we can."

"Okay, so now what? I don't want to be held prisoner in this house."

That's exactly what AJ wanted to do—keep her here, where he and Pax could watch her.

Teresa must have guessed where his mind was because she leveled him with a stare that should have frozen him solid. "Don't even think about it, AJ."

"It's the only way to protect you."

"I'll just have to take that risk. You can't keep me prisoner here."

"She has a point, AJ. The only way to flush this guy out of hiding is to put Teresa out there. Once he sees she hasn't been run off, he'll come after her again."

AJ shot a glare at Pax. "Exactly. He'll come after her again."

"And we'll be there to protect her this time."

"You know as well as I do there's no guarantee we'll be able to protect her one hundred percent of the time." AJ turned to Teresa. "We can't promise you that. You have to know this."

She gave a curt nod. "Understood. I can't hold you responsible if something happens to me." Then she laid her hand on his arm. "Any more than I hold you responsible for what happened to me five years ago, AJ. You have to let that go."

She knew. Somehow she knew about his guilt over her rape. "I don't feel . . ."

"Yeah, you do. I don't know why, but I can tell you feel that somehow you should have been here to prevent it."

He shrugged and stood, walked out back and breathed in the cleansing night air.

Teresa followed, wrapped her arms around his back and laid her head against him. "AJ, you can't control everything in your universe. You weren't responsible for those two guys raping me. That's on them, not you."

He turned and looked at her, needing her to see, to understand. "If I hadn't left—"

"It undoubtedly would have happened anyway. You don't know for sure, so let it go. I don't blame you for it any more than I blame Joey or any of the other people in my life who might have been there with me that night, who might have in some way been able to prevent it from happening. No one can change it."

The words sounded hollow in his head. He knew Teresa meant them, but he would never forgive himself for what had happened to her. He should have been there instead of dumping her and running off.

"Okay?" she asked, sliding her hands down his arms.

"Okay."

"So let's get me out there so the bad guy will show his ugly face."

AJ WEIGHED HEAVILY ON TERESA'S MIND AS SHE WENT TO WORK that night. She could tell from the look on his face that he still felt guilty about what had happened to her all those years ago, and nothing she said to him was going to change his mind.

Frustrating, for sure, but she was going to have to let it go for now. Later, when they had more time to sit and talk, she'd convince him otherwise. Now they had to concentrate on luring out the guy who was so eager to scare her away he was willing to shoot at her to do it. Being back at her job might make her visible enough to bring him out of hiding. She was at the front bar again, where everyone coming through the front doors could see her. AJ and Pax blended into the crowd so well she had no idea where they were, but she knew they were there, just like she knew she wasn't out of their sight for a second.

Even Russ and the Thorns had come in and hung out for several hours. Russ had found AJ, who had filled him in on what happened. After that, Russ made it a point to stay, had told her they were all concerned about her safety and would make sure to back up AJ and Pax in keeping watch over her. But the Thorns stayed out of sight, too, since they didn't want the Fists—or the guy gunning for Teresa—to spot them.

She felt safe in her cocoon of bodyguards, so she went about her business of serving drinks and interacting with her customers. Pax had told her not to leave her post unless one of them was with her. After the scare she'd had earlier in the day, she wasn't about to argue with him. She was independent, not stupid, and she stayed on guard, scanning every face she served. Had it been the bald guy with neck tattoos who had shot at her, or someone entirely different?

She wanted to save her brother, but she also wanted to come out of this alive.

So when the Fists strolled in as a group, she tensed and gripped the edge of the bar, ready to duck in case someone pulled a gun as they walked by. Which was a ridiculous thought. They weren't going to shoot her in this bar. It was packed. Too many witnesses. Still, she couldn't help her sweaty palms and knocking knees as the Fists strolled past her bar, and she had to force herself to keep her head up and focus on every face.

She almost missed him, had almost given up on him being there. She had to do a double take when he walked by, because his bald head was wrapped in a do-rag. But there was no mistaking those specific neck tattoos or the faint scar that ran through one side of his neck.

It was him, the guy who'd killed Larks. She didn't want to tear her gaze away from him as he boldly walked past her, but she had to alert AJ and Pax. She scanned the crowd, found Pax, and motioned wildly with her eyes toward the guy. Pax nodded and swiftly moved toward her.

"Which one?"

"He's wearing a black do-rag with white skulls. His neck tattoos are a tribal pattern, swirling up almost to his jawline and down his chest, and the scar on the left side of his neck that cuts through the tat. He's wearing a leather vest, no shirt underneath, sleeve tattoos on both arms, too."

Pax swiveled and viewed the area. "Got him," he said over his shoulder. "Stay put."

Excitement and nervousness interfered with Teresa's ability to do her job. Customers leaned in wanting drinks. She filled orders as fast as she could, but her gaze split to where Pax met up with AJ and they made a circle around the place, no doubt trying to corner the guy. Teresa lifted on her toes, trying to find the tattooed guy, but he'd gotten lost in the crowd somewhere.

Ten minutes passed and Teresa was beginning to think AJ and Pax had lost him, but Pax finally returned to her bar.

"What?" she asked.

"The Fists left and their friend went with them. We caught sight of them climbing on their bikes and taking off."

Dread felt like a rock in her stomach. "You didn't get him?"

"AJ and the Thorns are going after him."

Russ came up next to Pax. "I sent the guys to go with AJ." He turned to Teresa. "Pax and me are staying here with you."

"Why?"

"Because this might be a trap set to leave you unguarded," Pax said. "We're not going to let it happen."

"Okay. So we wait for—what? To hear from AJ? Are they going to just follow them or catch them or what?"

"They're going to follow them, and hopefully once they stop, AJ will alert the authorities and bring this guy in."

She shuddered in a hopeful breath. Maybe this was going to be over soon. Maybe Joey would be free.

Russ slid his hand across the bar and squeezed hers. "Stay focused. It's going to be okay."

She nodded and squeezed back. She'd known Russ as long as she'd known AJ. They'd all been friends forever, since they were kids. Russ was like family to her; he'd seen her through some rough times. She'd leaned as hard on him during that dark period in her life as she had on her brother—probably more so because she'd needed some distance from Joey after the rape. Joey had been so damn guilt-ridden about the whole thing that she'd pushed him away, had needed space from him because she couldn't breathe. But Russ had been there for her, to hold her hand and tell her everything would be okay, even though he'd seemed as hurt by what had happened to her as everyone else had been. He'd watched over her and kept people away when she wanted some time alone.

She didn't know what she would have done without him and the other Thorns.

And now he was here watching over her again. It was good to have friends, especially now when all she could do was watch the clock on the wall and hope and pray that AJ and the others were safe. They had no idea what they were riding into.

An hour passed and Teresa concentrated on work. The crowds hadn't slowed down; in fact they seemed to be getting heavier, which was okay with her. Keeping busy kept her hands—and her mind—occupied. Pax stayed out of sight and away from her, while Russ planted himself at the bar next to her, keeping a low profile by removing his Thorns jacket and wearing a knit hat low over his forehead. His gaze scanned everyone she served, which gave Teresa a measure of comfort—now there were two of them scanning the bar.

"So how close are you to AJ?" he asked during a lull in customers.

"We're just having some fun."

"Seems like more than that."

She wiped down the bar, then smiled at him. "Why do you think that?"

"I see the way he looks at you. Pax, too."

She flicked her gaze across the crowded bar, finding Pax right away. Yeah, he was looking at her, his expression unfathomable as their gazes locked and held. She could read just about anything she wanted into the way he looked at her—concern, desire, curiosity, frustration—the list went on endlessly.

She turned back to Russ. "I don't think either of them looks at me in any special way."

"Then you're blind. AJ's in love with you."

She laughed. "That was a long time ago, Russ. It's not like that anymore." Even if she wished it were, she'd been the one soundly preaching about not being able to go back to the past.

Russ took her hand. "Do you love him?"

She wasn't going to have this discussion with Russ. "That's not your business."

"What do you have going on with Pax, then?"

"Again. None of your business."

Russ lifted his chin. "What if I want it to be my business?"

The obvious shone in Russ's eyes. How could she have been so blind and missed it all these years? Russ hung out at her bar all the time—at the bar itself. Talking to her, not the other girls, not playing pool with Joey and the other guys, but hanging out with her.

She searched her memories trying to remember the last time he'd brought a girl around to meet her.

Hell. Never. She'd just assumed he was like a lot of the other guys, never settling down and always dating different girls. But now she knew.

She'd been oblivious, because she and Russ had been so close. Not a boyfriend—more like a best friend type of guy. She just didn't see him in a romantic way, and never had.

But apparently Russ saw her that way, and she'd totally, blindly missed it all this time because she'd had her head up her ass about her own issues.

She was such a moron. She laid her other hand over his. "Russ . . . I didn't know."

He half smiled. "Obviously. But now you do. Figured I'd better stake my claim since it looked like maybe AJ or Pax was going to."

Oh, God. She so wasn't good at this. "I don't know what to say. You and I have known each other so long. We're like—"

"If you say brother and sister, I'm going to puke on this bar."

She laughed. "No, I wasn't going to say that. We're friends. Good friends. You've been there for me when I needed you and

I appreciate it. But I just don't have . . . those kind of feelings for you."

"Feelings can change."

She hated this, hated having to hurt him. "And sometimes they can't."

He withdrew his hand, the hope on his face dying.

Her heart died a little, too. This sucked.

"I'm sorry, Russ. I need to be honest with you."

"No, it's okay. I get it." He swiveled around on his stool and resumed scanning the crowd.

She'd hurt him. That hadn't been her intent at all, but what was she supposed to do—lead him on? There was no way she was going to do that.

She filled a few drink orders, then tapped him on the shoulder. "Russ."

He turned around and smiled at her. "Hey. I get it, Teresa. You want someone else."

Yes, she did. Someone she wasn't going to have. She understood not being able to have what you wanted.

"I'm sorry, Russ. You know I care deeply for you."

He laughed. "That's not making me feel better right now."

His phone buzzed and he pressed his hand to his other ear to shut out the bar noise. His frowns as he listened made Teresa's stomach tumble, especially when he shot a worried gaze in her direction. Panicked, she sent probably not-so-subtle signals across the room to Pax, who hustled over and waited with her while Russ listened and didn't say much other than "when?" and "where?" and "how the fuck did that happen?"

Teresa chewed her lip and balanced on the balls of her feet until Russ closed his phone.

"What?" she asked, already knowing it was bad.

"Gunfight up in the hills."

Her heart crashed against her chest.

"Anyone hurt?" Pax asked.

Russ shook his head. "My guys managed to shake the Fists. AJ suspected a trap when the Fists led them into a deserted area."

"Okay. So what's wrong?"

"My guys have the Fists holed up in the hills, but AJ is missing."

"Missing?" Teresa's stomach dropped to her feet. "What do you mean he's missing?"

"He was with the Thorns, but as soon as the gunfire started they had to spread out for cover. After the Fists took off, my guys reconvened and AJ was nowhere to be found."

Pax took out his phone and dialed AJ's number. When he looked over at her and he wasn't speaking, her pulse kicked up about ten notches. Pax closed his phone. "He might be riding."

"Why would he do that? Why not stay with the Thorns?"

"I don't know." Pax rubbed his temple. "It doesn't make sense."

"He could be injured."

Pax turned to Russ. "Did they say anything about the terrain of the area? Is it possible AJ could have taken a hit and gone off a cliff or something?"

Teresa fought back the well of tears burning her eyes. She would not fall apart. They didn't know anything for sure yet.

"It was rocky and pretty steep. The Fists led them up there for a reason, so yeah, it's possible. They're still looking for him."

"Shit. We need to head up there and help them search."

"Shouldn't we call in the authorities?" Teresa asked.

"No. We can't," Russ said.

Pax frowned. "Why not?"

"Look, man. A few of our guys . . . they've got records. Some aren't even supposed to have left the state. They get caught in all this, they're going back in the joint. I need time to get them clear, ya know?"

Pax hesitated.

"Come on, Pax," Russ said. "They went up there to help. Don't punish them for it."

"Fine. But if we get up there and this is deep, I'm calling in the feds."

Russ nodded. "Let's go, then."

"I'm going with you."

Pax's gaze snapped to Teresa "No."

"There's no way you're going without me, Pax."

"It's too dangerous. You stay here."

"I have to agree with Pax, Teresa. You shouldn't be up there."

She had to think fast, had to make sure she went with them. "What if this is a trap? What if they want me left alone?"

Pax considered, scratched his head, then sighed. "You're right. But you ride with me. I don't want you on a bike by yourself right now. It makes you vulnerable."

"I still don't think it's a good idea," Russ said. "Teresa should stay here."

Pax shook his head. "Decision made. We're all riding together. The two of us will just have to watch over her."

Teresa laid her hand on Russ's arm. "I'll be fine."

"Joey will kill me if something happens to you."

She laughed. "I'm a big girl, and with the both of you looking out for me, I know I'll be safe."

That seemed to ease Russ a bit, because he nodded and they headed out.

The ride took seemingly forever. Teresa held tight to Pax, her lifeline, her strength, praying the entire time that AJ would be all right. Maybe AJ was hiding out, cut off from the others and unable to use his phone to let everyone know he was okay. She was determined to believe he was fine as Pax sped every mile through the curving roads leading into the hills.

It was late and not a lot of bikers were on the roads, especially when they turned off the main highway and onto a seldom-used two-lane. Remote, it seemed to stretch on forever as they rode higher up into the hills, the chill making Teresa's breath visible as she snuggled closer to Pax for warmth. She was glad she'd worn her gloves and a neck warmer along with her leather jacket to keep the cold air at bay at these higher elevations, and she was grateful Pax had made them take the time to climb into their chaps, even though Teresa hadn't wanted to spare a second before chasing after AJ. It was freezing up here.

This would have been a really great place for an SUV. With a heater. And a blanket.

Though there was nothing like an unobstructed view of the cloudless night sky, where it was just them and the stars and the thrum of the Harley's engines as they breezed through the night. If it wasn't for her worry over AJ, and her chattering teeth from the frigid cold, she could have enjoyed this ride. And even though she loved riding her own bike again, there was something to be said for having her thighs nestled against Pax's and the heat of his body keeping hers warm. Despite the reason for this ride, she was almost relaxed. Which made her feel guilty.

She wrapped her arms tighter around Pax and laid her head against his back, soaking up some of his strength. They'd find AJ. They'd get the guy who killed Larks. This was all going to work out.

She caught sight of Russ coming up just to the right rear of Pax's bike. She was about to turn and smile at him when she saw him lift a gun.

Panicked, she half turned in her seat. Was someone behind

them? No, he wasn't pointing that gun behind them at someone else, he was pointing it at them. What the hell was he doing?

She was about to scream his name when Russ zoomed up and fired. All she had time to do was grab on to Pax, but it was already too late. The bike swerved and everything tumbled into motion, including her. Pax hit the brakes hard, the squeal like a high-pitched scream. The rear tire went first, and they skidded toward the grassy embankment as the bike tipped over. Teresa flew off and had enough presence of mind to tuck herself into a ball as she tumbled down the grass, her body a living bowling ball rolling over and over.

She finally slid to a stop and flopped onto her back. Dizzy, sick, her lungs felt like fire as she cast her stunned gaze up at the night sky. What had just happened? Disoriented and out of breath, she fought for her bearings. And her breath, which seemed to come in shallow gasps.

She'd hit her back and knew it had knocked the wind out of her. She couldn't breathe, and the urge to panic was strong. The need to find Pax was stronger. She fought to maintain slow, calm inhales and exhales until she could breathe normally again, then she rolled to her side, careful to gauge for any injuries.

Other than feeling bruised as hell from her bumpy roller-coaster ride down the embankment, she was okay. Nothing was broken. She didn't feel any sticky wetness sliding down any of her limbs, so she wasn't bleeding. She removed her helmet and goggles and lifted herself on shaky legs, staying bent over to fight back the dizziness that still assailed her.

The gun. Russ had fired a gun at them. Why would he do that? And where was he? She searched the area around her, but dammit, it was dark and she couldn't see, couldn't hear anything.

No. Pax first. Pax had been thrown in the same direction. She had to find him, wanted to call out his name, but what if Russ was out there somewhere? He had a gun. He'd shot at them.

None of this made sense. She didn't know what to do.

Until she heard a hissing noise. She stilled, trying to determine direction. What was that sound? Pax's bike? She had to take the chance and start walking, though her legs felt like rubber. Unsteady, she maneuvered slowly across the steep terrain toward the sound.

There! Smoke rising and something metal glinting in the moonlight. She hurried as much as she could on her wobbly legs, Pax's overturned bike taking shape as she got closer.

It rested, crumpled and bent, against a thick tree. She scrambled around the tree and farther down the embankment and found Pax lying on the ground, unmoving.

Oh, God. She dropped to her knees next to him and felt for a pulse, relieved to the point of tears when she found one.

"Pax," she whispered, bending low so only he could hear her. "Pax, wake up."

Nothing. She didn't dare remove his helmet or try to move him, because she had no idea how badly he was hurt.

She pulled her hand away from his chest and lifted it toward the tiny sliver of moonlight.

Blood.

No. God, no. She unzipped his jacket and felt for injury, squeezing her eyes to blot out the sting of tears when she felt the blood seeping from his upper chest.

Gunshot. Had to be.

Dammit. Russ. Why?

She scrambled back up to Pax's bike and flipped open his saddlebag, pulling out a blanket, a bottle of water and—yes, thank God—a first-aid kit, the whole time lifting her gaze toward the road at the top of the hill, hoping like hell she wouldn't see Russ aiming a gun at her.

She hurried back to Pax and opened the first aid kit, then did what she could to staunch the flow of blood from his wound. But he needed to be in a hospital—now. She grabbed to pull her cell from her pocket, tears stinging her eyes as she realized it was in pieces, no doubt crushed during her fall from the bike.

Shit.

Pax stirred, his lids lifting.

She held on to his arms. "Pax."

He turned his head to the side and grimaced lifting his legs, and Teresa could have cried for joy that he could move.

"Don't move."

"What the fuck happened?"

"Russ shot you, and the bike went down a hill."

His eyes opened and he lifted his hand to her. "You okay?"

Her heart ached. He had a bullet in him and was lying on the ground, and he asked about her. "I'm fine. You're shot."

He moved his hand to his chest. "How bad?"

"I don't know. You're bleeding."

"Where's Russ?"

"Up there somewhere. I'm not sure."

"You need to get out of here. Call for help."

She shook her head. "I'm not leaving you."

"Get my phone. Right zipper pocket."

She fumbled with the zipper and yanked his phone out. It was in one piece, unlike hers.

"Call General Lee. He'll get the feds here. Then run and hide."

"I'm not leaving you."

He grabbed her wrist, his grip surprisingly strong. "He'll kill you, Teresa. You have to look out for yourself. Now, make the goddamn call."

She called General Lee, who was curt but listened to what she told him. He said he'd use the GPS on Pax's phone to get help their way as quickly as possible.

"Help's on the way," she said, zipping the phone back in his pocket so the authorities could find Pax.

"Now get out of here."

"No. I'm not leaving you."

"Teresa. He's coming down here to find us, to find you. You have to hide. I'm a sitting duck here. The bike will draw him to me and give you time to get away."

"He'll kill you."

"It's not me he wants. It's you." He shifted, hissing as he reached inside his jacket for his gun and handed it to her. She stared at the gun in her hand and then back at him.

"Take this and shoot the son of a bitch if he gets anywhere near you. Now, get the hell out of here and find a place to hide until the feds get here."

She didn't want to leave him there, injured and now unarmed. He was willing to die to protect her.

What kind of man would do that?

The kind of man she loved.

Oh, God.

"Pax, no." She laid her hands gently on his shoulders, realizing the impact of her thoughts. She loved him. "I can't."

He lifted his hand, cupped her cheek. "You have to. I need you to survive this."

But he wouldn't. He would lie there and bleed to death, or sacrifice himself so she'd be safe.

"Go. Teresa, goddammit. Go."

Crying now, she leaned over him and kissed him. "I love you."

Something shone in his eyes, a light she'd never seen before.

"Get out of here," he whispered. "Head east, and when you hear the feds, scream and run to them."

She nodded and stood, moving away, her tears falling so hard she could barely see. She swiped them away, knowing she was never going to see Pax again, that he would die because he loved her.

She held the gun in her hand and walked steadily away from him, her heart shattering with every step.

TWENTY

SHE HAD TO GET AWAY. SHE HAD TO BE SAFE.

She'd said she loved him. Was that because she meant it or because she thought he was going to die? Pax didn't know, didn't really believe in love, but damn, right now he really wanted to.

He'd shifted himself into a sitting position against the back of the tree, and now he reached up to pull off his helmet, tossing it to the ground. His chest burned like the fires of hell and he was weak as a baby, which really pissed him off.

But he'd gotten Teresa out of there, and that's what counted. He had to believe she was going to get out of this. She was smart, resourceful, and would do what it took to make sure she didn't get hurt.

He reached into his pocket and grabbed his cell phone, punching in AJ's number. Still no answer. Shit. AJ was fine, too. He had to be. AJ had to take care of Teresa because Pax wasn't going to be able to.

He would have liked that chance, though.

Now all he could do was lie here and wait to die. Not the way he'd imagined, going out in a blaze of glory, but not much of his life had turned out like he'd imagined.

He leaned against the tree and prayed like hell that Teresa was running.

TERESA LOPED ALONG AT THE FASTEST PACE SHE COULD UNTIL she couldn't run anymore, until her breath wheezed out and she had to stop, bend over and wait for oxygen to fill her lungs. Her chest hurt. Hell, every damn part of her body hurt. But she was alive and moving, and Pax had given her that chance. No way was she going to throw it away.

The thought of him lying back there, wounded, made her ache. Part of her wanted to go back there and be with him. She had the gun and she could fight off Russ, shoot him if necessary, but she'd never shot a man. Oh, sure, she'd taken the training and gotten her concealed carry license after the rape, wanting to make sure she could protect herself, but she'd always doubted she could pull the trigger.

Russ had shot Pax. She could pull the trigger. Lifelong friend or not, he had turned on them. And without her by his side, Pax was vulnerable. But if what he said was right, if Russ was after her and not him, then getting far away from Pax was the only way she could protect him.

She saw lights hovering at the top of the embankment. She froze, then scurried behind a tree.

The feds? The only thing she could see was headlights. Car lights, not a bike. And she hadn't seen Russ. Had he taken off after he'd shot Pax, thinking both of them were dead? She had no idea.

Then she saw two guys dressed in black come over the hill, running at a fast clip down the embankment. And they were headed toward Pax's location.

Teresa's pulse kicked up hard and fast, indecision wracking her. Suddenly hiding to save herself seemed cowardly. She had the gun. Pax was wounded and could do nothing to defend himself. What if those guys weren't the feds? If they were, she could go to them and lead them to Pax. If they weren't . . .

They were getting closer to finding Pax. Pax, who loved her enough to sacrifice himself to keep her safe.

She loved him, too.

She knew what she had to do—whatever it took to keep Pax alive, even if that meant calling attention to her location.

She stepped out from behind the tree, her hand, and the gun, in her pocket.

"I'm over here!" she called.

They turned and ran toward her, and she knew as soon as they got within sight that they weren't federal agents. Their leather jackets gave them away.

Panic bled through her, making her sweat.

She turned and started running, but she knew she wasn't going to be able to outrun them. She was bruised and sore, and her legs weren't going to be able to put up the fight she needed them to. The only alternative was to turn and shoot.

She pulled the gun out and turned around, but it was too late. They had gotten too close. One of them tackled her, the gun flying out of her hand as he did.

She landed with a thud and tried kicking the guy off of her, but the other one grabbed hold of her arm. She tried to wrestle away, but it was useless. They were stronger than her. The two of them dragged her up the embankment, tied her hands behind her and tossed her into the back of a black van.

And even worse, she had no idea if there were more of them down there looking for Pax, who was unarmed and vulnerable.

Dammit. Tears pricked her eyes as the van started up and

pulled away. She shoved the waterworks aside, letting anger settle in instead. She was still alive, and as long as she was alive there was a chance she could get out of this. If they hadn't killed her on the spot, they wanted her alive for a reason. She just didn't know what that reason was yet.

She should have shot them. Now she was in deep shit and no one knew where she was. She could only hope Pax was okay, that maybe by signaling to them she'd managed to at least save him.

AJ HAD BEEN IN THE LEAD ON A WINDING ROAD WHEN THE FISTS sprung their trap at the curve. AJ had gone one way, the Thorns had gone the other and the Fists were in the middle, effectively cutting AJ off from the Thorns.

While the Thorns fired back at the Fists, AJ had taken out his phone to call for backup, only to find his goddamn cell couldn't get service in this remote area.

He'd been in a ditch, and low ground meant sitting duck, and that just hadn't been acceptable. So while the Thorns leveled bullets at the Fists, AJ rolled out of the ditch and headed for the rocky hill behind him, staying low and out of sight. And maybe that would help his cell service so he could get them some goddamn backup.

It had taken him a half hour to climb the damn hill. Jagged edges, a few sheeted spots and sharp drop-offs meant he couldn't scale it fast. By the time he reached the summit, he was sweating and damn glad to have made it. And still no fucking cell service. Shit.

But he was on the back side of the Fists/Thorns battle now, which seemed to have turned into a standoff. The Fists were holding their ground and preventing the Thorns from breaking entrance into the compound. The Thorns were holding firm.

AJ saw a metal building at the crest of the hill. Looked like an abandoned warehouse, the faded red sign scrawled above the double front door proclaiming it a former auto salvage yard. A few hundred rusted-out auto body carcasses still littered the landscape behind the building, a graveyard for old Chevys, Fords and Dodges.

He'd counted six guys wandering around inside the building.

A van pulled up under the floodlights of the old metal building, and two guys dragged someone out the back and into the building.

Fuck.

It was Teresa. She was bound and struggling as they pulled her along.

Even worse, Russ had led the van into the parking lot in front of the building. He had to be working with the Fists.

Dammit.

Maybe it was lucky that AJ had found his way here after all. At least he knew Teresa was here. And she was alive. But where was Pax? It wasn't a good sign that he wasn't with them. It meant something bad had happened to him, because no way would Pax have let Teresa be taken by Russ.

Okay. He had to take a deep breath and clear his head. He had to figure out what the hell he was going to do, because he was outnumbered. And trapped. No point in heading back down to where the Thorns were. No way was he leaving Teresa.

And now the two who had brought Teresa wandered the outside perimeter. Eight total.

The odds weren't good at all, but what choice did he have? He wasn't going to take the time to make the trek back down to get to the Thorns, his goddamn phone was shit, his best friend was either hurt or dead, and Teresa was in trouble.

That left him only one option. He had to get in there.

twenty-one

SORE, TIRED, TRUSSED UP LIKE A THANKSGIVING TURKEY AND pissed as hell, Teresa sat on a threadbare sofa in a cold metal building and glared across the room at Russ the traitor as he talked to that asshole who had killed Larks. Russ occasionally shot worried glances her way.

If she'd had Pax's gun on her right now, she'd have shot him. She should have shot the two guys who'd come after her, should have had the presence of mind to do what Pax had told her to do in the first place. Then she wouldn't be here, tied up and waiting to be used as—as what, exactly? That she didn't know, but she was obviously here for a reason.

This was all her fault. But what choice had she had? Leave Pax as a sitting duck? They would have found him and killed him, and that hadn't been an acceptable alternative.

Better her than him. The feds would find him; he'd be fine. And she was going to get out of this and kick Russ's ass. He was Joey's best friend. He was her friend, goddammit. How could he do this to her? How could he even be having a conversation with the guy who had killed Larks and pinned the murder on her brother? If white-hot anger could melt rope, she'd be a free woman by now.

She surveyed the building. Two double doors in the front guarded by two men holding what looked like semiautomatic weapons. Two other guys guarding side exit doors, also holding weapons. One at the back door, similarly armed.

Russ the traitor headed her way, his expression wary.

Yeah, he should be wary. She held her tongue as he sat next to her on the sofa. "Are you comfortable?"

She shot a livid gaze to him. "Like a goddamn day at the beach."

"It wasn't supposed to happen this way, Teresa. Are you hurt?"

"Oh, I feel just great, Russ. Getting shot off a Harley and tumbling down an embankment is my idea of a fun night. I do it all the time."

He looked toward the front doorway, then back at her. "I'm sorry. I didn't know what else to do."

"You could have not shot at us."

"I had no choice."

She almost laughed at that. "What the hell are you doing with the Fists, Russ? Are you out of your mind?"

He dragged his hand through his thick shock of curly hair, not quite meeting her gaze. "It's . . . complicated."

"Complicated, my ass. That guy you were talking to is the one who killed Larks."

"I know." He shook his head. "It wasn't supposed to go down like this. None of it was. I'm sorry. I can't say that enough. I really am."

"It's a little late for sorry, isn't it? Why don't you figure out a way to get us both out of here? It's not too late for that."

"All those years ago. They told me I had to . . . to prove my loyalty."

She frowned. "What the hell are you talking about?"

He dropped his head to his chest and stared at his boots. "Never mind."

"Go ahead, Russ. It's time she knows the truth."

Teresa's gaze lifted to the man who'd come to stand in front of her. He looked familiar. She'd seen him around Larks a lot. Tall and thin, with long dark hair pulled into a ponytail, a sleeve of tattoos covering each arm. He was the Fists' second in command or something. "You're Walter."

Walter nodded and grinned. "Yeah, I am." He turned to Russ. "Go ahead, tell her."

Russ snapped his gaze to Walter. "Leave it alone, Walt."

Instead, Walt crouched down in front of Teresa and laid his hands on her knees. She lifted her bound feet to kick at him, but he just kneeled on them. She winced.

"No, I think it's time she knows the truth about who you are. Who I am."

She waited, certain she wasn't going to like what she was about to hear. She turned to Russ. "What truth, Russ?"

Russ shook his head. "They made me. Said I had to prove my loyalty."

"They made you what?"

Walt's fingers traveled up her legs. Teresa tried to shake him off, pushing her knees against him, but he didn't budge.

Walt laughed. "Just like last time, eh, Teresa? You were a little fighter then, too."

Her entire body went cold. "What did you say?"

"Don't, Walt," Russ said. "I mean it. Don't do it."

Walt ignored Russ; instead he kept his gaze trained on Teresa. "We needed Russ bound to the Fists, and what better way to do that than to take something from the Thorns?"

She turned her gaze to Russ. "What did you do, Russ?"

But Russ continued to stare at the ground, refusing to meet her gaze.

Walt continued. "You see, Russ saw things as we did, that there were possibilities for the Fists and the Thorns to expand. But your brother didn't see it our way. Unfortunately, the Thorns are loyal to Joey. Russ, on the other hand, liked our distribution idea, so he came over to our side. The only thing was, we wanted him to stay in the Thorns for a while, working the inside, scraping away at their loyalties to Joey."

Teresa laid a murderous look on Russ. "You son of a bitch."

"Oh, it gets better, Teresa," Walt said, his voice soft as he continued to move his hands over her legs. Tension coiled and tightened her muscles to the point of pain.

"You see, we needed Russ to prove his loyalty to us. And that meant something big."

She shifted her gaze to Russ again, a flicker of understanding beginning to swell inside her. It couldn't be. Russ would have never done that.

She turned her gaze back to Walter, who grinned. "Yes, I think you do know what happened that night your bike broke down."

Cold nausea roiled inside her belly. "No."

"Oh, yeah. We needed Russ to take what he'd always wanted, to hurt his best friend in the worst way, to prove to us he was loyal to the Fists. What better way to do that than through you?"

Tears blinded her, that night coming back to her in vivid detail. The two men holding her down, pulling off her clothes, violating her . . .

She would not cry. Not in front of this son of a bitch. She refused to say anything.

"So Russ 'fixed' your bike and we followed you that night, and Russ made sure Joey would be in no position to come to your aid. And when your bike broke down, we were there to . . . help."

Her body began to shake, her stomach violently ill as Walt continued to slide his hands up her legs. But instead of fear, waves of hatred rolled off her. Hatred for what these two men had done to her, especially the betrayal by one who'd continued to look her in the eye and call her a friend all these years, who claimed to love her. He'd betrayed her in the worst way possible.

She twisted around to look at Russ. "You make me sick, you son of a bitch. I want you dead."

Russ squeezed his eyes shut. "I'm sorry, Teresa. I'm so, so sorry. You don't know how much I regret what I did that night."

Fat tears fell onto Russ's hands as he kept his head bowed, his shoulders shaking with his silent misery.

Teresa had no sympathy. She was immune. His tears were meaningless to her. She wanted him to suffer like she'd suffered all these years.

But now she knew. And knowledge was power.

"So you see, once Russ had done that, we knew he was going to be loyal to us. And it's taken some time, but we finally hatched a plan to take down Larks, who was against the merger of the two clubs. Larks wanted to take the Thorns out by force, to muscle in on their territory and destroy the club. My idea was a merger— strength in numbers. Larks never was a smart guy, too much emotion involved, too involved in wanting to take down your brother and eliminate the Thorns entirely. We needed the extra muscle and influence the Thorns provided, so it was obvious that Larks would have to go, too. We decided to pin his murder on Joey and, with Russ's help on the Thorns side, unite our two organizations to become even stronger."

Unbelievable. She'd been a pawn and nothing more. "For drugs. You've done all this for drugs. You hurt me, my brother, even someone you claimed was your friend. And you talk about loyalty? Loyalty means nothing to you. This is all about greed."

Walt shrugged and stood. "It's all about free enterprise and moneymaking, sweetheart. We're businessmen."

"You're scum."

Walt laughed and stood, smoothing his hand over her hair. She refused to flinch even though his touch made her skin crawl. "Soon to be rich scum once we have access to the river."

He was going down. Somehow, someway, she was going to make that prick suffer for everything he'd done. And his weak-willed moronic partner Russ would be right next to him when it came time to pay. She had to keep her head clear and figure out what his angle was, buy some time and see if she could somehow finagle a way out of this.

"So why am I here?"

"Your friends AJ and Pax have to go. They're feds and they're a danger to my operation. Russ took care of Pax and we have AJ cornered outside somewhere, separated from the Thorns, who are being kept busy by my guys. He's hiding out, no doubt making plans to storm our location. He must have seen us bring you in here, and it's only a matter of time until he comes to your rescue." Walt pulled out a pistol and cocked it, looking down at her with a grin so menacing it made her recoil. "And when he does, we'll be ready for him."

Teresa looked down at the gun in Walter's hands.

She was dead. And so was AJ.

That wasn't acceptable.

IT WOULD BE DAWN IN ABOUT AN HOUR AND A HALF. AJ NEEDED the cover of darkness to sneak up on the Fists, so if he moved it was going to have to be soon.

He already knew it was a really stupid idea to take on eight guys by himself, but he'd be damned if he was going to sit on the rocks and do nothing when there was even the smallest chance he could save Teresa.

He pulled his Glock and checked the clip. Half full and one extra in his pocket. That wasn't going to take him far, but it was going to have to do. He'd just have to make damn sure every shot counted.

He inhaled and let the breath out slow and easy, focusing on what he had to do. First the two guys outside. He'd move around the backside of the cliff and take them out by surprise. Now would be a great time for a silencer, but he hadn't exactly left the house tonight thinking he was going to need to be armed for a stealth attack. He had his gun and a knife and he'd make do. If gunshots brought the others running outside, that would just make them easier targets to take down one by one, and he'd use the cover of darkness as his advantage.

He turned to move down the hill, spotting headlights along the road below him. He crouched down along the rock surface and watched as the dark SUV crept across the road leading to the Fists location.

More Fists?

The SUV stopped just before it rounded the corner toward the main road and cut off its lights. All four doors opened and figures in black poured out, followed by a limping, hunched-over Pax.

AJ exhaled a sigh of relief to see his friend alive. Obviously wounded, but dammit, he was alive.

And he'd brought the goddamn feds with him.

AJ started scrambling down the hill, thankful that down was lightning fast compared to up. Pax was the first to spot him, pushing down a rifle that one of the feds lifted in AJ's direction. By the time AJ hit the ground, he was wheezing and out of breath, his legs burning from his thighs all the way to his shins.

Pax tossed him a bottle of water and AJ gulped it down, leaning against the side of the hill.

"Glad to see you're not dead. But you look like shit," AJ said. Pax was pale as a ghost, blood coating his jacket and shirt. And he didn't look all that steady on his feet, either.

Pax grinned. "Takes more than a bullet to stop me."

"Still think you're Superman, don't you?"

Pax ignored the comment. "They wanted to airlift me to a hospital. We need to get Teresa first."

"How'd you find us?"

"Damn van they took her in is leaking more oil than Hansel and Gretel dropped bread crumbs. Feds arrived right after they took her, so once they stopped the blood oozing from my shoulder we just followed the oily crumbs. Found the Thorns, who filled us in on the status of the gunfight. Said they'd lost you somewhere, but they'd spotted the building and salvage yard and figured that's where everything was going down."

AJ nodded and filled him in on what he'd seen up at the salvage yard. Pax grimaced. "Fucking Russ. I can't believe he's working with the Fists."

"Nothing worse than a traitor in a motorcycle club. Joey's not going to be happy." AJ was relieved Joey wasn't here. Loyalty was paramount in MCs. Without it, a club fell apart. Punishment was swift and severe for those who broke that loyalty.

AJ sketched out the layout of the salvage yard and building. "We go driving up that long road and they're going to know we're coming," he said. "And they might kill Teresa before we get a chance to get inside."

Pax looked at the hill. "So the best way is to climb up and surprise them."

AJ didn't relish the idea of making that arduous trek up the hill again. "Probably." He looked at Pax. "But there's no way in hell you'll be able to scale those rocks in your condition."

"No." Pax turned and patted the hood of the SUV, then

grinned. "But I can sure ram this baby down their goddamn throats when the time is right."

TERESA TOOK EVERYTHING IN, NOT KNOWING WHAT INFORMATION might be useful, or when she might be able to make a move. Sure, she was outnumbered. She was a woman, physically weaker and held captive by eight men. They had the guns and she was tied up. But she refused to yield. Not this time, not ever again. She was going to fight them and do whatever she could to save AJ. She would even go so far as to manipulate Russ if she had to. She'd seen the guilt on his face. She could use that to her advantage.

In fact, that was probably a good idea. Guilt was a great motivator. She thought about Pax lying there in the cold darkness, wounded and bleeding, and what he'd given up for her. She thought about AJ walking into a trap and possibly getting riddled with bullets in an effort to save her. All it took for her eyes to well with tears was thinking about the men she loved. She let the tears flow and wept openly—and as loud as she could.

Just as she'd suspected, Russ came over to her and sat next to her. "Teresa. I'm so, so sorry."

She continued to weep. Russ awkwardly patted her back. She wanted to throw his arm off. His touch made her sick. How many times had he hugged her since that night five years ago, how many times had she allowed his hands on her? He'd raped her, had violated her for no other reason than to secure his spot in the Fists. What kind of man did that? His touch made her sick. She fought back the shudder and let her tears continue to fall. Russ wiped her cheeks with a handkerchief.

"If I could take it back, I would. I screwed up, Teresa. I shouldn't have done this. I should never have agreed to do anything with the Fists. I fucked everything up."

She tensed, wanting to scream at him about what he'd done to Joey. Russ had set up his best friend. He was going to sit back and allow Joey to go to jail for murder. He had no honor, no loyalty. She wanted to kill him with her bare hands. Instead, she had to play this game, to appear pathetic and weak when she was anything but.

He was bent near her now, whispering. She lifted her head and met his gaze, hoping she looked suitably miserable. "I don't want to die, Russ."

His eyes widened. "You're not going to die."

She sniffed. "They're going to kill me. I know everything now. They're going to use me to draw AJ in here, then they're going to shoot me."

He shook his head. "No. No, they're not."

"Russ, think about it. Use your head. The only reason I'm still alive is because I'm bait. I'm going to die here tonight. I don't want to die, Russ. Help me, please. You owe me that much."

He stared at her for the longest time. Teresa did her best to look miserable and scared.

"I'm not going to let them hurt you, Teresa. I hurt you enough."

Understatement, asshole. "Then help me. Untie me so I can get away when the time is right."

Russ turned to look around. No one was even paying attention to them.

"Now, Russ. Please."

He shifted back to her. "Okay. But don't move until I tell you to. Let me do this for you. I'll make sure no one hurts you."

"Okay. I trust you." *About as much as Dorothy trusted the Wicked Witch of the West.*

He reached around and loosened the ropes at her wrists and ankles enough that she could wriggle out of them within seconds.

"Now sit back and don't move until I tell you."

She sniffed and tried to look helpless as she sat back on the sofa. "Okay. Thank you, Russ."

"I'm going to go . . . see what's going on. I'll be back to check on you."

She nodded and offered up an encouraging smile. "Thank you for helping me."

He looked down at her with such guilt. "It's the least I can do."

Yeah, buddy. It is the least you can do. The very least.

If he thought untying her ropes meant all was forgiven, then he was dumb as a box of rocks. She would never forgive him for what he'd done to her, for betraying his fellow club members and especially his best friend.

Some things were unforgivable.

But she'd managed to manipulate him into untying her. Step one was successful. At least she'd be free and untethered now when it all went down; she could move around the building and possibly do something to help AJ.

She kept her eye on the guy she'd found out was named Magee, the one who'd actually stabbed Larks. He wore a knife sheath on his belt, and she saw the blade handle sticking out the top. She'd bet a million bucks that was the knife that he'd used to kill Larks. All she had to do was come out of this alive, identify Magee as the one who'd stabbed Larks, and they'd be able to test that knife against the wounds on Larks's body.

It was the whole "come out of this alive" part that was going to be difficult. But this time, she wasn't going to just lie there and be a victim. This time she was going to fight harder. Even if it killed her.

She heard shots outside and immediately sat up. Everyone went running to the double doors, weapons raised. The police must be here. Or AJ, but it sounded like a hell of a lot of firepower. Maybe AJ had brought an army with him.

For the first time since they'd grabbed her and tossed her in the van, she felt hope.

Someone killed the lights inside the building. Disoriented in the darkness but damn glad for it, Teresa stood and kicked out of the ropes at her feet and pulled away the ones at her wrists. She couldn't see, but she could move now, and she had to get the hell out of here before someone came looking for her. She knew there was a wall directly behind the couch. She headed for it, found it and used it to guide her toward one of the exits at the back of the building, figuring soon enough they were going to grab her to use her as a hostage.

She found the door and the knob, turned it and eased outside, shut the door and ran like hell. There were rusted-out cars littering the otherwise barren landscape, which at least provided plenty of places to hide. She wound her way through the automotive grave-yard, keeping her head up and her eyes focused for anyone who might be following her. So far all the action seemed to be centered on the front of the building, flashes of gunfire lighting up the dark night. All she had to do was climb inside one of these vehicles and hide until it was over.

Something caught her hair and jerked her backward. She screamed at the stinging pain in her scalp and reached up to hold her head. Strong arms circled her and she was tugged against a very hard chest.

"Where are you going, honey? The party is just starting."

Walter.

She screamed again, hoping someone would hear her. Walter turned her around and slapped her across the face so hard she fell. An explosion of pain hit her cheek and she rolled into a ball, cupping her face to shield it from the excruciating sting.

Walter grabbed her arm and hauled her up. Something cold and metal pressed against her temple.

"Scream again, bitch, and I'll put a bullet in your goddamn brain."

He dragged her out of the row of cars.

"Where are you taking me?"

"Shut up."

She tried to slow him down, make her body heavy as he propelled her down the side path and toward the front of the building.

"Move, goddammit." His fingers dug into her upper arm as he dragged her toward the door she'd exited earlier. He pulled it open and pushed her so hard she fell on knees already bruised from her tumble on the motorcycle earlier.

Gasping for breath, panicked and scared out of her wits, she tried to focus on what to do next, how to get out of this. It was dark in here, but she could see better now than she could earlier. Walter bent over her and grabbed her arm again.

"Get up. It's show time and you're the main event."

He dragged her toward the open double doors. She was going to be their bargaining chip, the way they escaped. She couldn't let it happen. Russ stood at the door, and when they got there, he cast her a worried look. She shook her head and Walter shoved her toward the open front door.

Teresa closed her eyes and waited for bullets to riddle her chest as she was thrust in front of the open door like an easy target, but nothing happened. She opened her eyes and looked around, but saw no one. They must be hiding behind those thick rocks in the hills, the only cover in the otherwise deserted landscape.

Walter came up behind her and put his gun to her head. "Listen up," he yelled to whoever was outside. "We're leaving and she's coming with us. She stays alive as long as we stay alive. One shot fired and a bullet goes into her head."

There was no response, so Walter walked out of the doorway, pulling her with him.

"T-Bone, back the van in. The rest of you, drag up the weapons and ammo. You—" He pointed at Russ and thrust Teresa at him. "Hold on to her and don't let her go. If she tries to get away, shoot her but don't kill her. Not yet, anyway."

Teresa relaxed a bit as soon as Russ had her. Now she had a chance to get away. As soon as Walter busied himself elsewhere, she lifted her gaze to Russ. "Please. Now's your chance to right all your wrongs."

Russ clamped his lips together, his gaze moving over Walter and all the guys scurrying around to load up their weapons.

"This is my only chance, Russ. He's going to kill me."

Russ looked down at her, tears filling his eyes. "I really am sorry, Teresa."

She waited and a black SUV screamed up the road toward them. Walter came running in their direction and Teresa shot a look at Russ.

"Go now. Run!" Russ pushed her, and she tore out of the opening like she was on fire. She heard shots but didn't stop to turn around as a barrage of gunfire exploded around her. She headed straight for the SUV, which circled her and protected her from the bullets. As soon as it was within range, she opened the back door and dove inside, shutting the door behind her.

"Get down on the floor!"

Pax? She lifted her head. "You're alive!"

"Yes, now get down on the goddamn floor. I'm going to ram this SUV down their throats. Feds are coming in right behind me."

She curled herself into a ball on the floor and jerked when the SUV accelerated, tires squealing as Pax drove it right into the devil's mouth. Bullets pinged off the side and Teresa broke into a cold sweat, praying the SUV's windows were bulletproof. Shattering glass told her they weren't.

"Pax!"

He didn't answer, and the SUV fishtailed as he crashed into the building. Suddenly gunfire was everywhere and Pax dove into the backseat, covering her body with his. It sounded like the Fourth of July all around them. Teresa knew any minute someone was going to yank open the door and shoot both of them. She felt his heart pounding against her back, knew he was worried about keeping her safe. She searched around and found his hand, laced her fingers with his, felt his body relax a bit against hers.

The gunfire finally stopped, and all she could hear was the sound of Pax's labored breathing.

"Pax."

"Yeah."

"You're wounded."

"Yeah."

"I think we should get up now. There's no more gunfire."

"Not until someone gives us the all clear."

"You're wheezing."

"I'm going to be fine, Teresa."

She felt something warm and wet against her back. "You're bleeding on me."

He laughed. "Sorry."

"Dammit. Don't be sorry. Let me look at you." She tried to shift but he wouldn't budge. "Pax."

"We're not moving until there's an all clear."

The door opened and Pax tightened against her.

"Is that all you two think about is sex?"

AJ. Teresa slumped in relief. "AJ, help him."

"I can get up on my own." Pax pushed off the floor, grunting in pain as he did. He slid out, though he didn't do it fast. AJ helped Pax out, then grabbed Teresa's hand and pulled her from the SUV, then jerked her against him. She wrapped her arms round him.

"Are you all right?" he asked, smoothing his hands over her.

"I'm fine. You?"

"Yeah."

"Pax is hurt." She pulled back and turned to Pax, wanting so much to go to him, but he was leaning against the car looking like he might drop any minute.

"Ambulance is on its way," AJ said, then he searched her face and frowned. "Who hit you?"

She wrinkled her nose. "Walter hit me. And Magee, the guy with the neck tattoo, is in there. There's a knife in his belt. It might be the same knife he used to stab Larks."

AJ nodded. "We'll be sure to tell the feds about that."

"What about Russ?"

"He's dead. Shot. Not sure whether it was us or the Fists who did him."

She nodded, waiting to feel remorse since he had set her free and for years she'd believed they were friends. She couldn't feel sorry for him. Not after what he'd done to her. Not after what he'd done to Joey.

She heard the scream of sirens and went to Pax, sliding her shoulder under his arm. He pressed his lips to her hair. "Glad you're okay."

"You saved my life."

He frowned. "You were stupid not to hide in the woods."

She smiled at him. "I was trying to save your life."

"I can take care of myself, Teresa."

"Uh-huh." She peeled back his jacket to see a bright stain of blood. "You do a fine job of that."

The ambulance pulled up and Teresa and AJ helped Pax over.

The paramedics got him on the gurney, and before long it took off toward the hospital. Teresa shuddered out a sigh. "I want to go to the hospital to make sure Pax is all right."

AJ studied her, then nodded. "Okay. You need to get checked out anyway."

"I'm fine. Just bruised and battered."

He grazed his knuckles across her cheek. "Yeah, you are fine."

"There's something I need to tell you."

"What?"

"Walter and Russ were the guys who raped me. Russ was in on the plan to merge the two clubs and Walter wanted Russ's loyalty. Raping me was Walter's way to ensure Russ would be loyal to the Fists—there would be no going back to the Thorns after that."

AJ raked his fingers through his hair. "Christ. I can't believe he did that to you. I'm sorry, Teresa."

She shrugged. "At least I know now. I know who and I know why. And I used Russ's guilt over it. He untied me inside so I could run. Unfortunately Walter caught me."

"Walter's got a lot to answer for," AJ said. "I wish I'd known this before the feds got hold of him."

She felt the rock-hard tension in AJ's arm. "Don't. He has to pay for his crimes the right way. And I'll testify."

"You seem so calm about it. Aren't you angry?"

She shifted her gaze to where Walter and the others were being loaded into a van, then back at AJ. "Anger ruled me for a long time, AJ. It prevented me from living. I can't let it do that to me anymore."

He put his arm around her and hugged her close. "You're an amazing woman, Teresa."

"No, I'm just human. I make mistakes. I made the mistake of letting the rape rule my life for too long. No more."

He brushed his lips across hers. "Let's go to the hospital and check on Pax."

TWENTY-TWO

PAX HAD FINALLY BEEN SPRUNG FROM HIS PRISON. TWO WEEKS of bed rest and house confinement and he was ready to climb the goddamn walls.

He was fine. They'd pulled out the bullet and sewn him up and claimed over and over again how lucky he was that the bullet had missed vital organs and arteries.

Whatever. He felt just fucking fine. Though he had to admit that recuperating at Teresa's house wasn't a bad thing at all.

He'd done the ER thing in South Dakota, and after the doctors had patched up his shoulder, he and AJ and Teresa had debriefed with the FBI. Walter and his Fists pals were going to be going away for a long time.

Teresa had been great, had given unemotional, detailed statements of everything she'd been through. Then they'd gone back to Grange's house where Pax had been loaded down with antibiotics and pain medicine so all he did was pass out for about two days. Grange had sent a car for them, since Pax's bike was toast after

Russ shot him off of it. It was a damn good thing Russ was dead, because ruining a guy's bike was a killing offense.

Teresa had insisted on trailering her bike and riding in the car with Pax, who refused to act like a sissy and be driven. It was bad enough he didn't have his bike to ride back, the least he could do was drive Teresa home. AJ had followed them and they'd settled in at her place.

AJ helped Teresa get her bar back up and running as well as covering things with the local authorities. Magee, the dumbass who had killed Larks, had kept his knife, and the uniquely custom-made edge matched the wounds on Larks's body, so Joey was released and Magee would face murder charges.

Teresa was elated and Joey was relieved, though shocked and hurt and pissed as hell at his former best friend Russ. But at least Joey wasn't going to jail for a murder he didn't commit.

All was well. Pax had been given the okay to leave town now. There was nothing keeping him—or AJ—here anymore.

Nothing but Teresa.

His first day sprung from the house, he'd bought a new bike. It gleamed black and silver and rode like a dream. He and AJ and Teresa had ridden a couple hours that day, enjoying the back roads and trails away from the city.

Now he sat at the bar with AJ while Teresa worked. Joey and his guys were there, too, but Pax was only interested in watching Teresa, who seemed much happier than she'd ever been before. She laughed and danced on the bar and smiled as if she didn't have a care in the world. He leaned against the back of the bar stool, sipped his beer and watched her as she served her customers, at home in her element once again.

Even in the short time he'd known her, she'd changed, grown into a woman who'd overcome a tragedy in her past. She didn't let it rule her life, refused to be labeled by her circumstances.

He'd learned from her, and maybe it was time he let go of the past, too.

He loved her. He'd never loved anyone in his entire life, but he loved Teresa. He and AJ had enjoyed a lot of women together, but leaving them had never been difficult. They'd all had fun together, and that's all it had ever been—just fun. Because that's all he'd ever allowed. Loving someone hurt, and risking that was just too much.

With Teresa it had been intense and hot and sexy and emotional and one big package of I-want-this-forever. And wasn't that just a kick in the pants, because he was the one who was always down on forever and commitment, and the one woman he knew he'd never have a chance at forever with was the one he wanted it with more than ever.

"You feeling okay, man?"

Pax dragged his gaze from Teresa to AJ. "I'm good. Glad to be out of the house."

AJ tipped his bottle against Pax's. "Amen to that. About time to hit the road again."

Pax lifted the bottle to his lips. "Uh-huh."

He'd always loved riding. The open road meant freedom to him. But suddenly, freedom didn't seem so damned exciting. If he told AJ what he was feeling, he'd probably laugh at him.

AJ COULDN'T TELL PAX WHAT HE FELT FOR TERESA. HE KNEW HIS best friend, knew he'd walk away from him if AJ told him he was in love with Teresa. Pax had the bonds of friendship down well. He wouldn't stand in AJ's way.

The problem was, AJ had been watching Teresa with Pax the past couple weeks since they'd come back here. She fussed over him, catered to him, and the looks she gave Pax made it clear that she was in love with him.

Plus she'd slept alone in her room every night, hadn't invited
AJ to share her bed since they'd come back from South Dakota.
She said she had to stay alert in case Pax needed her, but AJ figured
she just needed some distance and time to think after everything
that had happened up there, all the revelations she'd had to deal
with. Plus, try as she might to deny she was hurt, he'd seen the
bruises covering her body. He knew she was sore. He wanted to
offer her comfort, but he didn't want to pressure her into anything
she didn't want, so he stayed away.

Truthfully, he had no fucking idea what to do about Teresa.
Coming back here and being with her again had thrown him.
He'd thought visiting old friends would be easy, that whatever
he'd felt for Teresa long ago would be old history. It hadn't been.

He hadn't intended to fall in love with her all over again, but he
had. She'd grown more beautiful since the last time he'd seen her,
but it was more than her physical beauty he loved. She'd suffered a
major trauma, but had picked up the pieces and figured out how to
move on with her life, to not let what had happened to her define
her. Five years later she was still kicking the past's ass. So why had
he spent all these years running from his past, determined to never
take anything in his life too seriously, never set down roots. That's
why he and Pax had always meshed so well in everything they did.
They took it light and easy, neither of them wanting permanence
or forever. They lived for today, because they both knew promises
were often—always—broken.

But now AJ wanted tomorrow. And he wanted tomorrow with
Teresa.

What the hell was he going to do about that?

Nothing. She didn't want a life with him. Not his life.

He was going to leave, just like he'd always intended. He was
going to walk out of Teresa's life for the second time.

Only this time, he wasn't a kid chasing big dreams, or trying to protect her, or clueless about his past and his future and what that all meant to Teresa. This time he knew exactly what it would cost to walk away from her.

TERESA SHUT THE FRONT DOOR BEHIND HER. IT WAS STILL EARLY, but Heather had told her she'd close up and clean the bar tonight, that Teresa had been pushing herself too hard since she got back two weeks ago.

Maybe Heather was right. And it was nice to be back home before midnight, especially having Pax and AJ with her.

Pax finally had some color back in his face, and he looked plenty healthy. The man had amazing recuperative powers. After the first week he'd been grouchy as hell about being housebound, but Teresa had insisted he stay put. What was it about men thinking they were indestructible? She had even threatened to tie him to the bed if he didn't cooperate, but then Pax told her she'd have to stop talking like that because it made him hard and gave him ideas. She'd laughed, but it had spurred ideas of her and Pax together—ideas she shouldn't have been entertaining about someone recovering from being shot.

She'd kept AJ at arm's length, too, which had been difficult as hell, but she'd had a lot to think about over the past couple weeks. The revelation about Russ and Walter and what they'd done to her had left her feeling bruised, then empty inside. Plus she'd had to deal with Magee and the police and getting her brother freed. All of it had exacted an emotional toll and she'd needed some distance to think.

Now two weeks had passed and Pax was fine. But he'd almost lost his life over her. Russ tried to kill Pax to get to her, and Pax would have gladly died to save her. So would have AJ, who was prepared to storm the building single-handedly before Pax and the feds showed up.

She didn't know quite what to make of these guys, and she'd sure as hell never been in love with two men at the same time before. How was she supposed to handle emotions like this?

She knew they were leaving. Pax had been given the go-ahead to travel. They had jobs—careers they loved. It would be selfish to ask them to stay, and she loved them both too much to do it. So she already knew she was going to let them go, wasn't going to say a word.

But she had tonight with them.

"It was nice of Heather and Shelley to cover for you." Pax laid his keys down on the table in her living room.

She turned to him. "Yes, it was."

"You're probably tired." AJ came up to her and swept his fingers over her cheek.

"Actually, I'm not tired at all. I've gotten a lot of sleep the last couple weeks."

"Me, too," AJ said.

"Me, three," Pax threw in.

Her gaze shifted from one to the other. "So, we're all well rested. I don't know about you guys, but I have all this . . . pent-up energy from all this rest I've gotten."

Pax moved in and flanked her other side. "Is that right?" He slipped his arm around her and nuzzled her hair. "What do you want to do with all that energy?"

She turned to face him and wound her arms around him. "Fuck both of you. All night long."

AJ came in behind her, his hips bracketing her buttocks, his cock already hard as he pressed in and captured her waist with his hands. He pressed his lips against her ear. "I'm about to explode, Teresa."

Pax tipped her chin up with his finger, forcing her to look up at him. "I want to fuck you hard, Teresa. I want to come inside you over and over again."

"Yes. I need you." She reached back and wound her hand around AJ's neck. "Both of you."

Pax bent and kissed her, a hard, strong, passionate kiss that made her so damn glad he was alive, and that she was alive, too. She fell against him, rocking her hips against his, needing to feel his hard cock riding against her pussy. He grabbed her ass and pulled her closer, dragging her against his hard shaft. "I need to be inside you. I've waited too damn long."

AJ swept her hair away from her neck and kissed her nape, reaching around to lift her shirt and cup her breasts. Pax unzipped her jeans and slid his hand inside to cup her sex, his fingers sliding ever lower. She was wet, hot, and she wriggled as his palm grazed her clit and his fingers slid inside her pussy. AJ found her nipples and tugged them while Pax fucked her pussy with his fingers, both of them licking her neck and kissing her mouth. Her senses on overload, she rocked against Pax's hand, close to her orgasm, tightening against him.

"Yeah, that's it," he murmured against her lips.

She came with a harsh cry, tossing her head against AJ's shoulder.

She had barely come down off the lightning-fast orgasm when Pax dropped to his knees and pulled off her boots and socks, then jerked her jeans off while AJ lifted her shirt over her head and removed her bra. Pax put his mouth over her sex, shocking her with his hot tongue.

She was already pulsing and ready again. She threaded her fingers through his hair and spread her legs, lifting one to rest over his shoulders while he ate her pussy.

Watching him was wicked sin. Having AJ behind her, seeing

his hands against her breasts, pulling at her nipples, was taking her into the fires of hell itself. He cradled her against one arm and moved to her side to fit one of her nipples into his mouth, sucking the bud and flicking his tongue around it until she whimpered, unable to stand the breathless pleasure evoked by two mouths doing delicious things to her body.

Being pleasured by two men was heaven and hell combined, sensation pounding her top to bottom. She slid one hand around AJ's neck and the other into Pax's hair, wishing she could have an out-of-body experience, wishing she could see herself being licked and sucked by both of them. But she could only feel, as wicked pleasure wrapped itself around her like licking flames that started low in her belly and slowly burned her out of control.

"I'm going to come." She rocked her pussy against Pax, and AJ let go of her nipple to take her mouth in a slow, deep kiss that sent her catapulting into her next climax. She held tight to AJ as Pax lapped everything she had to give, until her legs couldn't hold her any longer. Then he stood and she fell against him, kissing him, tasting what he'd done for her. She shuddered, still wanting more.

She snaked her hand down the front of Pax's chest, feeling the solid wall of muscle that told her why he'd survived the gunshot and being thrown off his bike and tumbling down a steep embankment. He was unbreakable.

She lifted her gaze to his, then reached for the hem of his shirt and drew it up and over his head, placing both her hands on his chest, swirling her fingers over his skin, especially the deep red scar a mere few inches above his heart. If Russ had aimed lower . . .

She bent down and kissed that spot, letting her lips linger there. Pax hissed out a breath and tangled his fingers in her hair. She moved her lips lower, dropping to her knees, turning to grab hold of AJ's belt buckle and drag him over to her, too. She unzipped AJ's jeans and jerked them down. While he was climbing out of

RIDING THE NIGHT   291

them, she did the same to Pax, sliding his zipper down and dragging his jeans down over his hips, freeing his cock as his pants fell
to his ankles.

Both men were naked now, their cocks erect and at her face.
She took a moment to breathe in the musky scent of them, incredibly arousing in itself. Then she tilted her head back to give them
both a wicked smile, shuddering at the hunger she read on both
their faces. She reached up and circled their cocks with her hands,
stroking them, keeping her gaze trained on their faces.

Two men. She still couldn't believe she was having sex with
two men at the same time. It was something she'd never get used
to. She had to be the luckiest woman alive to have men this hot,
this sexy, this gorgeous, all to herself. She felt selfish, like she'd just
won the lottery twice. But she had no intention of sharing. They
were hers—both of them—at least tonight.

Tomorrow they were leaving.

She wouldn't think about that, not when she held all this hot
male flesh in her hands. She slid her fingers around their cocks,
leaned forward and licked the crest of AJ's, moving right to Pax's,
wrapping her tongue around his cockhead and closing her lips.
He groaned and slid his fingers in her hair, but she backed away
and moved back to AJ's cock, putting her lips over his to suck him
gently inside her mouth.

"Christ, Teresa," AJ muttered, rocking his pelvis forward to
feed her more of his cock. She opened her mouth and he slid his
shaft along her tongue, slid his cock inside her mouth. She pressed
her lips over him and squeezed, licking as she sucked.

She took AJ deep, rolling Pax's cock in her hand. Then she
switched, eventually sucking one and then the other in rotation.
Soon both their cocks were slippery with her saliva, glistening in
the low light of her living room. Hard and hot and ready for her
to climb on and fuck them.

Pleasuring them both made her wet, made her nipples tingle and her pussy quiver.

Pax pulled her to her feet. "Enough. I need to fuck you."

They went into the bedroom and Pax put on a condom. "I need a few minutes inside your tight, hot pussy," he said, sliding her onto her back on the edge of the bed. "Then I'm going to fuck your ass."

She shivered at the hot desire reflected in his brown eyes. "Yes."

He spread her legs and slid inside her, fucking hard and deep and taking her so close so fast she thought she'd die of the pleasure. AJ crawled onto the bed and dragged his tongue over her nipples, then along the column of her throat to take her mouth in a soul-shattering kiss.

Always connected, she thought as Pax thrust with his cock and AJ thrust with his tongue. She would always be connected to these two men. They were hers, and no woman would ever have them as she had. They might fuck other women, but no woman would love them like she did.

Tears stung her eyes, and she wrapped her hand around the back of AJ's neck, deepening the kiss just as Pax shoved deeper inside her pussy. She whimpered against AJ's mouth and he slid the pad of his thumb across one of her nipples.

This was torture, the sweetest kind.

Pax pulled out and AJ scooted to the center of the bed.

"Come here, babe," AJ said, pulling her on top of him. He put on a condom and Teresa slid onto his cock, her pussy pulsing as his buried himself inside her. Fully seated on him, she didn't move at all, just felt him as he thickened and pulsed inside her. She smiled down at him and leaned over to kiss him. God, how she loved kissing him, pressing her lips to his, letting him curl her toes by diving his fingers in her hair and moving his mouth over hers, his tongue licking across hers. His mouth gave her butterflies and his cock lifting up and down inside her rocked her world.

And then Pax climbed beside her. "Lube, Teresa."

"Bedside drawer."

Pax leaned over her back, kissed her neck. "You're in control here, Teresa. You're uncomfortable, you stop this."

She reached up and slid her hand across his cheek. "I want this. I want both of you inside me at the same time. Now fuck me."

She felt the cool liquid coating her ass, Pax's finger there teasing her as AJ thrust inside her. She lifted against Pax's finger, and he replaced his finger with his cock.

"Relax, baby," AJ said. "Exhale and push out when Pax slides inside. It's easier that way."

She nodded and AJ kissed her. She lost herself in AJ's lips and tongue as Pax pushed his cockhead past the tight barrier of her anus, then pushed his shaft inside her.

The burning pain made her hiss, but it finally settled and all she felt was full of cock, just as she wanted. She threw her head back and Pax leaned over her to lick her ear. "Ahh, you're so tight, so hot here, Teresa. Just like I knew you'd be."

AJ began to move again, the sensation unbelievable. She was filled by two cocks, both moving in tandem. She would lift a bit off AJ and Pax would drive into her ass. Then Pax would pull out a bit and AJ would thrust deep into her pussy. And when AJ began to circle his thumb over her clit, she felt the pleasure tremors inside, her body gripping them both in a tight vise. She shuddered and ground against AJ, raking her nails down his chest, her orgasm tunneling toward her like a runaway train she had no hope of stopping.

"I'm going to come. Oh, God, I'm going to come." She arched

her back and let her cries run free as her climax rocked her. She felt it everywhere, pulsing through her nerve endings like a strike of the sweetest hot lightning shooting through her, exploding over and over.

AJ groaned and shoved hard up into her, gripping her hips as he shouted out his climax. Pax gripped her hair and pulled as he came, too, the three of them locked together in the most intimate moment Teresa had ever experienced, coming together and forever bonding, the three of them.

She never wanted this moment to end; she still pulsed with the aftereffects of her orgasm long after it was over. Pax kissed her neck, AJ's lips brushed hers, and both their hands skated light and easy over her body.

At this moment, she felt treasured and cared for and loved.

Pax pulled out and drew Teresa from AJ's lap. The three of them showered together, Pax and AJ soaping her down gently, tenderly kissing her, rinsing her, drying her. They climbed into bed together and Teresa drifted off into a blissful slumber sandwiched between these two men she loved so deeply.

In the middle of the night, AJ woke her and made love to her again, slow and easy, without words, taking her to a low, rumbling climax that devastated her senses. After, she rolled over and found that Pax had been awake, watching them. She climbed on top of his steely hard cock and rode him to another blistering climax, neither of them speaking, just touching and kissing. Teresa was afraid to break the tenuous bond that still held the three of them together; she only wanted to feel them inside her, touching her, kissing her, loving her.

She fell asleep between them again, aching inside because she knew this would be the last time.

In the morning she made them coffee and they ate breakfast together.

"You packed up?" she asked as they helped her with the dishes.

Pax nodded, his expression solemn.

They put their bags on their bikes.

"So where are you headed next? Or is that some kind of national secret?"

AJ laughed. "Just back to headquarters for debriefing."

"Oh. Well, that's good." She twined the fingers of both hands together and clamped her lips shut.

Don't say it. It wouldn't matter anyway.

Pax locked his saddlebag. "I guess that's it."

She shuddered, then smiled. "I guess so."

"Teresa—" Pax came up to her, pulled her into his arms.

She placed her fingers on his lips. "Don't. Please. I'm having a hard enough time as it is."

He gave her a curt nod, then bent and put his mouth on hers, kissing her so deeply she couldn't hold back the tears. He let her go and turned away to grab his helmet, and AJ swept her into his arms to kiss her next, his mouth so soft, his kiss telling her so much.

She finally pulled away, blinked back the stinging tears and offered them a bright smile. "Ride careful."

AJ nodded and climbed on his bike. She stood outside in the driveway and watched them both ride away.

SHE HADN'T SAID ANYTHING TO THEM ABOUT HOW SHE FELT, knowing there were no words that would keep them tied to her. And she wouldn't have said so even if she could have figured out what to say.

Their life wasn't with her, could never be.

And it would be unfair of her to even attempt to change that.

She went inside, shut and locked her door, and then let the tears fall freely, let the ache and loss envelop her. She wrapped her arms around herself and sat on the sofa, knowing she was never going to get over loving them.

TWENTY-THREE

They made it back to Dallas, debriefed with General Lee, and unpacked their things. AJ couldn't stand being in his room. It felt claustrophobic. Apparently Pax couldn't either, because he was downstairs in the main room when AJ came down.

Everyone was here. There was a mandatory weekend get-together, which meant the whole group had to attend. All the guys had been out on assignment for a while, so it was nice to relax and catch up in between more official meetings and briefings.

Diaz and Jessie were there, and Spence, too. Spence had brought Shadoe along since they were about to start their own vacation, taking a ride out west. Mac and Lily came out of the kitchen arguing with each other about something. Rick and his new girlfriend Ava were snuggled in one of the oversized corner chairs.

It was good to see old friends again. Since Diaz and Jessie had gotten married, they'd bought a house and didn't hang out at Wild

Riders headquarters that much anymore. Shadoe and Spence were talking about getting married soon, too, though Shadoe said she might string Spence along for another year or two, which made Spence growl and Shadoe laugh.

"Heard about your vacation," Diaz said as AJ slid into one of the chairs. "You two manage to find trouble wherever you go, don't you?"

"We try."

"Got a new bullet wound to show off, I hear," Shadoe said to Pax. "That should impress the ladies."

"Uh-huh."

Shadoe's gaze shifted to Lily, and then to Jessie, who shrugged and asked, "What the hell is up with you two? You're usually the most talkative out of all of us and you've barely said two sentences."

"Just tired, I guess."

"It's more than that, AJ," Spence said, plopping his booted feet on top of the coffee table. "Spill."

AJ shrugged. "Nothing to talk about."

"I know that look," Jessie said, leaning on the arm of the sofa, her arm around Diaz. "I never thought I'd see the day."

"I think you're right," Shadoe said. "Dear God, the mighty have fallen."

AJ frowned. It was always like this when the guys got together. Now that they all had women, it had gotten even worse. "I have no idea what you're talking about."

"You're in love," Jessie said.

AJ didn't answer.

"Oh, my God, you are." Shadoe looked to Pax. "How's this going to affect your mighty twosome in the sex department?"

Pax didn't answer, either.

"Holy shit," Spence said. "You, too? Same woman or did you find two?"

"Am I missing something?" Ava asked.

Rick whispered in her ear. Ava's eyes widened, then she smiled. "Sounds fun."

"Not on your life," Rick said. "You're a one-man woman."

"I miss all the fun," she said, crossing her arms and affecting a pout.

"But Pax and AJ never did." Lily winked. "But I think their wildcat days must be over now that they're in lurrrrrve."

"Don't you all have places to go?" Pax asked.

"Not at the moment." Diaz leaned forward and clasped his hands together. "So . . . the old love bug finally bit the two of you, huh? And here I thought I'd be the last holdout."

"Hey." Jessie slugged him in the shoulder. "You fell hard and fast."

Diaz dragged Jessie onto his lap. "You seduced me."

She laughed. "Bullshit." But she kissed him.

The last thing AJ needed to be around right now was a couple in love. Or multiple couples in love. "Get a room."

"Hey, honey, you wanna talk about it?" Jessie asked, sliding off Diaz's lap to come over and sit on the arm of his chair.

"No, I really don't."

Shadoe stopped him. "We were just teasing you like we always do. We didn't mean to hurt your feelings."

He pulled her into a hug. "Feelings aren't hurt. Now go cuddle with that moron you seem to love."

She grinned. "Okay. Are you sure nothing's wrong?"

"Nothing a good workout won't solve."

Shadoe nodded. "I understand."

AJ went to the gym to beat the shit out of the punching bag.

After he'd worked up a sweat for an hour or so, he decided even a physical workout wasn't going to help.

"You miss her."

He grabbed a towel, not bothering to look at Pax. "Maybe."

Pax moved into the gym and took a seat on the metal chair. "Me, too."

Now AJ turned to Pax. "You love her."

Pax lifted his gaze to AJ. "Yeah, I do. So do you."

AJ leaned against the wall. "It wouldn't work. She's there, we're . . . everywhere."

"They've all made it work."

"Who?"

"All our friends here. Mac, Diaz, Spence, Rick. None of them ever thought their relationships would work. Now look at them."

"That's different. They're different." AJ pushed off the wall and moved toward the punching bag again.

"Bullshit. They're no different than you and me. They just wanted it bad enough to make it work."

AJ shifted his gaze back to Pax. "And you're saying we don't?"

"You and me aren't really the most experienced when it comes to love. We've always made it about sex, deliberately choosing women who we know were only in it for the fun. Teresa wasn't like that. She's a forever kind of woman."

AJ yanked off his gloves and grabbed his water bottle, pulling up the chair across from Pax. "You want forever."

"Yeah."

"With Teresa."

"I love her. I know you do, too. We've spent our whole lives running from what scares us, afraid those we love won't love us back."

"She let us leave."

"Yeah, she did. You know why?"

AJ sighed and leaned back in his chair. "Because she loves us."

TERESA SAT IN THE BACK OFFICE OF THE BAR DOING PAPER-
work, spitting out a curse when she added up the figures wrong
for the fifth time in a row.

"Goddammit." She crumpled up the paper and tossed it in the
trash can. "Pull your head out of your ass, idiot."

"You yelling at that piece of paper or yourself?"

Joey stood in the office doorway.

"What do you think?"

"I think you've been a miserable, snarling bitch since AJ and
Pax left a few days ago."

She stood and put the ledger away. "I have not."

"Sis, we're twins, remember? I know you. Sit down and talk
to me."

She slammed the door shut on the file cabinet and fell into her
chair, rubbing her fingers over the throbbing ache in her temples.

"You love him, don't you?"

She lifted her gaze to her brother. "I love *them*, Joey."

Joey's eyes widened. He came in and sat in the chair across
from her desk. "Both of them?"

"Yes. Both of them."

Joey laughed. "Tart."

Then she laughed. "Asshole."

"So what happened? You told them you loved them and they
left anyway?"

"Not exactly. I did tell Pax I loved him, but it was a near-death
situation. And I'm pretty sure he didn't believe me."

"So basically you didn't tell them. Why not?"

"They have their own lives, their careers. I didn't want to hold them back."

"Sometimes guys need to know you love them. We make terrible psychics, Teresa. It's just not in our genetic makeup. We like things simple and spelled out. Sometimes you even have to hit us over the head with it."

"And if I told them, then what? They would have just felt bad when they left. I couldn't do that to them. We went into this knowing they were going to leave."

"I think all of you were afraid of being hurt, so none of you wanted to take that first step."

She arched a brow. "Giving love advice now?"

"I love you. I want you to be happy."

Her heart swelled. "I love you, too. And I am happy."

"Not happy enough. If you want them, tell them. Then figure out a way to make it work."

TERESA THOUGHT ABOUT WHAT JOEY HAD SAID, AND HALFWAY through her shift that night, she realized maybe he was right. Maybe she'd given up, let them go too easily.

God, she missed them, missed their scent, the feel of their skin against hers, the way they kissed her and touched her, the way they made her laugh. She ached inside from missing them so much, and her bed was just so damned empty she hadn't been able to sleep in it since they'd left.

She popped a couple beers for a customer, then pulled her phone out of her pocket, her palms sweaty as she contemplated calling AJ or Pax and asking if maybe they'd meet her this weekend. They might be on assignment in another state by now. Would they hate being bothered?

And when had she become such a coward? She'd survived rape,

kidnapping and nearly being killed. She could damn well survive a fucking phone call and possible rejection. It certainly wouldn't be the worst thing that had ever happened to her.

She punched in AJ's cell number and waited, her heart in her throat as she heard it ring. And ring. And ring. No answer.

Stupid idea anyway.

"I'm right here, babe."

She frowned, certain he hadn't answered his phone. Yet she'd heard his voice.

"Teresa."

Her head shot up, her heart slamming against her ribs as AJ and Pax stood in front of her. She practically leaped over the bar and threw herself against them, planting her lips on Pax, then AJ, kissing them both with all the passion and need and longing she'd felt but hadn't said.

"I love you," she said, wrapping both of them in her arms. "I love you both."

"I love you, too," Pax said as he lifted her in his arms, then put her down and kissed her hard and deep, the kind of kiss she'd grown to love and expect from him. Then AJ pulled her to him and kissed her with that maddening softness that curled her toes.

"I love you, Teresa," he said, the emotion in his eyes so real it made tears well in hers.

She searched for Heather and Shelley, who grinned and waved at her. Shelley came over and hugged her.

"Get out of here, you lucky bitch. I've got it covered."

She grinned and nearly cried from the joy welling up inside her. "Thanks."

Outside, she turned to them both. "I can't believe you're here. Why are you back?"

"For you," Pax said. "We got back to Dallas and realized we couldn't make our lives work anymore without you."

"We both fell in love with you. And we both should have said so," AJ said. "But loving someone is hard. It's risky. There's a chance you'll get hurt."

She laid her palm on AJ's chest. "Yes, there is that chance. But it's a chance worth taking. And I should have said something to both of you, too. I didn't want you to go, but I was afraid to ask you to stay. I know you have a job that you both love, and I would never want to come between you and what you love."

"You're what we love," Pax said, hugging her so tight she thought she might burst with happiness. "Everything else can be worked around." He drew her away from him. "If that's what you want."

"Yeah, this is up to you, Teresa. If you want both of us, that is. It's not really a conventional type of relationship."

She linked her arms with theirs. "I'm not really a conventional type of girl. So this kind of relationship totally works for me."

"It works for us, too," AJ said.

"Good." She pulled away from them and looked at both of them. "Guys, I don't think I can wait until we get home."

AJ smiled and shared a look with Pax. "You want to do it right here?"

"It just so happens there's a very secluded spot behind the bar."

"Show us." AJ motioned with his head for her to lead the way.

She took them to the back lot where the overflow parking was. Since it wasn't a weekend and it was already late, the lot was empty. Behind the lot was a large oak tree and a rather sturdy fence with an empty field behind it, affording them plenty of privacy.

Teresa backed against the fence and spread her legs, already feeling the twinges of excitement skitter across her skin.

"So you've got a little exhibitionist in you." Pax said, skimming his hand across her breast.

It was hot out tonight. And humid. Teresa was glad she'd worn a skirt and a tank top, because her skin was on fire, especially when AJ put his hands on her, too.

God, she'd missed them both so much. AJ kissed her and Pax put his lips to her throat and she shuddered, embracing them, pulling them against her.

"I need one of you fucking me right now." She was panting, her pussy was wet and she ready to be fucked.

Pax turned her around and bent her over to face AJ. He lifted her skirt and jerked her panties down. She thrilled to his possession of her and raised her gaze to AJ, who was already unzipping his jeans and pulling his cock out.

"This is why we love you," AJ said. "Because you're perfect for us."

"I know," she said.

Both of them belonged to her now. She smiled at AJ and reached for his cock, drawing him closer so she could lick the wide crest as Pax nestled his hips against her and thrust inside her. She closed her eyes and felt her pussy convulse around him, then took AJ's cock between her lips, taking all of him as he thrust deeply into her mouth.

"Ahh, baby, it's going to be so good," AJ said, holding on to her hair and sliding his shaft along her tongue. "I love you so much."

She loved that he felt free enough to say it to her now, that he caressed her hair as he fucked her mouth. Pax bent over her and held her hips, stroked her breasts and nipples and kissed her neck while he fucked her.

"I love you, Teresa," he whispered as he stroked his cock inside her. "You're ours, forever."

He reached around and found her clit and started to rub her. "Now come for us, honey. Come on my cock."

She was so tightly wound, so filled with love and desire for them, that she felt the sensations deepening inside her. Pax kept the pace of massaging her clit while pounding his cock inside her, and AJ lifted her chin, forcing her gaze to his.

"I'm going to come in your mouth when you come, Teresa. We're all going to go off together."

The way he looked at her, the tension on his face, the love in his eyes, set her off. She kept her focus on AJ and let go, moaning around his cock, grabbing his shaft with her hands and stroking him into her mouth as she rocked back into Pax. Pax groaned and dug his fingers into her hips, pressing himself against her as came inside her in a couple hard thrusts.

AJ let go and came inside her mouth. She took all he had, holding on to his shaft and swallowing what he gave her.

They lifted her, held her while she licked her lips. Pax withdrew and pulled her panties up, helped her put her clothing back into place. Then they came together and kissed her, held her while she gathered her balance.

She wrapped her arms around both of them. "I love you."

"I love you, too."

They had both said it.

She closed her eyes and felt like the luckiest woman alive. She'd had to go through hell to get here, but she had survived and she deserved this happiness with these amazing men. She was never letting go.

PAX'S HEART SWELLED WITH MORE EMOTION AND MORE LOVE than he'd ever felt in his life. He had everything he'd ever wanted, and he was almost afraid to believe it was real. His best friend and the woman they both loved.

"So now what? How do we make this work?"

They sat at a coffee shop in town and ate, sipped coffee and talked about the three of them.

"AJ and I will still have to do our jobs, but Grange has gotten used to his people moving on with their lives and changing locations."

AJ nodded and took her hand. "Which means we can live wherever we want, but we'll have to travel on assignment."

"I can live with that," Teresa said.

"We did ask that unless there are so many assignments that all the Wild Riders are out, AJ and I won't be assigned at the same time. That way one of us will always be here with you."

"I thought the two of you always went out on assignment together."

AJ nodded. "We do. We did. Now we have a woman to take care of, so we'll change that."

"You're our first priority now, Teresa," Pax said. "We want to be here for you."

Her eyes glittered with tears. She reached out and grasped their hands. "I don't know what I did to deserve you two."

The waitress came over and refilled their cups, glanced down where Teresa had her hands linked with both of theirs, looked over at Teresa and winked, then walked away.

"I supposed not everyone will think me being with two men is acceptable."

AJ grinned. "The waitress thought it was just fine."

"What if—"

"What?" Pax asked.

"It's jumping the gun. Never mind."

"Teresa. If this is going to work, we need to be able to talk about anything."

"What if I get pregnant?"

The thought of her carrying his child . . . Pax's chest damn near burst with pride and excitement. "Do you want kids?"

"Yes, I do. Very much. I thought I'd never have them after the rape, thought I'd never be whole enough to let a man touch me. Now the thought of it—yes, I do want children."

"Then what's the problem?" AJ asked.

"Whose baby will it be?"

Pax looked over at AJ, and they both nodded. "It'll be ours," Pax said.

Teresa closed her eyes, and when she opened them again, a tear slid down her cheek. "I love you."

Pax knew whenever she said the words, she meant she loved them both. And that would always be good enough.

"Come on," he said, puling out his wallet to pay the bill.

They headed outside to climb on their bikes. Teresa grabbed her helmet.

"Oh, Pax?"

"Yeah, Teresa?"

"AJ's name is Adirondack Jolon."

Pax's eyes widened. He looked over at AJ, who cringed.

"No shit?"

Teresa grinned. "No shit. Now that you know, it's kind of like a secret bond. You're sworn to never to reveal that to anyone."

Pax shook his head. "Dude. I'm sorry."

AJ slammed his helmet on. "Not as sorry as I am."

Pax laughed and fired up his bike. "Let's go home."

He finally had a home to go to, and a woman who loved him as much as he loved her.

THEY TOOK OFF, AJ TAKING UP THE FRONT, LAUGHING AS HE realized he now had the family he'd always wanted. His best friend, and a woman they both loved.

Families were never alike from one house to another, from one generation to another. He thought of the children he and Pax would give Teresa, and realized he was nothing like his stepfather, any more than Pax was a product of the world he'd grown up in, any more than the children they'd create would be anything like they'd been.

Things were going to be different. Tonight was their new beginning.

He rode the night with a wide grin on his face and led his family home.